14.00

How to
Marry
a
Warlock
in 10 Days

How to Marry a Warlock in 10 Days

Saranna DeWylde

B
BRAVA

KENSINGTON PUBLISHING CORP.
www.kensingtonbooks.com

BRAVA BOOKS are published by

Kensington Publishing Corp.
119 West 40th Street
New York, NY 10018

All Kensington titles, imprints, and distributed lines are available at special quantity discounts for bulk purchases for sales promotions, premiums, fund-raising, educational, or institutional use.

Special book excerpts or customized printings can also be created to fit specific needs. For details, write or phone the office of the Kensington special sales manager: Kensington Publishing Corp., 119 West 40th Street, New York, NY 10018, attn: Special Sales Department; phone: 1-800-221-2647.

BRAVA and the B logo are Reg. U.S. Pat. & TM Off.

ISBN-13: 978-0-7582-6916-4
ISBN-10: 0-7582-6916-1

First Kensington Trade Paperback Printing: October 2012

10 9 8 7 6 5 4 3 2 1

Printed in the United States of America

ACKNOWLEDGMENTS

Thanks a million to Jessica Leach for her tireless research and constant support.

A huge thank-you to my critique partner for not having a stroke when I deleted half this book and started over.

And of course, all my family, friends, and readers (some who fall into all three categories) who've supported me in so many ways.

CHAPTER ONE

The Centerfold

Midnight Cherrywood didn't feel the least bit guilty as she grinned like the most jaded of lechers over the new centerfold in *Weekly Warlock* magazine. Even though said centerfold just happened to be one Dred Shadowins, dark warlock and bastard extraordinaire. The dark part had never been proven, but she definitely had proof of the bastard part.

Back at the Academy, he'd called her "Cherry-Would-If-She-Could." He'd dipped her braids in a potion that had turned them into snakes for three days; he'd cursed her fig yogurt to sour if she looked at it; and had compared her legs to those of a horse/mule hybrid more times than she cared to count. It should be a sin for such a nasty warlock to look so good, but she supposed that one man, even a warlock, couldn't be allowed to have everything.

"On your back, woman!" Dred's image demanded, looking every inch the conquering barbarian.

The special thing about the warlock publications was that she could see the articles play themselves out not on the page, but in what mortals would call 3-D. In fact, for an extra subscription fee, the magazine came with a special feature so she could have the likeness of any centerfold act out scenarios. She could feel everything she wanted him to do to her just as if he was there in the flesh.

Middy sighed in expectation of the pleasure to come. She liked it when he was bossy; she'd programmed him that way after a few days of experimenting. She was going to dress him in a kilt later. This magazine was like a real-life Fuck Me Ken doll with none of the messy attachments. He didn't come with the Ducati broom or the mansion, but that was all Barbie's shit anyway. She was the doctor, the lawyer, the astronaut . . . he was just the ditzy arm candy.

She'd paid the extra fee for image interaction gladly. Unfortunately, the program wouldn't accept anything that was squick-worthy or that the owner of the image found offensive in reality. The first time Dred had done a pictorial, she'd tried to make him walk around on a leash and bark like a dog. She'd only had success in making him lick her boot and call her "mistress."

Middy found it to be a sad state of affairs when even her fantasies wouldn't do as they were told. She wouldn't argue too much though because for all of the program's recalcitrance to be humiliated, it was more than happy to provide images of dipping Dred's almost white-blond head between her aching thighs.

Dred Shadowins was just arrogant enough to think that every woman in the world wanted to ride his face like a show pony. Middy couldn't blame him though; he really was delicious as long as he had his mouth full.

Yes, Dred Shadowins was going to have a mouth too full of her to be saying much of anything, let alone something hateful. Middy leaned back on her mountain of overstuffed pillows, fanned her hair out behind her just so, and closed her eyes.

She knew it was a sad thing that she had an ongoing affair with a centerfold when the real thing was at all of the same social functions she attended. Of course, her presence at those soirees was more out of duty than any actual desire to go. The Gargoyle War had left many families impoverished and Middy felt the magickal world should support the families of soldiers on both sides, so she organized charity functions and solicited donations.

Middy wished that she could stop thinking about the actual man and just jill-off to his tasty likeness. Not that she wanted the real thing. That would be stupid. Aside from the rumors about his ties to dark magick, he was also one of the richest warlocks in the world. Hell, he was one of the richest people in the world, mortal or warlock, and that made him one of the most eligible bachelors on the planet. He went through women and witches like dental floss.

Middy was amazed at how real it felt when he ran his fingers over her thighs, when he . . . When her damned Witchberry went off, vibrating like a jackhammer and interrupting her recreation. She was tempted to put all that vibration to better use. It wasn't as if she could turn it off though. In the magickal world the Now Network meant RIGHT NOW. There was no lost signal, no "reject" button for magickal calls. The vibrating was just to let you know that you needed to be prepared. The chancellors used Witchberries for video conferencing on demand.

Middy closed the magazine and straightened herself, which put her dreamboat on pause. He was still looking at her and licking his chops lasciviously. Thank the Goddess he couldn't do anything else while he was on pause or she'd be screaming in tongues at Chancellor Vargill. He'd get to know her in ways that just weren't necessary for their professional relationship.

"Cherrywood!" Chancellor Vargill's voice reverberated through the little machine.

She had the urge to trill back, but composed herself. "Yes, Martin?"

"Are you busy?"

If that mattered, he wouldn't have called on the Witchberry, the pompous ass. "What can I do for you?"

"The funding for the Gargoyle Masque just fell through. We need donations and we need them now. Who on your contributors list can we hit up to sponsor something of this size?"

The universe was conspiring against her. There was only one warlock who could part with that kind of scratch on a moment's notice. The warlock of her fantasies, Dred Shadowins.

"What do you mean the funding 'fell through'? It doesn't just *fall through*. What happened?" Middy demanded.

Martin Vargill's face colored and it seemed that his collar was too tight. He shoved a finger between the garrote of the material and his neck before answering. "Chancellor Butterbean was caught, let us say wand out, with Aloe Hugginfroth."

Aloe Hugginfroth was a notorious escort and pariah. Gavin Butterbean's career would implode on itself not because of Hugginfroth's reputation, but due to the fact that it was his wife who held the purse strings. Unfortunately, Ginger Butterbean also knew that the Gargoyle Masque was one of Gavin's favorite charities and she would have snatched the funding right out from under it. The selfish bitch couldn't care less about the women and children she'd be helping, only about drowning her husband's political career. Without the networking from the Gargoyle Masque, he was sure to lose his chancellorship.

"Maybe I can talk to Ginger," Middy said weakly. Even though she knew that it wasn't a viable option, she didn't appreciate the chancellor's loud cackle. He honked like a goose.

"Middy, you need to go see Dred Shadowins. We both know that without him, the Masque will be a no-go this year. Remember the starving kids, Cherrywood."

Middy huffed. Those damned kids got her every time. "I'll call his secretary."

"He's expecting you in an hour."

An hour? One miserable little piss-ant of an hour? Was he high? "If you call the secretary, you can deliver the pitch."

"Already tried, Middy. He wants you."

He wants you. If only that were true. Want in one hand and well . . . the rest was obvious. She knew which one filled up first and with the same material that was going to be spewing from his gloriously decadent mouth in exactly one hour.

"Why? Is *he* high? I know you must be."

"You do carry on so, Midnight. What's the big deal? You pitch our cause all day long. It's your bread and butter. Dred Shadowins is no different. Unless you're one of those screaming debutantes who think he's the bee's knees in Armani because he's rich. I really thought better of you."

"Martin, you are cordially invited to fuck yourself sideways."

"I hope you won't be kissing Shadowins with that mouth."

"So help me, Vargill, I'm going to reach through this phone and . . ."

"Fifty-five minutes and counting, Middy." Vargill hung up.

Even being a witch, she wasn't sure she had enough time to make herself presentable and still be on time for her meeting. Why had Dred Shadowins asked for her? He'd probably run out of small animals to kick.

Middy knew she needed to suck it up and go prostrate herself before the almighty Shadowins, anything to get those children into homes. It was worth the blow to her pride to help the children.

She was tempted to put on something frumpy and dowdy to prove to him that she didn't care what he thought. Middy had to admit that she wanted him to see her and be completely taken by her beauty, floored by how kind the years had been to her and, not to mention, the great shape of her ass. Something she hadn't had at the Academy.

She hadn't had this rack back then either; Middy had been a late bloomer. Though bloom she had. She'd gone from a carpenter's dream—flat as a board and never been nailed—to 1940s Hollywood lush. The never-been-nailed part still applied, much to her displeasure. She found that she liked her fantasies more than anything reality had to offer.

In the end, she gave in to her vanity. Middy decided it would take a big enough kick in the taco by swallowing her pride to go see Shadowins. She chose a tight-fitting skirt that came to just above her knees and a feminine blouse. It was work chic, but sexy, too. The black bra she wore beneath the pink silk gave it just enough edge. She may have been a quiet sort of witch, but that didn't mean she didn't know how to dress.

Corralling her hair was another matter entirely. Not that it was ratty, unkempt, or even had split ends. It was just a riot of curls and they wanted to hang where they wanted to hang. There were no mergers or suggested courses of action; it had to be a straight up hostile takeover to get it up into a bun. Even then, it was a loose bun, but she liked how it looked on her with fey little wisps framing her face.

Again, she was thankful that she was a witch or the amount of product she'd have to dump in her hair would be enough to glue a polar bear to an ice cap. She was mostly satisfied with her look and charmed her makeup on.

Not too bad. She looked a little bit like Snow White, but that had always worked for her. It was what she'd dressed as for every Samhain since she could remember. Now, if she could just find her damned broom. The thing had been in the shop twice already in the last three months. She hoped it didn't dump her in Bangladesh. That would not be good for her complexion or the Gargoyle Masque.

She looked at the closed copy of *Weekly Warlock* and sighed heavily. She'd much rather be dealing with this version of Dred Shadowins. Not only did she have to deal with Dastard Dred, as she'd called him, but she had to deal with her broom. Her broom was a timid little thing, afraid of heights. Pretty much worthless, but every time she tried to trade him in, his bristles quivered tearfully and she couldn't bring herself to do it.

Middy found her broom hiding from her in the back of the shoe closet. She knew she was lucky to have found him because the back of that thing led to another dimension. At least, that's what the sock gnome had told her when she'd caught him stealing one of her thigh-highs. She'd threatened him with dirty gym socks; they never wanted those. For good reason, she supposed.

Middy soothed the broom out of the corner and got him ready to go. She hopped on him sidesaddle because he had traditional sensibilities, not at all like some of the newer models who were more than happy to have witches' thighs clamped tightly on both sides of the steering shaft. And she wondered then if Aloe Hugginfroth's broom could apply for hazard pay. That, too, could possibly have been a black hole to another dimension.

CHAPTER TWO

The Appointment

Shadowins Towers were located on the mortal side of Kansas City, Missouri, because Dred liked to be in the middle. He found that the middle was always the easiest road to travel and he could veer off to either side at a moment's notice. This applied to politics, business, magick, and women. He especially liked to be in the middle with women, in the middle of two women if he had his way.

And he usually did.

He wasn't sure what perversity had caused him to demand Miss-Cherry-Would-If-She-Could bring the pitch for the Gargoyle Masque. Dred already knew that he was going to give her the money. Even he couldn't resist all of those sad-eyed, snot-nosed little creatures who were oddly endearing with their pleas for help. He wouldn't go so far as to say that he liked other people's spawn, but they were interesting in their own way, and unpredictable.

He was also aware that at times, he was indeed a twisted bastard. Of course, that hadn't stopped him from making his demands when Vargill had called sniveling about Butterbean's dumbassery. How in the name of hell he'd gotten caught with that slag Aloe Hugginfroth was beyond him. It wasn't that he hadn't had his turn with the talented witch, because he had. All warlocks had their share of vices, but that didn't mean they needed to be displayed like Solstice lights on a tree.

He hadn't really thought much about Middy Cherry-wood since their days at the Academy. Dred had been such a spoiled little shit, and now that he thought about it, he wasn't sure that much had changed where he was concerned. He'd realized that plenty had changed with Middy when he'd seen her a month or so ago at a luncheon and damn if she wasn't mouthwatering. Of course, there was the fact that her panties might be the only ones that he hadn't been in as far as the magickal world was concerned. He was running out of new dishes to try and she was most definitely a dish.

He'd always thought Cherry-Would-If-She-Could, but now he wondered if Cherry-Had, and if she would again with him? Dred knew that she was going to be a challenge and that whetted his appetite for more, much more.

He knew she would be prompt so he waited for her in what they called the Broom Closet. It was a small room where magickal folk could travel back and forth between the mortal and magickal worlds unmolested.

Dred wasn't disappointed. She arrived with one minute to spare looking like she'd just crawled out of his bed. Her lips were plump and pink, as if she'd just been kissed thoroughly, and her hair was slightly mussed. Wait, no. If she'd just crawled out of *his* bed, her hair would look like she hadn't brushed it in years and she wouldn't even be able to sit a broom. He flashed his trademarked Shadowins's smirk. That was how she was going to look tomorrow morning.

She was going to be wearing that same berry-pink silk blouse, but it would be buttoned wrong. They usually missed one or two after a night with a warlock of his prowess. He'd bet that the tail of the blouse would just skim the tops of her thighs and would be an enticing invitation to see what else she had to offer in that exact shade of pink.

Middy leaned over as she dismounted her broom with the ladylike comportment that the Academy had beaten into her head. He remembered the days when a broom could buck her if she even looked at it too long. Dred caught a glimpse of a lace-edged, black satin bra as she shifted.

He was instantly hard at the sight of the soft swells of her creamy breasts over that naughty black lace. Dred wondered if she liked how that silk felt like against her bare skin, if it taunted her nipples and, further, what shade of pink they were.

Dred decided then that pink was his new favorite color. Especially when her cheeks flushed the same hue. He would have to endeavor to keep them that way.

He extended a hand to help her from the platform and she looked at it like it was covered in the Ebola virus. Dred looked down at his hand again to make sure that it wasn't in any way offensive. No, it wasn't covered in griffin shit, . . . He'd been petting them before her arrival, but he knew he'd washed his hands. There would be no stealing of corporate secrets here; his griffins would rip out the hearts of anyone set on espionage against Shadowins holdings.

"May I, Miss Cherrywood?" It had been really difficult not to call her Miss Cherry-Would-If-She-Could. He knew that the epithet would light her on fire and her eyes would flash and those tasty blouse gnomes would heave and . . . It would be like a sensual storm for his senses, getting her knickers in a knot.

She was flustered again, but she took the hand he offered and stepped down beside him.

"I didn't expect you to meet me yourself," she said as she

smoothed her skirt with one hand. Middy tried to pull the other one back, but he wasn't inclined to let go.

"I can't have you wandering these secret halls, now can I? The griffins might think that you were up to no good."

"No good? I'm not the one who has been accused of unpleasantries," Middy replied calmly.

"Miss Cherrywood, I wouldn't call murdering a whole village for a Hand of Glory an unpleasantry," he said, referring to one of the atrocities he was thought to have committed in pursuit of dark magick. Although, if the truth were known, he was actually in possession of that particular item, though he had not acquired it by murdering anyone. "If that's what you consider unpleasant, I would hate to see what you'd call evil."

She gasped. "Are you admitting it?"

"Of course not. Why? Do you think I did it? Are you afraid to be alone with the wolf in his den?"

"Should I be?"

"Oh, yes, Miss-Cherry-Would-If She-Could. Be very afraid." Fuck it. He couldn't help himself; he wanted to see her face flush and that fire spark in her eyes. Not to mention she deserved it. If she wanted to play hardball, he could play.

It made him almost sick that most of the magickal community believed such horrors about him. He could be a right bastard, to be sure. But if these people really thought that he'd murdered a whole village for one cursed object . . . Yet, they still came groveling because of his money and position. He hadn't thought that Middy was one of those.

It occurred to him that he wanted her to think better of him. Dred had this sudden urge to tell her everything that had happened, how *he'd* been the hero of Shale Creek, not Tristan Belledare. It was true that he'd gone to Shale Creek to get the object, but to destroy it, not to use it. Then, it had gone supernova and taken half the population of Shale Creek with it—it would have taken half of the warlockian world if not for Dred's magick. It had never mattered to him before that anyone knew he was a good warlock, but he wanted Middy to know.

And not just because she'd narrowed her eyes and he thought for a moment he could see curses brewing in their depths. He was surprised and a little intrigued by what she said next.

"Really, I thought we were past all of this juvenile behavior, Mr. Shadowins. Especially since you requested that I come with the pitch from the foundation. Was it just to torment me because you're still the school bully?" She tapped his chest with a folder of papers that held her presentation.

Oh, he was going to torment her further, all right. He was going to do things to her that would make her scream his name like he was the second coming of Merlin. If he had to bedevil her into it, then so be it. Dred was surprised, almost to the point of heart failure, that she hadn't melted right there in the Broom Closet when he'd offered her his hand. Most witches did. Hell, most women fell on their backs like any number of shelled creatures and seemed to get stuck, but not Miss-Cherry-Was-Going-To.

He tried a different tack. "I apologize; I didn't realize it bothered you. I was merely attempting to make you more at ease by bringing up our childhood memories." Dred was surprised that he hadn't choked on that word. He never apologized and if he had to for social reasons, it was always a double-edged jibe. In this case, though, he found that he was actually a little sorry. Or that's what he assumed the heavy feeling in his gut was.

He didn't like it one bit.

She rewarded him with a smile. "Thank you, Mr. Shadowins. Now, if we could just go to your office, I will try not to take up too much more of your time."

"I was actually thinking we could do this over lunch. My schedule is very full today and this is the only time I have between meetings. I made reservations at a lovely little winery." Most women loved the winery. He preferred a good, solid beer himself, but whatever.

She looked torn and unsure of herself. "I don't think that's a good idea."

"You have to eat, right? I know I do. I thought we were past juvenile behaviors, Miss Cherrywood." He'd had to bite down to keep the other name from coming out of his mouth. He loved to say it and he loved the look on her face and the way her eyes flashed with fire. . . . "We're two adults having a business lunch." When she still looked unsure, he whipped out the big guns. "Think of the children."

She sighed and agreed. Dred had to wonder how long that little line was going to work. He knew he needed to play with it until he broke it. Hopefully, he'd have her screaming in tongues beneath him by then.

CHAPTER THREE
Lunching and Midnight

As soon as the words were out of her mouth, Middy regretted them. He pulled her flush against the hard expanse of his body and secured his forearm just beneath her breasts. The heat of his arm burned her and she wanted to get away from him, but she wanted to get closer, too. She wanted to rub herself against him and make him ache the same way she ached. Middy was hyperaware of his breath on her neck, the way she could feel his every touch, every casual brush of skin to skin, and how her body fit into his in just that perfect way that said they were meant to fuck.

She almost tittered aloud. It made her giggle to refer to it that way. Middy still wondered how people could do all of those things to each other and still look one another in the face in the morning. She'd heard some wild stories from her friends that had to do with the chocolate starfish and someone's tongue. It disgusted her and intrigued her at the same time.

After thinking all of those dirty things about Dred Shadowins, she had a tough time looking him in the face. Those were just dirty little fantasies, she reminded herself.

He smelled so good, just like sandalwood, patchouli, and something else that she couldn't name. She wondered if he was having the same kind of reaction to her. Scratch that with a brick—she *wanted* him to be having the same kind of reaction. *Needed* would have been a better word still, but she wasn't quite ready to admit that where even her own brain could hear it.

On the plus side, she had recourse that he didn't. She could go home and play with Centerfold Dred to her heart's desire. Or, more accurately, her clit's desire. Her heart certainly had nothing to do with it.

Teleporting usually made her nauseous and she was glad that it wasn't a power she'd been gifted with. For one horrible moment on the way to the winery, she thought she was going to spew all over Dred. It would serve him right, of course, but it would be her very own brand of chunky humiliation. It actually wasn't so bad—the teleporting, not the spewing—when she had that hot, hard body behind her.

She felt so small and safe. Probably because he was a scary, enormous Viking-looking bastard with those shoulders and that jaw. . . . He had snowflakes in his eyes. Or maybe it was steel? He was the thing that went bump in the night. The monsters under the bed were worried about coming home from a long day at work and finding *him* under their own beds.

It wouldn't be so horrible if she found him under hers.

Okay, that was it. The final straw. The next time she had an impure thought about Dred Shadowins while in his presence, she was going to go home and light both of those issues of *Weekly Warlock* on fire. So help her, Circe!

His fingers splayed across her stomach and she felt lightning through her veins that ended between her thighs. Middy was so hot for him, she was sure that her hair was going to burst into flames.

She was so acutely aware of his every breath, she didn't even notice how they got into the winery, whom they spoke with, or even how they'd been seated. He was looking at her now like he expected some sort of answer.

Middy was still lost in the rapture that had been his hand

on her body. She was suddenly afraid. If just that simple contact had done that to her, what would a full-on encounter achieve? Could one die from an orgasm?

She supposed it had to be possible. What brought her back down to earth was the knowledge that if he succeeded in murdering her by orgasm, there would be no containing his ego, and women would line up around the world twice for that kind of death.

No, no. She couldn't have that. After all, he was still a dark warlock and evil right down to his perfectly manicured toenails. She'd read that in the magazine, too. He liked pedicures. How metrosexual and un-Alpha was that? Yeah, she just had to keep her brain on that train of thought.

He smiled at her and she fell out through the baggage car and the train left without her. He was angelically handsome when he smiled. The warmth crept up into his eyes, melting the arctic tundra there and making him almost human.

He was talking to her, but she still had no idea what he'd said. It was completely unacceptable for her to have this reaction to him. That was it, the magazine had to go. No more jilling-off to real people. Then situations such as these could be avoided.

"So, you were saying, Miss Cherrywood?"

"Middy, please." Every time he said "Cherrywood" she kept expecting to hear the last part of that thrice-damned taunt.

"Middy? That's rather old womanish of you." He took a sip of wine.

"Oh?" She took umbrage. Middy liked her name. "Dred is any better? You sound like some emo goth hanging out at Hot Topic to pick up a suitable princess of the night to share your darkness, or some other tripe."

Of course, she wasn't going to tell him that the shoes she was wearing had come from Hot Topic. Nope, or the fairy pen she had in her purse. Of course, the magickal model could hold a real fairy. She didn't keep hers stocked; it seemed wrong to keep them there just to light up her pen when they had the stars to look after.

"You've got me there." He smirked at her again, the corner of his mouth curling up. "Though I have to say, I like it better than Mordred."

"Mordred does have that dark warlock ring to it."

"It's a family name. My mother says she can trace our family's roots back to Arthur through Mordred and LeFey. If you prefer it to Dred, then you may use it."

"Now you've got me," she said smiling.

"Do I?" he asked casually, but his eyes were like hot coals as they burned into her.

"I was just going to say that I like Dred better."

"Is Middy a nickname?"

"For Midnight."

"Now who's hanging out at Hot Topic?" Dred smirked again.

Middy swore his face was going to freeze like that if he kept doing it. Not that it would be awful because it wasn't like he was slack jawed and algae toothed or anything. It was that devastating smirk.

Couldn't the man have had a bad hair day in all of his life? He'd probably had grooming charms since birth. All of the highborns did. Hell, this one might have had it in the womb given how beautiful and forever perfect his mother, Aradia Shadowins, was rumored to be.

She'd never seen the witch up close, so Middy couldn't say with any certainty. Looking at the fine specimen of the son, she had to imagine the mother was beautiful. Aradia contributed money to various charities herself, but didn't attend social gatherings much since the Gargoyle War.

"I love their music selection."

Dred Shadowins had just admitted that he did, in fact, shop at Hot Topic. She'd dated one warlock who'd teased her mercilessly about it. It was mortal alternative culture couture, something most of the highborns frowned upon. Not to mention that she was years older than most of the other shoppers. That's what was embarrassing. Dred's admission could be a trap to get her to admit something else about herself that he could use to taunt her.

"Shall we get on with it?" Middy knew the sooner she was done with this, the sooner she could get away from him.

He was looking at her as if he knew what she looked like naked and was pleased with what he saw. She'd dreamed of this, but she'd never thought it would actually happen. She wasn't sure that she wanted it to happen. Some things were better as a fantasy. There had to be more to his interest than his suddenly waking up and deciding he had to have a piece of Miss Midnight Cherrywood.

Even if there wasn't, which there had to be, she didn't see herself falling into bed with Dred Shadowins. Middy was smarter than that. Plus, she didn't even like him. It was important to like the person that you let into the holiest of holies, wasn't it?

She pulled out her folders and packets of information about the foundation and the work it did. Middy was sure that he already had the research, as he'd donated before, but since this was a much more sizable amount, he would have gone digging with a fine-toothed comb.

"I'm going to be blunt. We need the Gargoyle Masque. If it doesn't happen, many of our projects are going to fall through. Lots of needy children won't get clean drinking water, food, or a chance to go to school. We haven't even begun to talk about sending these kids to Academy. This is just a mortal education, simple things that we take for granted, but that could change circumstances for these kids in a dramatic way." Middy pushed the figures over to him.

"What about health care?"

"We have a witch and warlock team who go to these places and offer mortal and magickal treatments to the populace on a monthly basis, but it's not enough."

"What about the gargoyle population?"

"I'm not going to lie. We offer care and treatment to all magickal folk. We also offer integration classes and other services to help promote acceptance on both sides. I hope that's not a problem for you."

"No, it's not a problem, Midnight." He flipped through the papers she'd given him. "You've got your cost estimate planned down to the very cent."

"I'm thorough and efficient. Full disclosure of how your donation will be used is part of my charm," she said with a smile.

Stop flirting. Right now.

"It certainly is. Tell you what. I'll double my donation if you go as my date to the Masque."

Middy choked on the apple-cranberry spinach salad she'd ordered. Time seemed to stop as did that devil-spawned cranberry that had been between her molars, but was now somewhere between her throat and her tongue.

She inhaled deeply, but that didn't help. It seemed to make that satanic berry quadruple in size and she hawked like a lumberjack with too much chew, trying to dislodge the thing. It was to no avail. She knew the other patrons were looking at her, but she couldn't breathe. Dred was going to be no help because he was watching her quizzically as if she were a new sort of bug under glass. Middy hawked again with such force that it sent the berry on an ill-fated path, bypassing her mouth and up into her nose just as she was managing a particularly forceful exhale.

That cranberry shot out of her right nostril like a bullet from an M-16. It hurt like, well, shooting a cranberry out of your nose. Too bad that wasn't the end of it. The cranbullet shot straight at Dred's wineglass. With the amount of

force behind it, Middy watched in slow motion as it connected with the delicate glass. She was expecting the glass
to shatter and stain the tablecloth. Embarrassing, yes. But
not the sort of mortification that would make you pray for
an asteroid the size of Los Angeles to end it all so no one
else would ever know about this particular misadventure.

No. The glass didn't break; the cran-bullet bounced from
its clear and delicate surface like a rubber ball and was cat-
apulted right into Dred's eye. She saw his eyes widen as it
sped toward impact, almost as if he were giving it a better
target.

Middy watched in horror as he leaned back, as if he
could escape his impending doom. He'd leaned so far back
that his chair was perched in a precarious position at the
moment of impact. He flipped the chair over backwards
and landed with his hand over his eye and his ass in the air.
His chair dropped into a sort of makeshift shelter over his
head. Ironic, given it was after the fact.

Middy didn't know whether to laugh or cry. She was
frozen to her chair as waiters and management came running to the rescue.

She didn't mind all the commotion though; as long as
they were fussing over him, they were ignoring her. Too
bad Dred had teleported them to the winery. If she'd had
her broom, she could have made a very quick escape and
never, ever had to look him in his good eye again.

Because Middy was sure, he would only have one good
one left. The bastard would probably wear an eye patch and
get even more ass because he looked even more dangerous.

Dred had regained his seat and was now perched across
from her with only one, steel-gray eye open, appraising her.
Middy was sure that if her cheeks got any redder, she'd look
like a Red Hot.

"You were saying?" Dred said casually.

All Middy could do was shake her head. She couldn't pry

her mouth open with a crowbar. Not that it mattered in any event. No sound would be issuing forth.

"Miss Cherrywood, I asked you a question. Please do me the courtesy of answering."

He still wanted to go with her to the Masque? What perversity was this? She wanted to ask why, but the look on his one-eyed face was enough to strangle that question in its infancy.

She pried her mouth open and was surprised that it didn't make a sound like a rusty hinge. Middy told her voice to say no. She demanded it, but her vocal cords were ever rebellious organs. No sound came out, but she realized that she was flopping her head around in the affirmative.

"I'm glad that's settled. Now, if you please, could you get your meal to go?"

He was so polite, it was making the situation worse. She felt a little titter tickle the back of her throat. It was a giggle. He was so correct, so proper, and he still had one eye closed. It was swelling now, which she felt bad about, but she could see it growing like a tumor as she stared at it, daring her to laugh.

"Miss Cherrywood, if you laugh right at this moment, there will be certain hell to pay."

That made the tickle grow to more of an itch and she tittered out loud this time, but with her teeth biting down on her bottom lip.

"I am allergic to cranberries."

She snorted again, choking on her cough, and damn the man if he didn't duck. Middy didn't even see him fly around the table and she didn't even realize that he'd dragged her from the dining room and out through the front door, it all happened so fast. She did realize when his arm was around her again and she was plastered to his body.

Middy prayed to anyone that was listening that she didn't hurl on this trip either. Again, being next to him was so nice, but she'd already shot an allergen right into his eye. She didn't quite wish she was dead yet, but that was all it would take.

Then she realized she'd just challenged the universe. The path of her thoughts was just the same as muttering aloud that it couldn't get any worse. It could *always* get worse. She made bargains and pleaded, she promised never to jill-off to Dred again, even though she knew it was a lie, if she could just make it through the teleportation without spewing apple-cranberry-spinach horror all over his Cavallies. Her stomach settled and she prayed the universe wouldn't hold her to her promise.

They appeared in the Broom Closet and he did not offer his hand this time to help her mount her broom. She wasn't sure what to say.

"Thank you for lunch and your donation," Middy said weakly.

"I'd like to say my pleasure, but I won't. I will see you at six o'clock on October thirteenth."

Middy let out the breath she'd been holding when she'd departed, but found that she didn't want to laugh anymore. She had a date with Dred Shadowins. A casual lunch had resulted in a disaster that could live on in infamy with its own name, like a war movie with John Wayne. What did the Masque have in store?

Nothing good, of that she was certain. Especially when she got home and found her housemate, Drusilla "Tally" Tallow, waiting for her.

"Martin told me that you were having a pitch session with Mordred Shadowins. Quite frankly, I'm surprised you're back this early." Tally eyed her with disapproval. "And looking so fresh and uncorrupted."

"Oh, it's Martin now, is it?" Middy teased as she kicked off her heels and they marched themselves back to her closet.

"You have to cast that spell on my shoes. They just won't obey me." Tally sighed. "And yes, it's Martin. I rather like him."

"Do you?" Middy asked, a warm happiness suffusing her. Tally had been lonely and unhappy for a long time. "Last I knew, you were still calling him Chancellor Vargill. Spill. I need details."

"Well, you knew he flew me home after that Beltane charity thing." Tally bit her lip, as if there was something else she wanted to say and for a moment, Middy thought she saw a shadow in her eyes, but it was gone as quickly as it had come. Midnight chalked it up to everything Tally had been through with her shitty taste in warlocks. They used to joke that she could bring out the zero in any hero.

"You said nothing happened." Midnight raised a brow in faux disapproval.

"It didn't. Not that night. He asked me out to dinner and it went from there." Tally smiled. "I didn't tell you because he thought it would be akward if you knew. But I can't help myself, Middy. I really like him."

"I'm happy for you." She smiled.

"And he gives the best—"

"I really don't need *those* details, Tally. I need to be able to look him in the face," Middy interrupted with a blush.

"No, you don't, do you? Not unless you're planning on stealing him away from me." Tally eyed her again.

"Goddess, no!"

"Just checking. I know he's incredibly reserved and not just a little bookish, but he's so kind." Tally got a dreamy look on her pixie features.

"I know you need someone to be good to you after that crap cauldron of an ex-boyfriend, Tristan Belledare. War hero, my ass," Middy said. "A man who says 'I love you' just to get in your pants certainly wouldn't sacrifice anything to save someone else."

"So, dish, girly! You're not getting out of it by changing the subject to my ill-fated hookups."

"I might have to kill myself."

"Why? What did he do?" Tally sat up straight and started looking for her book of hexes on the coffee table. She found the proof of the latest copy of her magazine, *Witches Waxing Wicked.*

Tally could craft amazingly diabolical hexes. In fact, she had a disclaimer on every issue that stated her hexes were just novelty items and for entertainment only since she'd been sued four times in the first year of her magazine's publication.

"No, he didn't do anything. Except call me Cherry-Would-If-She-Could." Middy rolled her eyes.

"Maybe Cherry should." Tally raised her eyebrows and then, at Middy's scowl, said, "Come on! It's Dred Shadowins. Are you seriously going to tell me that you haven't thought about just throwing yourself on his wand in wild abandon? What witch hasn't?"

"Exactly. What witch hasn't?" She looked at her friend pointedly.

"You. That's who. And me." Tally sighed.

"I was kind enough to bring up his reputation," Middy offered.

Tally gasped. "What did he say?"

"Not so much. I mentioned unpleasantries and he said if I thought murdering a whole village for a Hand of Glory was 'unpleasant,' he'd hate to see what I thought was evil."

"Don't stop there. Then what?"

"Um, he asked me to the Masque," Middy said quietly, dreading what was coming next.

"So, he's going to donate the funds? Have you called Martin? He'll be thrilled! He was so worried you'd . . . Oh, my Goddess! Wait, why are you making that face? What did you do?"

Middy shrugged and turned her mouth into awkward little moue as she struggled with the words. Tally grabbed her shoulders and shook her, as if the action would rattle the words out of her friend's mouth.

"I tried to assassinate him with a cranberry."

"How did you do that?" Tally squealed at a decibel that made dogs everywhere cringe.

"I choked on it."

"I still don't understand." Tally's hands moved to her hips.

"It flew out of my nose and hit him in the eye over lunch."

"Shitballs."

"Exactly. And he still wants me to go to the Masque with him."

Tally was screaming now and still shaking Middy like a maraca. "You are getting laid like tile, baby!"

"Hold on, I said yes because he offered to double his donation. I'm not sleeping with him. That would be too much like hookery."

"Oh, yes, you are! But I bet there won't be any sleeping." Tally smirked. "He's just what you need. It will be a great experience. You're going to lose your virginity to a sex god. Not only that, but you won't have all of those uncomfortable attachments. You know what the deal is going in and given that you don't even like him, hell, it couldn't be more perfect."

"No! Absolutely not."

"Well, Middy. What else are you going to do with it?"

"Fall in love maybe?"

"You've been reading too much again. Fall in love later after you've gotten this complication out of the way."

"Maybe."

"No, there is no 'maybe.' You're going to ride him like a mechanical bull. He uses witches as nothing more than a means to an end. Why not give him a dose of his own medicine for all of womankind? It's just a stupid bit of flesh anyway and it's in the way."

Middy had to say that her friend's argument did make sense. She wouldn't have to worry about looking Dred in the face again after the Masque. Maybe this was the answer she was looking for? She knew better than to fall in love and, like Tally said, she didn't even like him anyway. Of course, there was the fact that she'd had his likeness dancing like a Chippendale in her bedroom in the dark of the night.

Even better, maybe she'd get over this obsession with him. She could just work it right out of her system. Her pride wouldn't let her keep thinking about someone who'd put his proverbial sword in her sheath and never call again, and she knew he wouldn't if things progressed that far.

What a hell of a way to decide to lose it.

She wasn't sure if she meant her mind or her cherry.

CHAPTER FOUR
Cranberry Crush

Having a cranberry pried from his ocular orifice was not exactly how Dred Shadowins had envisioned the rest of his day after lunch with Midnight Cherrywood. It had plenty to do with orifices, but not so much this one and certainly not his own.

Unless she was really into that kind of thing? Then maybe there could be negotiations of a certain— He wasn't going to think about that now.

Explaining to Magick Medic staff how he'd gotten the damn cranberry stuck in his eye to start with hadn't been easy. Neither had it been easy to summon a look intimidating enough to quell their snorts of laughter with one freaking eye.

He'd done it though and they'd gone about their work silently. Of course, he was sure that he'd be the topic of discussion over dinner for many weeks to come. It wasn't anything new that he'd be the topic of discussion, but it was usually about how rich or handsome he was. Not how this idiot had strolled into Urgent Care with a cranberry sticking out of his eye. Especially when the debutante witches all seemed to titter on about his "penetrating gaze" or "piercing eyes. Not so engaging as a cyclops, he was sure.

It had taken a very expensive potion, three charms, and a cleric's prayer to get the swelling to go down and he'd have to wear an eye patch for a week. If he'd been a mortal with that kind of super allergy, his throat would have promptly closed and he would have been dead.

Damned cranberries!

At this point, it was impossible not to notice that disaster followed Middy Cherrywood wherever she went. She was a right little mess, that one. Yet, Dred was intrigued. She'd not acted like the other skirts he'd hunted. Again, he had to suppose it was good that she was going to be a challenge because after he was done with her, he'd have to start over. He'd shagged every witch known to the magickal world. Or so the tabloids said.

Which brought him back to Midnight Cherrywood—a witch who needed a good pounding if there ever was one. Dred decided that he was just the warlock to give it to her.

His Witchberry started buzzing and he looked at the screen for a moment. It was High Chancellor Godrickle.

Fuck.

"Shadowins." Hubert Godrickle's face appeared pinched and pale on the screen.

"What's happened?" Dred knew that the High Chancellor wouldn't be calling him unless something serious had happened. They avoided each other like the plague, but for the appearances at social functions that were expected.

They didn't want to give away Dred's secret.

Dred Shadowins wasn't just a billionaire playboy. He was a war hero, the kind that no one ever hears about. Not like that pompous cock, Tristan Belledare, who'd convinced the Magickal Senate that he'd saved the world from certain doom, et cetera and so forth. Dred moved in shadows and mystery; he was a secret operative, a spy. Not for the Magickal Senate either, but for his people, specifically for High Chancellor Godrickle.

Witches and warlocks, gargoyles, fairies, dragons, and other magickal kin had their own governments, whose leaders met monthly in the Magickal Senate, which was much like the days of Rome and just as corrupt. Right now, from the look on Godrickle's face, Rome was burning.

"You look like someone shat in your Eye of Newt." Dred raised a brow, uncertain if he even wanted to hear about this latest installment of fuckery.

"The Gargoyle Council did. Twice," Hubert said. "What do you know about cursed or dark objects?"

Dred shrugged in response. What didn't he know? Cursed and dark objects were items crafted in pain and suffering that often led to more of the same. They could be used to channel immense power—though that power often came with a blood price—sometimes even a life price. He'd trafficked in them briefly as a young warlock, when he'd still had his head up his own ass. Nothing too serious had crossed his palm, and for that, he was thankful. The junky rush of power that came along with the cursed and dark objects was too much to resist and many a witch and warlock had met horrible fates.

"Someone is moving some major merchandise through the U.S. and we're not sure how they are getting it in or out."

"We knew that, Hubert. Why do the gargoyles care?"

"Their national museum was plundered and, if that's not the worst of it, they're sure that whoever did this is trying to resurrect a lamia." Hubert inhaled a shaky breath. "They're using hatchling gargoyles as sacrifices."

Dred almost dropped his Witchberry. "A lamia? What evidence did they find that would point anything so foul? Hatchlings? I know that their breeding numbers have been down since the war, but how is that automatically linked to dark magick or a cursed item? I suppose they are blaming us because of the war." The Gargoyle War had been over for five years, but that wasn't long enough for either side to forgive or forget the atrocities they'd committed against each other, all in the name of amassing more magick.

If someone actually managed to raise a lamia in the filthy flesh . . . He shuddered to think of it. Those bitches were nasty. They had the torsos of women, the sex organs of women, but with the lower body of a bird, and teeth more like an alligator's than a human's. They lived off the meat of the innocent.

"I've met with Moonfire Glee this morning. She's says that they're not accusing us, but would like our help. Moonfire thinks that there is someone else to blame who is trying to implicate the warlocks. A broken wand was found at the museum break-in."

"We don't even use wands anymore, for the most part. It's like putting bunny ears on your spelltop for better Internet reception."

"Dred, there was something else."

Dred knew from his tone that this was definitely something he didn't want to hear. He'd seen some atrocities in the war and he'd even done things that he wasn't proud of: killing, maiming, sometimes even torturing prisoners for information, but they were things that had to be done.

"Just get on with it. All of this dramatic buildup does nothing for my attitude."

"Or your complexion," Hubert attempted a joke.

"Now you're joking? This must be like deep-sea shit diving if you're trying to be funny."

"I'll just send you the file."

"Well, what do you want me to do about it, after I see this great horror?" Dred felt something akin to trepidation coiling like a snake in his belly, even though he spoke casually.

"You need to find out who is doing this and stop them. Before anything happens to more hatchlings, or this bastard succeeds and manages to raise a lamia. I know you run in certain circles, but you're going to need to expand your horizons to the calmer set. This guy isn't going to do anything that's going to draw attention to himself. He's going to be living in the suburbs with a yard and a dog. He's going to be married and they will be well-to-do. Your normal playboy broom-set party folk are not going to cut it."

"Okay, not a problem."

"You say that now."

"What the hell is that supposed to mean?" Dred furrowed his brow.

"Dred, you need to become a part of that group. Intrinsically. You can't just show up and blasé your way through this like you do everything else. They are naturally wary of those that aren't their kind."

"Their kind? Are they another breed of warlock I've yet to hear about?"

"Yes. Actually, I think they are," Godrickle said thoughtfully.

"What kind is that?" Dred said, unimpressed.

"Married."

If Dred had been imbibing, he would have shot it out of his nose like Middy Cherrywood's cranberry. "Look, I'll do a lot for my people, but marriage?"

"You're escorting Middy Cherrywood to the Gargoyle Masque, aren't you? She would be the perfect witch for your cover. Innocent. Sweet. You don't have to marry her. Just get engaged. Do the rounds of parties and social functions that will be required when a warlock of your station gets engaged. Present it before the Chancellors' Council. It will be approved. It will allow you to move in circles that you didn't even know you wanted to move in."

"That's for damn sure."

"We believe that a member of the Witches' Auxiliary and of the Warlocks' Club are involved. It could be a spousal team. Only married folk are allowed to join. Look at the file. Then tell me you're not going to do it," Hubert said with a sigh.

"I didn't say I wouldn't do it. I'm just not happy about it."

"Just look at the file, Dred. Look at the file." Hubert's image went dark.

Dred's Witchberry beeped to notify him of the file he'd received. His stomach turned and he took a breath to steady himself before he opened the file.

What he saw was indeed horrible. The file was full of pictures that were nothing but carnage. Dred Shadowins had seen death; he'd dealt her cold kiss and even felt it himself upon his cheek in the bleak hours before dawn. He'd never seen anything like this.

There had to be hundreds of gargoyle hatchlings, all broken and bloody. Dead before they'd had a chance to experience the world. Some lay entwined with one another, trying to protect the smaller ones. Wings and limbs had been torn off, presumable to feed the lamia. Or an army of them.

Dred couldn't look at those little faces frozen in horror, the wide innocence of those dark eyes forever open. . . . He could feel his stomach revolt and he managed to make it to the bathroom before he threw up. Those images burned themselves into his brain; he kept closing his eyes, but they were still there. He'd seen horrors in the war, yes. But never anything like this.

Dred knew that he was going to do as Godrickle had asked. He knew that he'd do anything to keep such an atrocity from ever happening again. All of those hatchlings were babies, they were someone's children.

During the war, they'd been told that gargoyles didn't have the same emotions as warlocks and witches. They were told that because gargoyles hatched their young, they were cold-blooded in every sense of the word. Dred knew otherwise; he'd seen mothers and fathers weeping over fallen warriors, he'd seen . . .

He felt his stomach twist again and he closed his eyes and

leaned his head back against the cool, marble tiles. Dred knew he would have to move on this and fast. He also knew Godrickle was right. Middy was just the right witch to help in this little charade. She'd do it for the children. Midnight Cherrywood had a heart. Something he wasn't so sure that any of the other witches of his acquaintance knew anything about.

This also meant he wasn't going to allow himself to break it. If she agreed to this, he'd do her the favor of not fucking her blue. He felt an acute sense of loss that he was sure was just disappointment. He'd talk to her at the Masque.

He sighed. His choices of costume had narrowed considerably with this recent cranberry incident. Dred had been having trouble choosing what to go as. Both costumes included breeches and Hessians, but only one included an eye patch.

Dred knew both looked good on him, as did everything. What would look really good on him was Midnight Cherrywood riding him like a broom. Of course, his brain wasn't supposed to be going down that particular path anymore, but it refused to listen to him.

He felt like every kind of a bastard for thinking about his own pleasure after having just looked at those images. Not just his own, but Middy Cherrywood's. Middy with her head thrown back, her lips glistening from their kisses, and her mouth open, begging him for more while straddling . . .

Bastard!

It didn't matter anyway. She was going to agree to this and he wouldn't use her after that. Dred had a code that he lived by. It wasn't so much society's morals, but his own. There were rules and he'd learned the hard way that to break them was a one-way ticket to self-destruction.

CHAPTER FIVE

The Gargoyle Masque

"What part of *I'll wear this when you shit four blue kittens* was unclear, Drusilla Tallow?" Middy screeched as she discovered that all of the clothes in her closet were gone, her drawers had been stripped as naked as she was, and all that was left for her to wear was the pleather catsuit, hooker boots, and the black-framed glasses of The Baroness costume from the *G.I. Joe* movie.

"Middy, you're wearing that costume and that's final," Tally said with determination.

"I am not!" Middy honked like a goose that had sat on a rake. "No one will even know who I am supposed to be."

"Warlock and mortal alike have all had a hard-on for The Baroness for almost thirty years. I promise they will all know who you are. Warlocks do go to the movies, you know."

"I can't show my face in this, Tally. I'm serious."

"Honey, I hate to break it to you, but no one, and I mean no one, is going to be looking at your face."

"They'll see my panty line."

"Not if you don't wear any."

"Tally! If I don't wear any it will . . . It will . . ." she tried.

"I'm on the other side of the door and you can't say it?"

"The flora and fauna of my nether bits will not take kindly to direct contact with material like this."

"Flora and . . . Oh! Will it be like pulling apart a grilled cheese?" Tally smirked.

"You are so crude."

"Yeah, and I bet you're still blushing. Come on! Live a little. You're just going to be at this thing for a few hours and then you can change into something comfy. I bet the donations will go up," Tally added.

"Fine." Middy wouldn't admit that she'd wanted to be talked into it. It would serve Dred right for demanding that she be his date to the fund-raiser. Though, perhaps the cranberry in the eye had been punishment enough.

Maybe. She couldn't help feeling that insisting on her company was some sort of perversity to appease his boredom. If so, he deserved everything she could dish out. Especially showing up in a supernaturally tight costume where all of her attributes were readily visible, as well as her flaws.

She'd been told that her hips were too wide, her breasts too lush, and her ass too big. Tally didn't seem to think so; the rail-skinny witch had told her on countless occasions that she was endlessly jealous of her ass. She said that in certain mortal circles, she had what was called "ghetto booty." Now, Middy had seen a few music videos and she thought that ghetto booty was kind of hot. Why was mortal society obsessed with models who could turn sideways and disappear? They didn't look like women. They looked like cabin boys who'd been made to dress like girls and starved to show their ribs. Apparently, that was the standard of beauty.

Middy didn't get it, but she didn't really care too much. If she were a warlock, not that she wanted to be, but if she were, she would want a witch that looked like a witch, not another warlock. After all, these were enlightened times. If a warlock wanted another warlock, why not have one instead of a witch that looked like one?

She wasn't quite sure that it was okay to display her assets so obviously in polite society though. This was a fund-raiser not a strip joint. Though, she knew of a few witches who went to these things husband hunting and everything they had to offer was splayed out like a selection in a candy store. Of course, there was nothing sweet about them. They were all back-biting bitches who'd take your head off with their claws as soon as say anything genuine.

Middy didn't want to be mistaken for one of those.

"Sweet Merlin with a ball gag! What is taking you so long? You're not getting out of this."

"You try charming pleather to smooth up your thighs and see how far you get," Middy snapped as she shimmied and contorted, trying to urge the costume up over her body.

Suddenly, she was dressed and feeling much like she imagined a wench at a Renaissance fair. Middy didn't know how these women did it. She didn't think that her rack was supposed to be up that high. She could use if for a shelf, set her drink on it, and her Witchberry. Maybe even one of those monstrous (tasty) turkey legs.

"Is that better? I was always better at fashion charms than you. Now open the door. I need to see your hair to charm it appropriately."

"I'm thinking that will be more like a hex," Middy muttered as she opened the door.

"Hell, Mids. You look good."

"You say that like it's a surprise." Middy frowned.

"No, I knew it would look great on you. It's just you're really beautiful. Now, hold still."

Tally began the incantation that forced Middy's hair into smooth, silky lines and added just a bit of length to make it fall to her hips, and she perched the glasses on the end of Middy's nose.

"You want a mirror?" Tally asked.

"No. It will be easier if I just don't think about what I'm wearing." Middy wasn't sure how she could forget, not with that slick material rubbing right on her clit. Tonight was going to be torture. "I really don't want to wear this, Tally."

"If you don't wear it, you're just going to be Snow White," Tally growled. "Again. Like you have been every year since Academy." Tally's extreme distaste at the prospect was evident on her face. In fact, it was as obvious as a pile of elephant poop next to a Dodge Dart.

"It looks good on me."

"It's bor-ing." Tally dragged it out like it was two words. "Okay, so theoretically I let you out of this costume— what would you be?"

"A fairy princess."

Tally snorted and sounded like a cat with a particularly vicious hairball. "A fairy *what*?"

"Princess." Middy was resolute. "I want snowflakes in my hair and fairy dust on my cleavage and a pretty, sparkly dress. Oh, and a crown. I want a crown made out of ice."

"And you're going to use this costume to entice Dred Shadowins, how exactly?"

"I'm not! I don't want to!"

"Of course, you do." The hairball was back.

"Okay, I do. Women throw themselves at him all the time though. I am going to be different."

"You already shot a cranberry in his eye. Isn't that different enough for you?"

Middy tried to sit down, but the pleather wouldn't bend. So, it was more of a leaning over and then the rest was gravity. She was stuck on her back with her bosoms up to her chin and legs that wouldn't bend.

"A little help, Tally?"

"Maybe it was a little tight. I had the best intentions."

"Make with the fairy princess right now. Dred is going to be here any minute and I am flat on my back, dressed like a dominatrix from Hell."

"I don't want to." Tally pouted with her arms crossed over her chest.

"You do it or I will hex all of your birth control potions. Every last one," Middy promised.

"You fight dirty."

"How else am I going to hold my own with Dred Shadowins? Now, do it," she demanded.

"Fine, but you're not getting any panties."

"What! Why?" Middy realized that she was out of time as the buzzer rang. "Fine. Just fix it."

Her fairy princess costume made it no easier to be upright; her bosoms were still launched out into space, the space between her chin and where they should have been. If she arched her neck far enough she could almost touch her nose to her breast. They were glittery as she'd asked and she touched her hand to the top of her head and almost cut her finger on the sharp points of her crown.

Middy finally managed to roll herself into an upright position and gain her feet. Tally had given her four-inch heels, which she immediately shrank an inch. They now put her at exactly six feet even. She knew from Dred's centerfold bio that he was four inches taller than that.

Instead of the ball gown she'd wanted, she ended up with what could only be described as a tutu. It wasn't exactly that short, but it was close enough for frog tossing and hex bombs. Middy had to admit that her legs looked really good, especially in those heels with the laces that twined up her calf. What there was of the skirt was white and glittery with a layer of crinoline underneath that was a lovely ice blue.

She supposed it would do, even though she felt very naked without her panties. It was sort of empowering though, a much better feeling than all of that plastic-pleather horror.

The doorbell rang again, a large sound that practically shook the foundations of the old Victorian house. She'd assumed that Tally had gone to answer the door. Apparently not, since he'd felt the urge to ring the bell a second time.

Middy took gingerly steps in her new heels and opened the door. She usually checked through the peephole first and was now heartily sorry that she hadn't. If she'd peeked, she would have been able to take in Dred's costume without gasping like she had the first time a boy had put his tongue in her mouth.

He was wearing breeches. Sweet Morrigan have mercy, breeches! They hugged his strong thighs with extreme prejudice and disappeared down into Hessian boots that she so loved to read about.

It was worse because her perusal of *Weekly Warlock* told her exactly what was under those camel-colored breeches. She immediately wondered what it would feel like to be straddling him in her current, knickerless state with him still wearing those. They were a soft fabric, not cotton, but textured. Middy almost reached out a hand to touch them, but was able to curb that disaster before it happened.

Middy was finally able to tear her gaze from the package and look up. He was dressed like a pirate. His white-blond hair curled just a bit under his ears and out from beneath the red scarf he'd tied around his head. Usually, she would find that incredibly lame, but it just seemed to work for him. Especially the eye patch, which she was sure was not part of the costume.

It gave him an air of danger that was just enough to twist her nipples. They were hard against the silky material of her bodice and she was thankful that it had been reinforced with a touch of padding so it wasn't obvious.

He looked at her like he was the Big Bad Wolf and she was prey. Yes, that's exactly what she felt like, a sacrificial offering. Or a steak.

It was a heady feeling to know that he wanted her. No

matter what was up his sleeve, a warlock didn't eye a witch like that without carnal intent. It didn't matter that he was a bastard extraordinaire as she was so fond of saying. She had talked herself into losing her cherry tonight and she was going to do it. It didn't matter that she didn't like him. She liked his body and he was supposed to be talented in bed, so she wouldn't get caught up in any weird virginal/stalker attachment. Then, she'd be more confident as a lover when she did find someone she cared for. It made sense, sort of.

"You look lovely, Midnight."

"Thank you." She blushed. "I should have expected something dashing from you. Like a pirate."

"It was in the running before the eye patch, but since I already had it on . . ." He shrugged. "Are you ready to go?"

"Just let me get my bag." She held the door open for him to come inside while she tried to think of the spell to make her current bag match her costume.

Tally came out of the bathroom in just a towel and gasped when she saw Dred. "Shame on you, Middy. I didn't know you had company." She let the towel gape just a bit.

"Ah, the infamous Drusilla Tallow. I see you and Middy are still close," Dred said as he pursed his lips.

"Tally, please." She smiled.

"I don't kiss and tell. A man's tally is a private thing and I don't think I know you well enough just yet to talk numbers."

Tally, rather than getting upset, giggled. "*Call me* Tally. It's my name. You are so bad."

"I can't help myself."

Middy glared at Drusilla, wondering just what the hell had gotten into her. Tally had helped her decide that Dred was the one. This was going to happen and now her roommate was wandering around half naked trying to get his attention? That was obviously what she was doing.

Why else would she be flapping around in nothing but a towel?

"I'm ready," Middy offered casually, as if the sight of her best friend trying to undermine her efforts hadn't pissed her off like a prized bull with a bee stinger in its nut sac.

"Are you going to the ball, Tally?"

Oh, if he asked her to come with them, she was going to . . .

"No, no one asked me." She pouted.

Middy almost choked, but it was Tally that was going to get the throat hug in three . . . two . . .

"That's too bad. Perhaps Middy will bring you one of the gift bags." He placed his hand on the small of Middy's back to guide her out the door.

She wasn't sure what to do with that. He'd chosen her over Tally. That was unusual. Or maybe he just wanted her to think that and, later, he'd be sneaking into Tally's room after he left Middy's. And Midnight wondered if Tally would let him. She'd said she was happy with Martin, but she wasn't acting like herself.

Middy didn't know why she'd gotten upset to start with. She didn't even like Dred Shadowins, so what did she care if Tally flaunted her wares in his direction? What concerned her more was her friend's actions and the motivation behind them. She'd always trusted Tally, so she must have had a good reason for acting as she had. Tally had never let her down. She wasn't going to start mistrusting her now.

Dred Shadowins, however, was another matter entirely. Especially when it became apparent that they were going to have to teleport again.

"Dred, I think I already mentioned this, but teleporting does unnatural things to my stomach. I don't want to hurl all over you before the Masque. I feel bad enough about the cranberry."

"Here, let's try it this way." Dred turned her around so that her cheek was pressed against his shoulder and . . . and he smelled like Bay Rum. It was different from how he'd smelled before, but it was a warm and languorous scent that made her think of that feeling in her stomach when she drank warm, buttered rum. She almost felt that sweet warmth spreading throughout her senses every time she breathed him in.

His arms closed around her and anchored her to him. She hooked her hands up over his shoulders and held on for all she was worth. He smelled so good and he was so warm that she gave a happy sigh.

He let go then and his fingers trailed lazy paths up and down her back and finally to the bare skin of her shoulders beneath the cascade of her hair. His touch on her exposed flesh sent erotic shivers tingling through her.

"You better not let go when we teleport," she murmured into his shoulder.

"I didn't, Middy. We're here."

She sprang away from him like a cherry-chocolate pop tart erupting from a toaster with a too-tight spring. "I, um, knew that."

"Didn't that make for an easier trip?"

Middy opened her mouth to answer, but Chancellor Vargill pounced on them.

"Shadowins, so good of you to sponsor this little soiree." His ruddy features colored further, making him look like a shiny Solstice ornament.

"So good of Middy to make it happen." Dred nodded to her.

"Ah, yes, Middy. She's been a jewel to give so much to the foundation. Much of this was done on her own time." Martin Vargill clapped her on the back with the enthusiasm of a rabid soccer fan.

Dred's eyes were immediately drawn to her glitter-dusted

breasts as the motion from Vargill's good-natured backslapping almost rattled them out of their restraints. She looked up and met his stare and if it was possible, his gaze burned hotter. She felt like she was going to burst into flame if he stared any harder.

He didn't even care that he'd been caught! Most warlocks would look away and then try to steal another peek when she wasn't looking. Not Dred Shadowins, he appraised her boldly and with blatant appreciation.

Martin was not oblivious. "I see you young people would like to enjoy your evening. I'll expect you tomorrow to go over donations, Middy."

She was alone with the viper! Well, as alone as one could be at a charity event.

"Dred, you're still staring." She slapped his arm lightly.

"Sweetheart, you wouldn't have doused them with glitter if you didn't want me to look."

He did have her there. She just hadn't expected his looking to be so . . . so intense. She felt naked. "Just because I may have invited a glance doesn't mean you can strip me naked with your eyes."

"When I strip you naked, you'll know it."

Middy blushed furiously. "Didn't I just say with your eyes? I didn't say you'd done it."

"You'd allow it, though?" He pulled her close to him. "Care to dance?"

"I don't know what game you're playing, but I don't want to play."

"Don't you want to hear the rules first?" he asked.

"I didn't think you played by any rules," Middy said, but did let him lead her to the dance floor.

"I play by a very rigid set of rules, though they are my own." His hand slid down to the small of her back and he pressed her more intimately to him.

"So you can change the rules as you play for your benefit?" She smiled up at him, the sweetness on her face a cover for the sharpness of her words.

"How is it you know me so well?" Dred didn't answer her question.

"I read," she quipped before she could think better of it. They moved across the floor. "Oh, really? I've said that in only one interview I've given, but I'm sure a good little witch would not be caught dead with her nose in such a publication."

Her face flamed. She started scanning her brain for everything she'd read about him in *Weekly Warlock*. She didn't remember that particular interview and she'd read them all. No, he couldn't know. Could he?

She was forced to look up into his face as he bent her back for a dip. "I don't read that." It squeaked out of her mouth like a mouse with a brick on its tail.

He pulled her flush against him again so that he could whisper in her ear. "Of course, you don't. *Weekly Warlock* isn't a magazine that a witch such as you would find interesting."

Oh, that bastard! He knew.

He couldn't.

Well, he does now, you sloppy bitch! After all, she'd just admitted as much to him. Sometimes she was amazed that she was allowed to leave the house by herself. Really, she was aghast at her own incompetence.

Dred pulled her out of the dip.

"Exactly. What do I care what kind of conditioner is best for a warlock's hair? I don't bother to condition mine half of the time." She was finding that she did care, very much, since her hand was on the back of his neck and his hair seemed to be curling over her fingers of its own volition. It was like silk, damn him.

Why did such an arrogant ass of a man have to be wrapped in so fine a package? Speaking of packages, wow!

It had been one thing to look at in the magazine, but another matter entirely having it there, in the flesh. Not to mention touching her.

Okay, so it wasn't *really* touching her. There were several layers of fabric between her and it, but damn if she didn't know it was there and, oh, my Circe, *awake*. She was very aware of her own bare state beneath her skirt.

"You don't?" His hand tangled in her curls and seemed to cup the back of her head. "It's so soft and . . ."

She thought for a second that he was going to kiss her. That's how they did it in every novel she'd ever read. He would tangle his hands in her hair, he'd stare at her mouth, and she'd chew her bottom lip and her breasts would be heaving and he'd . . .

Be interrupted by Tristan Belledare. "May I cut in?"

No, no, no! Middy could have growled in frustration. She'd picked her irritating gentleman for the evening and it was Mordred Shadowins, not Tristan Belledare. How dare he ask anyway, after the way he'd treated Tally?

"It's up to the lady." Dred smiled.

Double damn! Why did he have to pick now to be a gentleman? A little voice piped up like a screaming teapot, telling her that he'd been a gentleman all along. He'd still been kind enough to teleport her back to her broom with a cranberry in his eye. That was downright chivalrous.

It just would have been extremely convenient if Dred could have felt the least bit territorial, if only for a moment. She didn't like saying no to something so simple as a dance. It was rude, but she didn't like Belledare.

That hissing voice started talking again and reminded her that she didn't like Shadowins either, but she had made up her mind to have wild, passionate sex with him. So, a dance with someone else she didn't like couldn't hurt. Could it?

"Come on, Mids. Are you still mad at me for this thing with Tally?"

She was still very mad at him for the "thing with Tally." He'd not only broken her heart, he'd broken Tally's trust in people in general. Middy turned her face into Dred's shirt.

"Reporters from *Magickal Mayhem* are watching. Unless you want your face splashed all over tomorrow's paper as the witch that was too good to dance with the local hero, I suggest you do it," Dred whispered in her ear.

Middy found herself being pulled into Tristan's arms. He was just as warm as Dred and smelled almost as good, but it wasn't the same. There were no cracked-out butterflies slam dancing in her stomach when he touched her.

"Smile," Tristan said before he turned them to face the photographer.

She was too startled to refuse and found what seemed to be a hundred lights flashing in her face. Middy was sure she was going to look like she'd been chewing on tinfoil, from the pained smile she'd plastered to her face.

Great. Now she was going to get hate mail from screaming fan girls who all thought that Tristan Belledare was some kind of saint. Then there was Tally, but she expected to be there to explain the situation to her friend when the paper arrived. It had taken Tally a long time to deal with what Tristan had done to her. Middy wasn't sure if Tally had ever really gotten over him. Now, this was going to be shoved in her face. It would look like the worst kind of betrayal. Tally had been so in love with him and she'd thought Tristan loved her, too. He'd said he did. Then she'd caught him with another witch and when poor Tally had asked him if he'd ever really loved her, he'd said no. It had shattered her friend's heart into a million little pieces.

"Thanks, Tristan. Now, even Tally is going to hate me tomorrow. What do you want?"

"To warn you," he said, still smiling for the reporters. "Keep smiling, Mids."

"My face already hurts from smiling, you witchinizing bastard. Spill." She'd hear him out because he'd been friends with her older brothers when she'd been a witchling, but that was all he was getting from her.

"Dred Shadowins is evil," he whispered in her ear. "It doesn't matter that he gave you the money for the Masque. He has it to spare. Don't let him fool you."

"Fool me into what, Tristan?" She fought the urge to add: "The same way you fooled Tally?" But she didn't want to give the reporters any more ammunition than they already had about Tally's humiliation. It had already been splashed over the headlines enough when it had happened. Middy still remembered the pain in Tally's eyes that it had been front-page news. It made her sick.

"I just don't want to see you get hurt." The way he touched her changed, his fingers lingering on her cheek, his breath was still soft against her ear. It was more intimate. A caress and Middy didn't like it. "What about Tally?" She hoped that would be a sharp slap of reality. If she didn't know better, she'd say that Tristan was trying to make her think that he had feelings for her. Tristan was handsome, but even if she'd been interested, he was the bastard who'd betrayed her friend. That wasn't a line Middy would ever cross.

"Don't trust her either. Your life is in danger."

She laughed and it was genuine. "Tristan, are you drunk?"

"Leave with me, leave right now," he pleaded earnestly.

"No. You haven't even told me *how* I'm in danger. I'm not some silly girl who is going to be enamored of your charms and just leave with you because you feed me a romantic line about how you're going to save me. I'd think you'd be more original."

He moved her even closer to him. "Mids, I won't deny I'd love to get you naked. In fact, I'm pretty sure you're not wearing panties and I can't tell you how hot that is, but I'm serious."

Her face flamed. "How would you know if I'm wearing drawers or not?"

"My hand is almost on your ass, love. But that's beside the point. The point is that you are in danger and you're being really contrary about letting me save you."

"You have to keep that hero image fresh, don't you? Do you have reporters waiting outside to catch shots of you spiriting me off into the night away from Dred Shadowins? For my own safety, *of course*." She sneered.

"Middy, he's involved in smuggling cursed objects. The rumors about what happened in Shale Creek are true."

They couldn't be. Dred might be a bastard but . . . But what, exactly? But she didn't want to believe that his hands were capable of such atrocity because she wanted them on her body?

She didn't trust Tristan either. From what she'd seen, he'd never done anything that didn't benefit him somehow. She'd always thought there was more to Shale Creek than what he'd let on. So why was he telling her this? What exactly did he hope to get out of it?

"I don't trust you."

"Don't trust me, fine. Don't trust Shadowins either."

"Who says that I do?"

His hand slipped lower on her hip. "Definitely no panties. Is that for Dred, then? Have you already slept with him?"

This line of questioning was really starting to piss her off. "Tristan"—she smiled sweetly— "I can honestly say that I haven't done any *sleeping* in Dred Shadowins's bed."

It was the truth. Of course, she'd twisted it to sound like a lie.

"Middy, since this may be my last chance to say it, I have to tell you. It's always been you. Even when I was with Tally." He leaned closer to her, and dipped his head to whisper against her lips, "I would be good to you, I'd take care of you . . . ." he trailed off.

By the Morrigan's corset, he was going to kiss her! Not what she'd been hoping for. She tried to turn her head to the side, but there was no avoiding it. He had her locked in an iron grip and it was more of an invasion than a kiss.

He had her locked against him so she couldn't struggle and she was vaguely aware of the furious snapping of camera shutters and the blinding waves of flashes as they all fought to be the first to snap a picture of Tristan Belledare and his witch of the week. Which was definitely not her.

Suddenly, he was unceremoniously plucked from her like a nasty little specimen of lice. Seemingly flicked away with the same disgust.

Dred to the rescue!

Middy would have to ponder that bit of incongruity later. The cameras were still flashing with a sick intensity and caught the entire exchange.

"What the hell, Shadowins?" Tristan said with a smirk.

"I'm afraid I'm going to have to assume the role of the offended party, here." His cold, perfect smile was brutal.

"Are you going to challenge me to a duel or something?" Tristan asked lightly.

"Not quite. I am within my rights to do so under magickal law though," Dred offered with the same casual demeanor, but he pulled Middy close to his body.

"It's not like you're engaged," Tristan snorted.

"Actually," Dred began and the corner of his mouth turned up in a wicked smile. "Midnight just agreed to become my magickally wedded witch."

Middy wasn't sure how she kept her mouth from dangling open like a broken door with one rusted-out hinge, but Tristan wasn't so lucky. She imagined the pictures in tomorrow's paper would be less than flattering.

She didn't know what the hell Dred was playing at, but

she decided for the moment to just go with the flow. She could have slapped him, hexed him, made a big show, but his announcement could benefit her *and the charity* later.

After all, he'd claimed her as his fiancée in public, in front of witnesses, the silly warlock. She'd have him over a barrel when he tried to get out of it and then she could guarantee his support of the Gargoyle Masque for years to come.

Plus, Tally would get a great kick out of Tristan's startled face on the front page of *Magickal Mayhem* tomorrow.

The reporters rushed them in the middle of the dance floor and security had to push them back outside. They were all madly hooked on Dred Shadowins's announcement and the look of total devastation on the hero's face.

CHAPTER SIX
Down and Dirty

"The car's magickally sealed, we can talk inside," Dred whispered in her ear as he pushed her to a waiting limousine.

She wasn't sure if she was thankful or disappointed that they weren't going to teleport again. Middy had liked being pressed up against him and smelling his cologne and . . .

"Are you listening?"

No, not really. Just watching your mouth move, that strong jawline, those sensual lips, and thinking about using you like a gigolo.

"Huh? No, sorry. I was a little distracted."

If she'd been thinking correctly, she would have sat next to him instead of across from him. Why? Because he was the only place that there was to look and she'd been jilling-off to him for so long that she was wet just looking at him. She felt like a Pavlovian dog, setting her girly bits to slobbering when the bell rang. Middy wondered if she was going to soak through her dress and leave a spot on the leather. Or worse, she was going to have to sit with her legs clamped together. If she relaxed her knees, he'd be able to see up to her muffin.

Damn Tally for making her go sans panties. She was going to choke that witch twice when she got home.

"I'm going to tell you something that you can't tell anyone else. I need your witch's word. On your magick."

She didn't think that Dred Shadowins knew anything that was worth her witch's word. He made it sound like he was about to drop a state secret on her or something. There was a weighted intensity about him that hadn't been there before, a seriousness.

"I swear on my magick that I won't tell anyone else." Middy felt the binding of her vow slide through her.

He seemed to relax a little bit. "Obviously, I need you to pose as my fiancée."

"I gathered that much from your oh-so-sudden announcement. You're lucky I didn't hex your balls off for that."

"You weren't enjoying Tristan's slug of a tongue in your mouth anyway. I thought you'd be happy for the save."

"You shoved me in front of the paparazzi like a sacrificial lamb."

"Sorry about that and I'm equally sorry to say that for the run of this charade, that's not going to change." He shrugged.

"A little warning would have been nice."

"Hence our discussion here, in a magickally sealed conveyance instead of teleporting. You were amazingly cool under pressure, by the way," he said as he pulled his eye patch off.

"Thank you, but can we get to the whys and wherefores? And it better be for a good reason, or I'm not doing it."

He took a breath as if to fortify himself. "I'm a spy." Dred watched her carefully and when she didn't respond, he continued. "I need a fiancée to move about through certain social circles to find out who is smuggling dark objects. These warlocks are doing horrible things and if I don't stop them, we could end up at war with the gargoyles again."

"You're planting stink pickles."

"Pardon me?" Dred looked offended.

"Shit. This is shit and you're full of it." Middy rolled her eyes.

"I swear on my magick that I am a spy for High Chancellor Godrickle."

Middy didn't know if she should scoff some more or be very afraid because he was delusional. Dred was obviously insane; there was no other way to explain it. Perhaps from the guilt he felt over Shale Creek?

It was then that another vehicle slammed into the rear of the limo and the force sent Middy hurtling through the space between them and she found herself straddling the deliciously hot and unfortunately insane warlock across from her.

It really couldn't have been more horrible and perfect all at once if she'd planned it. She was mortified because his hand just happened to catch her bare ass. She was surprised she had enough blood left in the upper regions of her body to color her cheeks.

But she didn't think that he was wearing anything underneath those breeches either. He must have liked what he'd found because his cock was hard and if not for that thin material between them, it would have been inside of her.

That would have been just her luck, too, to go flying through the air and land impaled on the most notorious dick in the magickal world—to lose her virginity to a fender-bender.

"All right back there, Sir?" The chauffeur's voice echoed through the speaker, though it did nothing to cut the tension.

"I think we're just fine," he said, his gray eyes now like mercury, liquid with lust.

"It will be a moment while I exchange information with the mortal, Sir."

"We've got everything in hand." Dred splayed his hands wider on the flesh that had been unceremoniously shoved into them to punctuate his meaning.

Middy didn't know what to do.

It felt so naughty to feel her bare skin against his clothes and to know that he was just as hot for her. He shifted and the friction sent a jolt of pleasure through her. She wanted to rock her hips against him and demand he continue.

On the other hand, she wanted to run screaming from the limo because he thought that he was a spy. His elevator clearly stopped a few floors from the top. Right now, all she could think about was what was stopped at the juncture of his thighs.

Of all the things that she would have expected him to do, wrapping his arm around her waist and pulling her tighter against him was last on the list. He didn't taunt her or use her desire like a weapon; he seemed just as driven as she was.

Dred didn't look away from her, didn't close his eyes. He knew exactly what he was doing and watched her face with expectation as he moved against her. She wanted to look away, to bury her face in his shoulder, or even close her eyes, but his gaze held her.

Middy dared to push back and damn if she didn't just want to yell, "Take me now." How did a witch ask a warlock to plow her like a cornfield? Especially if that warlock was crazier than a shithouse rat? She wondered, as she rolled her hips, if this was the conundrum that warlocks faced. There were some crazy witches out there who plucked bristles from brooms and hexed bodily functions. . . .

Anything that felt this good had to be worth it though. She didn't think she wanted to be on top when it happened. She was sexually active only with herself and wasn't sure if that irritating little veil of flesh was still there or not, but she'd heard that losing her virginity could hurt like hell.

She wanted him to kiss her, but he was still intent on her face.

That's when she realized that technically, nothing had happened that they couldn't back away from. He obviously wanted her, but right now all they were dealing with was her naked muffin against his very hard cock.

She was a modern witch; she could make the first intentional move. Flying across a seat from the inertia of a horny Jeep with an eye for a sleek limo's rear end couldn't be construed as the first move. Not really. Middy pushed a stray lock of white-blond hair from his forehead and his grip tightened on her when she traced down his jawline with the pad of her finger.

Dred closed his eyes, but didn't let go of her. "You don't want this," he whispered.

"I'm a witch grown, Dred Shadowins. I know very well what I do and do not want." She rolled her hips to make her point.

"No, not this, not me." His hands spoke a different language from his mouth because they moved to her hips to anchor her to him.

"If you don't want me, Dred, that's one thing."

Middy found herself on her back, and Dred's mouth just a breath away from hers, His hips were between her thighs, his cock still thick with desire.

"I am such a bastard," he said as if he were resigned to it. Then his mouth crashed into hers.

He had no talent for romance, but heat bloomed wherever he touched her. She was on fire. Dred's kiss was devastation; so much more so than the pale imitation of his centerfold. The centerfold catered to her ideas of romance and desire. It tingled centers of her brain that would have been stimulated by the act, but it wasn't the act, it wasn't real.

This was stark reality—she was splayed beneath Dred Shadowins and he wanted her. He wasn't a fantasy; his mouth didn't move over hers with a practiced tenderness, his hands didn't touch her with a devoted reverence. No, this was much more visceral and blatantly animal.

His kiss was brutal, but she met his onslaught with her own demands. Middy arched up into him and wrapped her legs around his waist. Dred slipped his hand between them to touch her slick heat.

Dred's fingers felt so good, so right.

Until they didn't.

She shrieked at the sharp pain and Dred froze.

"Is that what I think it is?" he asked in a jagged whisper.

"Depends on what you think it is."

"Now is not the time for banter. Middy, are you a virgin?"

"Does it matter?"

It was at precisely that moment when Middy realized Dred could fly. That was the only logical explanation for how fast he moved away from her. She didn't think he could have moved faster if she'd been on fire.

Literally, not figuratively. Because figuratively, she was still burning. She could see from the bulge in his breeches that he was, too, but she didn't understand what the problem was.

"Hell, yes, it matters."

"Merlin, Dred. Everyone comes with issues. You're insane and I'm a virgin. Whatever."

"Whatever? How can you be so cavalier about something that important?"

"It's not important. It's in the way. You should be flattered."

"Maybe I would have been if you hadn't just said I was insane."

"I thought all men, warlock and mortal alike were eager to be first and last. Kind of like how cats feel they need to be the first one to mark the litter box."

"Midnight! Your virginity should not be compared to cat litter." He sounded like a scandalized grandmother.

"Why do you care, honestly?"

"Because you're a nice witch, Middy."

"Oh, puke. Is that the 'friend zone'?"

"Look, I really need your help and I can't risk fucking it up with the old stick and move."

Stick and move? What the hell was . . . ? Oh. So, he didn't want to fuck her because he needed her. Middy was sure that his reasoning was backwards somehow.

"Are you a bad lay?" It hopped out of her mouth like a gerbil on an escape mission.

Dred choked on the sparkling water he'd just opened. "Pardon me?"

"Well, why else would it be an issue? You think that if you sleep with me, I won't help you. Logic leads me to believe, based on the criteria, that you're a bad lay. Simple, really."

"I'm just not looking for a relationship."

"You're such a pompous bag, you know that? Why would you assume that I want a relationship? I don't even like you."

His mouth hung open again and he looked a bit like a large-mouthed bass the way his chops were opening and closing in rapid succession.

"But you're a virgin," he managed.

"Which means exactly what? I was thinking I could just get it over with. I assumed it would be good since you're you. I mean, I've heard things." Middy shrugged and gave him a knowing look.

She wasn't sure what had gotten into her, but she found that she enjoyed the startled look on his face more than cheesecake. He was speechless and unsettled. The combination made her smile.

Perhaps the filter that had been installed between her brain and her mouth had been overrated. From now on, she was just going to say whatever she felt like. Middy would have to work on the not blushing part later. She had the cherry for his sundae in more ways than one.

"You know what? You want me to help you by posing as your fiancée? Then you're just going to have to put out."

"And I'm the one you think is crazy? You don't know what you're getting into on either count. I'm the dark warlock, remember?"

"I didn't say I wanted to marry you. I just want all of the perks that I would get if I was really your fiancée. I want your continued support of the Gargoyle Masque until you die, and I want the use of your wand; though Merlin knows the odometer has been turned over at least twice on that thing. I suppose it's like a car really: You don't buy a brand-new car for a brand-new driver. There's bound to be dings."

Yes, Middy had to say that she was feeling very pleased with herself.

"That's it, that's all you want? You'll do this, details unspecified for a ride on my wand, as you so delicately put it, and my support of the Masque until my death? I agree to these terms and do so swear. Do you swear it?"

"I swear it," Middy said with confidence. After all, what's the worst that could happen?

Chapter Seven
The Worst That Could Happen

It was that worst thing that could have happened! Dred Shadowins had found scruples in some bargain bin at the thrift store. He'd actually dropped her at home without even getting out of the limo.

That lout had actually tried to refuse the great and wonderful gift of her virginity. As she'd told Dred, she thought that warlocks were like her cat: They wanted to be the first to mark in a new territory. It didn't matter if they were going to stay there or not.

She should have known better than to make a deal with the devil or Mordred Shadowins. Middy realized after the deal had been sealed and he'd pressed that lukewarm kiss to her cheek that she should have specified *when* she wanted to avail herself of his "passion wand."

Now that she'd actually had his hands on her, she didn't think the centerfold would do. No, nothing but the infuriating warlock in the flesh could satisfy her now.

This nasty little revelation caused her to rethink her plans.

If she was already addicted to his touch from a Seven in Heaven makeout session like a witch still in Academy, what would it be like when she got the whole package? Middy was feeling a little light-headed at the prospect.

Maybe demanding coital bliss from a sex god hadn't been the brightest idea she'd ever had, but Middy was never one to do anything halfway. If she was going to have someone butter her muffin, she wanted it to be a quality product.

Now what to say to Tally when she pounced on her and demanded details? News of her "engagement" was bound to travel fast.

Unicorn balls in a pastry puff! What was she going to tell her mother? *Hi, Mom. I know I didn't tell you I was dating Dred Shadowins, dark warlock and filthy rich sex god, but we're getting married. Yeah. Oh, and . . .* She couldn't even tell her mother that the engagement was a ruse. She'd sworn on her magick.

If Middy hadn't been sure that she would have knocked herself on her ass, she would have palmed her forehead at the very deep pile of unicorn dung that she was standing in.

Never mind her mother! What in the name of Avalon was she going to tell her brothers?

Falcon, Hawk, and Raven were going to curse her fiancé's balls off. They'd be hanging on the Yule tree like faerie bells. Why hadn't she thought of this when she'd been considering the ruse?

She looked at her Witchberry, and her brain was frantically thinking of ways to murder it before her mother could call. The garbage disposal seemed to be the best option. Dred Shadowins's engagement was breaking news. All of the warlockian channels would have coverage and it was only a matter of time before the mortal gossipmongers smelled blood, too.

Middy knew the right thing to do would be to call her family before they saw it on the news. That way, she might be able to save Dred's wand. Otherwise, she'd be getting stiffed at the end of this deal and not in the way she'd bargained for.

She had a flashback to senior year at the Academy. Middy's date had come to pick her up for the winter formal, but they'd never made it to the dance. Her brothers, otherwise known as the Trifecta of Doom, had gotten their claws into him and he hadn't lasted long. He'd run screaming from the house before Middy could make it down the stairs.

She was just going to have to put her foot down.

Where the hell was Tally? Middy had quickly taken inventory of the house and discovered it to be sans her partner in crime. Why wasn't she home? On the one hand, she was thankful that the witch wasn't there to pounce on her, but on the other, she needed her to pounce on her brothers.

Middy was going to have to take charge.

Right now, apparently, because her lovely elvish-carved door splintered in half and melted away as the aforementioned Trifecta filled the space.

In that moment, Middy was struck with the realization that her brothers looked like Simian blowfish. She knew other witches found them handsome, and she supposed they were if they could keep from dragging knuckle and puffing up like gorillas.

The same with that huge vein in each of their foreheads that pulsed with testosterone. Middy thought something was going to burst from them like in a mortal horror flick.

"Midnight Marie, what the fuck?" Raven growled.

He was the youngest of her brothers, though only by ten minutes. But those minutes made all of the difference in the world. Raven was the hothead, as was obvious by the way he careened through the door like a rabid St. Bernard.

She narrowed her eyes at him and put her hand on her hip. "I could ask you the same thing."

"You could, but this isn't about him," Hawk stated, trying to take charge.

"You think? It sure as shit is now. Have you seen my door? No? Oh, that would be because . . ."

"Now, Midnight." Falcon eyed her sternly.

"Now Midnight nothing!" She stomped her foot.

"Are you going to invite us in?" Raven said more softly.

"Would it keep you out if I said no?"

"You'd think that you'd be a little more grateful." Hawk was surly.

"Grateful? For what exactly?" She eyed them all with displeasure. "What if I'd been entertaining?"

She knew, of course, that would be the thing to say to get them to inflate again. Middy knew she was kicking the junkyard dog, but she didn't care. She'd had enough of their well-intentioned interference.

This lot just had to learn that she was an adult.

Which was going to be a long time in coming, judging from their reactions. Three identical jaws set with purpose and three chests filled with air and puffed, ready for battle. Three sets of biceps bulged with the adrenaline that shot through them at the thought of their baby sister "entertaining."

Not just entertaining, but entertaining Dred Shadowins.

They would have charged her like Hannibal's elephants if not for Falcon. He held out his arms to block his brothers' advance. If it had been anyone other than the level-headed Falcon, they would have broken ranks and charged anyway.

"So, it's true? Where is the bastard?" Falcon said, his lips tight like rubber bands.

"At home, I imagine. Sleeping like any normal warlock would be at this hour of the night." Her irritation was rising and her other hand made it to her hip.

"Dred Shadowins. Butcher of Shale Creek?" Hawk's nostrils flared and his jaw ticked.

"He is not." Not that Middy knew anything about it, but she felt the need to defend him. She almost cringed because when they "broke up" and ended that little charade, it would all come back to bite her in the ass with really sharp teeth. It would be a chorus of "I told you so" and pitying looks; not only that, but the breakup would forever and irrevocably seal her fate in their eyes.

This would make it obvious to them that she couldn't be trusted to manage her own life. If Middy thought they were a pain in the ass now, after this debacle, they weren't even going to let her have tampons for fear of poking out her eye.

"Oh, no, Middy. No." Raven's hand fluttered to his chest like an English miss.

"No, what?" she demanded.

"You're serious," Raven whined.

"As a heart attack." She grinned. Middy was enjoying his discomfort.

"I thought this had to be some sort of joke," he whimpered again. "I knew we shouldn't have let her get that magazine. I told you no good would come of it."

"What do you mean by 'let me'?" Middy's ire was raised now and her hair began to stand on end as her power gathered around her.

"Uh, Raven," Hawk started.

"What, you didn't think we knew about your dirty little magazine? I told them that we should . . ."

Raven was promptly cut off as a Cornish hen flew from Middy's freezer and tried to work its way into his mouth, seemingly of its own volition.

"The magazine was Mom's idea," Hawk offered.

"What?" she shrieked again.

He opened his mouth to say something else, but thought better of it as he watched Raven trying to battle the Cornish hen's stubby appendages.

Falcon was ever the voice of reason. "Midnight Marie, behave yourself. We're just here to take care of you."

"When are you going to realize that I don't need you to take care of me?"

"Now that you've got Dred to do it?" Falcon said, rolling his eyes.

"No. Now that I am a woman grown. If I need your help, I will damn well ask for it."

"It was Mom's idea anyway," Raven said as the hen dropped lifelessly to the ground. "She's the one that got you that subscription, but I swear if any of us knew that you were going to fall in love with the centerfold . . ."

"Why didn't you tell us, Mids?" Hawk interrupted, giving her his best impression of a kicked puppy.

"I didn't know myself until last night." Middy didn't feel bad for that one because it was true.

"If you want to have a fling with Shadowins, by all means. But do you have to marry him?" Hawk asked.

"Look, it was all very sudden. Tristan couldn't keep his hands to himself and . . ."

The three of them puffed again like balloons at the mention of Belledare pawing her.

"There were reporters at the Masque, it turned into this whole thing and . . . Why weren't any of you at the Masque?"

This drew a collective silence from the trio.

"I see."

"We're here to talk about you," Hawk said.

"You keep saying that. I suppose you may as well come in." She spun on her heel. "And you'd better magick my door back hale and hearty if you want to keep your mouth free of dancing hens and used cat litter."

A plain, not to mention ugly, steel door replaced the gaping entryway where her brothers had stood.

"*My* door! The one carved by elvish hands with the ancient sigils."

"Why couldn't they have impressed the symbols on steel?" Falcon asked.

"That would be safer," Hawk added.

"Because they carved them into Holy Oak. Now!" Middy demanded. She was about to invoke the kitty litter. . . .

Her door appeared hale and hearty just as she'd demanded and with a wave of her hand she summoned coffee and tea on her guest china. She even went the extra mile and conjured chocolate pumpkin cookies. Those were her brothers' favorites.

Falcon was the first to sit down. "So—" He paused as he took a cup of coffee and crammed two cookies into his mouth. "When are you bringing him home?"

It sounded more like a drunk with a harelip trying to recite Shakespeare, especially amid the crumbs falling out of his mouth, but she knew what he was asking.

"I'm really not sure," she demurred.

"Midnight, it's not just us asking. Mom wants to know. In fact, it took something just short of tying her down to make her stay home," Raven said as he crammed three cookies in his mouth.

"Hell." This really was the worst that could happen. "I need to check with Dred's secretary and take a look at his schedule."

"If he wants to marry you, he can damn well clear it," Falcon shot back.

"If he wants to live to make it to the wedding," Hawk said under his breath.

"I heard that, Hawk Cherrywood. If any of you lay one hand on him, no, one finger . . . One breath! Just one whisper of hexes or curses and none of you will have any grandchildren to tell this story to. Do you understand me?" Middy looked at each of them pointedly and in turn until they hung their heads.

"I can't wait until one of you decides that you've found *the one*. I'm going to make that witch wish she'd never been born." Middy gave them a wicked grin. "All for your own good, of course. Have to test her, make sure she can go the long haul, right, boys? Everything that you dish up to Dred, I'll be taking notes."

"Go ahead, Mids. I don't think any of us is the marrying kind," Raven snorted.

"Yeah, remember that. And don't forget to repeat that little gem in front of Mom."

They all cringed.

"Yeah, so you better get onboard with this Dred thing. If someone has to give her grandbabies, wouldn't you rather it be me? Of course, that will only get you a temporary stay of execution, but it's better than nothing."

"You drive a hard bargain, Midnight Marie." Falcon seemed to get some sort of kick out of using her full name.

Her face flamed; she couldn't help thinking of her *hard* bargain with Dred.

"Oh, son of a two-headed hydra." Raven was rubbing at his temples as if the act could push the newly budded pain out of his head.

"What's your problem now?" Middy snapped.

"I know where your mind went. I was right there with you. Not about Dred, of course, but you're a witch. You're not supposed to think like a warlock."

"And why not? I'm allowed to have a healthy sex drive."

Middy was sure that if Raven could have plugged his ears just then and sung something really loud to keep those words from ever reaching the processing center of his brain, he would have.

"No, technically you're not. We remember when you were born, Midnight. We were seven," Falcon said. "You were the sweetest baby. So pink and happy." He scowled then, his brow furrowing in displeasure.

"But I'm not a baby anymore, Falcon. I'm a witch grown. And normal red-blooded witches have sex. With warlocks. Or other witches if that's what moves them—"

"Middy, I'm sorry about the door. Really, I am. Heartily and forever. Please, can we not talk about sex?" Hawk begged.

"This is a new Middy. You've never been like this before." Raven shook his head.

"Well, it's all about coming into my own, I guess. See, I liked that look of startled confusion on Dred's face so much that I've uninstalled my filter. I find I quite like the look on all of your faces, too. That and—" She paused for the maximum effect. If one of her brothers didn't fall over in a dead faint, she'd be surprised. And disappointed. "I got laid. Does wonders to loosen the tongue, don't you know."

She thought for sure that it would be Raven who reacted first to her lie, but it was Hawk. One eyelid fluttered up and down, almost like he was having a stroke. The other eye was glassy and staring at some far off place in the distance where baby sisters didn't say words like "laid" and much less knew what they meant. Middy wondered what he was going to do the first time he heard "fuck" come out of her mouth.

Hawk grabbed at his chest and she heard his breath catch in his throat as he fell over. It was like knocking down a redwood. If not for the fact that he obliterated her chaise longue with his body mass, she would have thought he was being a drama queen. But no, he lay there in a stupor with bits of longue and splintered wood splayed out behind him like a collage.

She giggled.

Raven and Falcon looked like two horrified maiden aunts.

"Oh, yes, my darling brothers. The pasty is on the other . . ."

Raven clamped a hand over her mouth. "We get it. Really, we do." He was pleading with her now.

Falcon snatched Raven's hand away just as she was considering whether to bite or not to bite. He must have seen something in her eyes. They backed away from her slowly, dragging Hawk with them.

"Remember to call Mom and tell her when Dred can make it to dinner," Falcon added before shoving them all through the door behind him.

Yes, indeed. If one were to ask Falcon, Hawk, or Raven, this was the worst thing that could have happened.

CHAPTER EIGHT
Dark Alley Assignation

A certain chancellor pulled the musty velvet of his father's cloak over his head and ducked into the Banshee's Bawl—a bar on the warlockian side of St. Louis. He nodded his head to the familiar bartender and palmed the key for his regular room above the bar.

His round cheeks were numb from the chill in the air, but it was nothing compared to the icy feeling that slid down his spine. He was in a world of shit and didn't see a viable way out. He huffed and puffed like the horny werewolf from Little Red Riding Hooker as he navigated the twisted and curved staircase.

The cloak gave him a sense of security, a sense of invincibility. The tighter he pulled the cloak, the stronger he felt, and the more he believed this plan would work.

It was about time that someone knocked those pompous warlocks off their pedestals. He'd thought for sure that the Gargoyle War would have done it. If the warlocks had lost, they'd have been slaves to the gargoyles, forced to serve just as he had all those hundreds of years ago. Born half-jinn, he'd been hunted when the council had seen what he was capable of. They'd chained his magick, bound his power to serve only their will, and when he'd rebelled and killed his jailers, they'd sentenced him to an eternity in Chaldonean Hall.

As if he ever would have let that stop him. He stifled a laugh. He'd sold his soul for his freedom. They'd all pay for their ancestors' crimes against him. He'd crush this world under his boot until every witch and warlock knew what it was to suffer as he had suffered.

His masterpiece had almost been within his grasp. Oh, how he'd schemed and plotted. A casual word here, an implication there, and the world had erupted into a bloody dream. The Gargoyle War had been a delectable manifestation of his talent.

Then, in a single moment, Shale Creek had ruined him. A single act of selflessness had thwarted years of political cock-sucking and maneuvering. It had been no easy feat to push the council into war. The absolute destruction of the mixed gargoyle/warlock community of Shale Creek should have been the boiling point. Each side would blame the other and they'd both pull out everything in their armories.

And out of the destruction would have emerged a new world order, one where he ruled over the mortal world and magick alike. Instead, someone had been willing to die to deactivate all that black magick.

Now, he just had to figure out which one of those fuck-bags had done it, which one of those pretty boy media whores had screwed him over. Shadowins or Belledare?

It was a conundrum, really. Shadowins was a shiny prick, but he'd trafficked in dark and cursed objects. He had the knowledge and the magick to defeat a Hand of Glory—the most powerful of all cursed objects—a candle made from the hands of six hanged warlocks who'd all murdered for their dark power. But Belledare was the war hero. It was he who'd come crowing from the shadows and the ash about saving lives.

And it was he who'd whispered in the dark about the Butcher of Shale Creek—that Dred Shadowins had killed hundreds for that Hand of Glory.

Given Shadowins's reputation, perhaps he had. But no one had accused him before the high court. This was what made him pause in his assignment of blame. Why hadn't Shadowins been tried as a war criminal like so many others? Had he performed some secret and heroic duty for the Warlock Council? Why else wasn't he rotting inside a painting in Chaldonean Hall?

If he wasn't careful, that's where his own hide was going to end up. Cursed to serve out his sentence under glass watching the world go by while spectators came to stare at him in his magickal cage.

Never again.

He didn't have another soul to trade, so if he were to be caught again, he was beyond fucked. It gave him a perverse pleasure to hand down sentences to Chaldonean Hall. It gave him even more enjoyment to carry them out, to walk amongst the damned knowing that his own prison hung empty.

Perhaps he'd just kill Shadowins *and* Belledare.

He couldn't do it outright though, no. He was so much smarter than either of them—so much apart from the rest of the warlockian world that he knew he was meant to be their god. And like a god, he would destroy where and as he wished.

He wanted to see just what it would take for Shadowins to kill the hero. Or perhaps it would be more interesting if he could coerce the hero into a wanton act of murder?

The key was Midnight Cherrywood, virginal witch and universal good girl. There was magick in her blood, magick older, stronger, and more pure than what had been seen in centuries. The echo of it reverberated through him any time she was within ten feet of him. It stung him like a thousand killer bees, but he coveted it just the same.

His cock was hard at the thought of corrupting her.

He was brought back to the world by the graze of sharp

teeth on his neck and the touch of cold, reptilian skin. Those teeth lingered on the meat of his shoulder where the tendons stood corded and ready for her assault. This was what he was here for, after all.

The creature slithered around him like a python, but then released her hold only to kneel in front of him and push the heavy cloak up to his thighs so her eager fingers could find the small cock hiding beneath his milky paunch. Her lips closed around the wormlike appendage and suckled. He wanted to grab her hair, but he didn't dare. Already, the mouth full of teeth grazed the tip of his cock, already he was flirting with death just by allowing her this.

He was confident she wouldn't actually consume him; a lamia could only take nourishment from innocent flesh, preying mostly on women and children. And he was soured and bitter; his flesh would taste like the dark.

It was his semen that she was after. All of the unformed possibility of life was what kept her in the body she'd stolen.

She looked up into his eyes, and her mouth split in a wide razor as she smiled. Her tongue curled around his member and pulled it deep into her throat.

When he came, he was thinking of the scalding purity that burned inside of Middy Cherrywood like it did no other, that light that made her the only weapon of any use against his lamia. He was thinking of what it would be like to snuff the brightest light that the warlockian world had seen in an age.

He gave no thought to the body of the witch the creature retreated into when she was done.

CHAPTER NINE

An Invitation to the Castle

Midnight Cherrywood looked at her spelltop. She wasn't sure if she wanted to check her magickal mail or not. Not since the Dred Debacle had exploded across mortal and magickal media alike.

Suddenly, shy little Middy was the center of attention. Suddenly, she was Someone and everyone wanted a piece of her. She'd had to shut off the m-mail alerts to her Witchberry because the damn thing had been spasming like an epileptic under a disco ball at a rave. Middy knew she'd have to respond sooner or later. After all, she was a society witch now. She had more social obligations than just the foundation and the Masque.

Oh, what this could do for the Masque!

Perhaps she could build support for the orphanage idea that she'd been cramming up Vargill's rump every time she got him to sit still. She could use some of these reporters to her advantage. . . . Middy found a new tenacity.

She was empowered.

She was going to network.

She was going to use her social connections to save the world.

Resolved, Middy powered up her spelltop with an incantation and connected to the Warlockian World Web. Middy settled in to answer the four hundred m-mails that she'd received. The first few were gingerbread, a lot like mortal spam, and so she deleted them right off. She had to get a new gingerbread filter now that she wasn't actually going to open them all.

Then she saw one that almost made her pee her pants. Her whole body went numb with shock, so she might well have christened the chair. She'd have to check later.

It was from Barista Snow.

She was so thankful that she'd had the foresight to put down her morning cup of cinnamon tea. Middy would have sprayed it out of her nose all over the shiny screen of her spelltop. Barista Snow was the wife of Chancellor Roderick Snow and she was to the Warlockian world what Almack's had been to the *Ton*. Witches did not run in the upper circles of magickal society without her expressed approval.

The m-mail was on a beautiful animated background. It filled the whole room with the likeness of falling snow. The scene was so real that Middy could feel it on the tip of her nose. Each flake was fat and thick, like frozen lace.

It was an invitation to a house party at Snow Manor for the coming weekend!

Her head almost fell off when she realized that she didn't have Dred's Witchberry number. Merlin's Hemorrhoids! What was she going to do? She had to get in touch with him. What if he had plans this weekend?

Oh, his plans could go hang. This was a pass to Olympus by way of Snow Manor. Hell, Snow Manor was better than Olympus. It was a large, crystalline castle that sat nestled in the Swiss Alps. Invisible to mortal eyes, it had been a stronghold of magick for centuries, but it looked like something right out of a fairy tale.

A castle fit for a princess. Or Barista Snow.

That witch used the ice theme in everything she did, but somehow, anything that bore her stamp was perfect.

She also had the best anti-aging charms. She was a witch of one hundred and twenty, but looked no more than a mortal thirty. Most witches who lived that long looked at least forty-five.

Bitch.

Goddess.

For Middy, it would be the chance of a lifetime just to see the inside of the manor. Let alone stay there for the weekend and be entertained by the legend herself.

She'd need a new wardrobe! Middy was an unusual witch in that she hated shopping. Hated it with a singular burning like she did cramps. Not to mention she was just balls at shopping.

Midnight Cherrywood had been born without the shopping gene. Every nice piece of clothing she owned either her mother or Tally had picked out for her. She could put it together after it was in her closet; it was just choosing things in the store that was the problem. Then there was the issue of fabrics. Warlockian fabrics always had the best wrinkle release, but most were dry charming only.

If Middy hated anything more than shopping, it was dry charming.

It was then, as her mind wound the myriad tendrils of her thoughts into a noose, that Middy realized she'd promptly spazzed right the fuck out.

"Fuck," she whispered out loud. "Fuck!" It tasted good on her tongue. The word just rolled off like melted butter.

Of course, that really wasn't the imagery she wanted. In fact, it grossed her out. But damn was it ever fun to say.

"Fuck!"

She was still a few monkeys short of a barrel of fun, but she was feeling much more in control of herself after a few "fucks." Middy giggled. She'd been told it only took one—fuck that is—to feel better.

"What the hell are you giggling about, sitting here in the

dark all by yourself?" Tally asked her as she flipped on the light and strolled into the room looking sated and full.

"Nothing," Middy sighed. "I'm just losing my mind."

"Dred?"

"Barista Snow."

"What did the witch do now?" Tally refilled the wobbly teacup in Middy's hand and lounged beside her.

"She invited me to a house party this weekend."

"You're shitting me blue. Seriously?" Tally perked up.

"Duties of the wealthy affianced." Middy shrugged her shoulders.

"Shopping!" Tally cried and was on her feet.

"Uh, no. How about you shop and I will stay here?" Middy flashed her roomie a pleading look, but the effort was wasted. Her friend would have done it anyway.

"I want to go! I would die to see the inside of Snow Manor. I wonder if all the chancellors have been invited? Maybe I should ask Martin? What if he's not going? Or what if he's going and he doesn't want to take me?" Tally frowned and then suddenly put her hand on her stomach and grimaced.

"Tally, what's wrong?" Middy watched, unsure of how to help her friend as she watched her face contort.

"Oh, nothing. I'll be okay. No worries. It's a new cleanse tea I tried. It's giving me the most horrible gut pains."

"Maybe you should lie down."

"And miss out on shopping? You're going to Snow Manor and I won't have you wearing whatever horrors are currently hanging in your closet." Tally managed a real smile. "Plus, those society witches are vicious. I'd never forgive myself if you went into that nest of vipers unprepared. A good dress and designer shoes are better than armor."

Middy wasn't convinced. It was more than a bad cleanse. Tally hadn't been herself for weeks. "Tally, don't drink the tea anymore, okay? It's obviously not good for you." Middy didn't want to pry, whatever was going on with her friend was something she obviously didn't want to talk about, and it was obviously more than tea. "If you want to talk about—"

"There's a good sale at Kate Spade. I'd better go so I don't miss it. We'll have you shipshape in no time." She was gone in the blink of an eye to bury herself in the holy communion of trade. And to avoid any further conversation.

Middy was once again alone with her thoughts and though she was worried about Tally, her thoughts continued to turn to Dred. She rationalized that Tally had basically told her to butt out by cutting off her offer to talk, so it was okay if Middy filled her brain with Dred instead. His hands, his face, his mouth.

That limo ride.

Her slit ached as she remembered how wantonly she'd splayed herself, how hard his cock had been for her, and the heat of his mouth on her skin. She remembered the taste of him on her lips and her fingers fluttered across her mouth.

How dare he be the best almost lay she'd ever had!

It was false advertising that he was nothing like his centerfold. Of course, if his centerfold was as good as all that, witches would have no reason to put up with him in the flesh.

The very fine and utterly delicious flesh.

She thought about her recently neglected copy of *Weekly Warlock* and figured that since Tally was gone and she was all alone, what better way to pass a few hours? She'd make him call her "mistress" again and this time, maybe she wouldn't just be riding his face like a show pony.

Middy Cherrywood had a dirty little secret.

It wasn't that she used *Weekly Warlock* to jill-off. She'd made that right in her head a long time ago. It was that she'd never let her fantasy do the actual deed. She'd had him perform every deviation known to man and warlock with his tongue and fingers, and she'd inspected his package at length, but she'd never wanted to let it anywhere near . . .

It was supposed to feel real, so would it hurt? What if she got attached? He was just a 3-D pleasure program and not the real Dred. These were the questions that she'd asked herself.

But she wanted to be prepared for the real thing. She didn't want any more surprises like what had happened in the limo. He'd seemed downright maiden aunt about the whole thing. Totally unacceptable.

Middy pulled the latest centerfold out from under her pillow. Merlin, but if that wasn't a fine piece of warlock. The witch that actually got to marry him was going to be a very lucky creature. Of course, she'd have to put her foot down about him displaying his parts far and wide for any who cared to see. Or fantasize about pillaging. At least, that's what Middy would do.

She turned to Dred's page and he appeared just as naked and hard as she'd left him. Just as willing to fulfill her every desire.

"I want this to be like it was really you," she informed the naked Dred charm.

"Really me, Mistress?" he answered, a dazed look on his normally sharp features.

"Stop with the 'mistressing.' I want this encounter to be like it would if I were really with Dred Shadowins. Not touching me how I've programmed you, but how he would touch me."

"I'm afraid that's impossible." He shrugged his massive shoulders. "Otherwise, why would witches bother if they could get the real thing in a centerfold? You're a smart witch; I'd think you'd know better." The program looked at her with blatant disapproval.

"Damn," she swore. It didn't make her feel better and it didn't solve her problem either.

"I guess you'll just have to use your tongue instead." Middy splayed her legs wide, exposing the soft flesh that yearned for his mouth.

"I guess so." The corner of his mouth turned up in a trademark Shadowins's smirk.

"I'm getting back talk from a centerfold. Shut up and be objectified," she demanded.

"Yes, ma'am."

Middy decided that she liked *ma'am* even better than *mistress.*

The Dred charm didn't kiss her, didn't trace his fingers along the contours of her skin, and he didn't maneuver her to his pleasure. All he did was put his tongue to her. Leave it to Middy to find something to complain about in a cunnilingus charm that she'd written herself.

She knew that she was in big trouble. Middy had been almost addicted to this Dred charm, and now it really wasn't doing much for her. It looked like him; hell, it even smelled like him, but it wasn't him.

Middy pushed her fingers through his hair. It felt the same, it was so silky. The sensation was so real. She felt the tongue flicking faster and harder and she let her mind drift back to the limo, always back to the limo, when she'd been in his lap. The naughty feel of her nakedness against his cock, the way her hips had moved instinctively against him, the intensity between them when their eyes had met and the sensation of being beneath him.

She'd felt so completely possessed by him and he hadn't even been inside of her yet. Middy cried out as the charm responded to her need and filled her with sensation. It was delicious and decadent, but it was nothing like what Dred had wrought.

Middy squirmed against the tireless tongue, arched her

back to meet his mouth, to demand more. Her demands turned into pleas as she reached a plateau. Release was just out of her grasp.

She imagined Dred inside of her, and opened her eyes to look at the head bent down between her thighs. But even as he looked up and met her gaze, it was still not enough. So many times before, that was all that it had taken to send her spiraling through an endless sea of pleasure—to see his eyes darken as they met hers. To know she had power over him, but this was something else.

She whimpered, "Dred!" It was an entreaty and a demand both. It was a benediction from lips that longed to sin more wholly.

Her fingers were curled around the duvet and her body was taut and straining. She let out a frustrated high-pitched sound that had started out as a sigh and ended in a scream. Middy grabbed the closest thing to her, which was the *Weekly Warlock* and sent it flying across the room.

Too bad Tally had forgotten to lock the damn door because there was Dred Shadowins, in the flesh.

Middy's mouth fell open and her jaw seemed to unhinge itself. She desperately wanted to say something that would make this go away. She knew that he'd seen everything, Middy Cherrywood jilling-off with his likeness because the real thing had turned her down. It didn't get any more humiliating.

In that moment, she wished that she was Tally. Tally would have had something to say that would put him on his ass quicker than a junk punch. She'd say something like, "Want to help?" or "Fuck me now," or any number of other things that had to sound better than the creaky sound of her jaw trying to close.

"Poor Midnight," he said. "You just need the real thing."

Coming from any other mouth that would have sounded trite. It would have sounded like a letter that had been

typed one-handed to *Cauldron Forum*. But it wasn't. Not
with the way his eyes were like a twilight storm, the hard,
determined set of his jaw, and the measured exhale of
breath against her skin when he sank to his knees on the
bed.

He didn't allow her to protest, didn't permit her to shatter the moment with her embarrassment. The first touch of
his tongue sent an electric jolt through her such as she'd
never felt before.

Middy would like to say that she'd made him work for it,
but she'd been so close for so long. She tried to fight her orgasm because she wanted it to last longer, but it was just too
good to resist.

"So sweet," he whispered between strokes.

He was talking about her. Talking about tasting *her*! She
spasmed and tightened; Dred was just what she needed to
push off of that plateau. His mouth sent her careening over
the edge and she was screaming his name and who knew
what else. There could have been some Latin in there
somewhere, she wasn't sure.

When her eyes fluttered open, he was watching her intently.

Middy had assumed that after he'd worn her muffin like
a hat, maybe he would want to do other things. He seemed
content just to watch her, but she was not content with that
state of affairs. Twice, he'd been diving into her nethers and
twice, he'd demurred.

Was she dirty? Did she smell? Was it not tasty? She'd
never tasted it, so she didn't know. It couldn't be the whole
virgin thing, could it? He'd made a deal though, given his
word. It was a magickal binding. He had to put out even-
tually.

He was still staring at her.

She was afraid to say anything for fear of what would
come out of her mouth or that she'd be rejected again. A

witch could only ask to be plowed like a field so many times before it was just embarrassing. Not that it could get any more embarrassing than having the object of your lust walk in on incontrovertible proof that he was the entirety of the deposits in the spank bank.

Middy realized her legs were still wide.

Did she have something strange down there that was different from all of the other witches he'd . . . She looked at him with the question in her eyes, even though it hadn't passed her lips. Her traitorous mouth couldn't be trusted to stop with one question.

He shook his head and grimaced. "I just can't, Middy. By Merlin and the Morrigan, how I want to." Dred moved up the bed to lie next to her.

That made no sense to her whatsoever. She'd thought warlocks were always eager. At least that was what she'd always heard. Dred was supposed to be a sex god. So far, he'd been acting like a monk. It was bad for her self-esteem.

He licked his lips and closed his eyes, his snowflake lashes brushing his cheeks. Dred looked as if he were savoring some divine dish.

Middy had to clench her thighs together when she realized that the divine dish was the taste of her witchy bits.

"Then why don't you? I thought that you indulged in all things hedonist," Middy said as if she were the most experienced and inviting of tarts.

"Because my cock is killing me."

Middy hadn't expected so blunt an answer.

"Why? Did you sprain it? Or did you break it off in Aloe Hugginfroth?"

"You know what? Never mind. Plotting is more important. Did you get an invitation from Barista Snow?"

"I did, actually."

"Don't you think it would be nice to discuss why I need

you to pose as my fiancée? Or maybe what you're going to say to my mother when you meet her?"

"See, I would have called you. If I'd had your stupid Witchberry number. And speaking of calling, you could have called before you came over. Or, I don't know, knocked? What is it with warlocks and knocking? Are you allergic to it?"

"What other warlocks have been over here without knocking?" Dred narrowed his eyes and in them Middy could see horrible fates awaiting those trespassers.

She found that she rather liked it. Her "fiancé" was feeling protective.

"My brothers, actually. Raven incinerated my door. Douche bag."

"Brothers as in plural? You have more than one?"

Middy rolled her eyes. "Falcon, Hawk, and Raven Cherrywood: the Trifecta of Doom."

"Seriously? Those are your brothers?"

"What, like there is more than one Cherrywood?" Middy rolled her eyes again.

"Damn it."

"I think that warrants stronger verbiage."

"Only you could sit there sky clad and discuss verbiage." He looked thoughtful for a moment. "Well, you and Mrs. Tinterbox from AP Lit senior year."

Middy took stock of herself and pulled the duvet over her nakedness. "I'm not even going to ask. I don't want to know."

"Why does it warrant stronger verbiage, as you so eloquently put it?" Dred asked. He seemed genuinely curious, as if he didn't already know that meeting her brothers was a fate worse than death.

"Why do you think? For such a brilliant businessman, sometimes I think you're half stupid."

"Only half? Thanks," he snorted.

"They want to meet you."

"I'd assumed." Dred shrugged.

"My mother wants you to come for dinner."

"That's what comes with being affianced. I thought you witches knew all about this sort of thing?"

"You don't understand." She sighed heavily.

"Explain it to me."

"My brothers. The Trifecta of Doom. Back at the Academy, I never had a date make it past the foyer."

"Well, I'm not just any date. I'm—"

"The warlock they want to slice into little pieces and make into Solstice gravy."

"It's not that bad. I'm rich and I have pull with the council. My lineage can be traced back to Avalon. Why wouldn't they approve?" Dred shrugged again.

"Infamy, maybe?" Middy thought she was going to get seasick from how many times her eyes had rolled to the back of her head of their own volition. "I still think you're insane, but since I gave you my witch's word, I can't really explain it to them, now can I?"

"No, Midnight. I'm sorry, but you can't."

A small, frustrated sound escaped her.

"I brought something to show you—" He appraised her for a moment. "I'd meant to show it to you before lunch, but . . ." He shrugged his shoulders as if it were all out of his control and winked at her.

Before lunch? They hadn't eaten yet. Middy cocked her head to the side as if the motion could rattle her cogs loose and help realization set in. She didn't know what there was to wink about either. He was just talking about . . .

He meant her muffin!

Sweet Circe, this warlock was trying to kill her. It would be death by muffinquake. Everything he said was candy-coated with sex and each of those syllables out of his mouth made her body clench.

This was really it. She was lighting *Weekly Warlock* on fire. No more jilling-off to him. Not that it got her anywhere anyway. Not after this blatant show of "cunning linguistics."

She really meant that this time, unlike the previous four times when she was just vowing for effect. Really.

"I am coming to enjoy that shade of pink."

In that second, Middy realized she'd had enough. He had all the power here and she was going to get some of it back. Or she was going to die of embarrassment trying.

"Coming?" She repeated the word for effect. "Doesn't look like it to me. You're not even breathing heavy." Middy smiled and reached over to put her hand boldly on his package. "Doesn't feel like it either."

Dred made a sound low in his throat and Middy realized that the previously mentioned package had just become a special delivery. It hardened beneath her touch and she was curious to know more.

He caught her wrist. "Midnight! Sweet hell, no."

"Tell me more about why you're on the injured list," Middy said. "I think I deserve to know what's keeping me from my payment."

Dred gritted his teeth and closed his eyes; he took a deep breath. "That's going to be just as bad, Midnight." He pulled her against him and he shifted his weight so that their mouths were only seconds apart. "It was the night of the Masque."

"The night when you abandoned me to find my own pleasure?" Middy couldn't believe the words that had just fallen out of her mouth with no care as to where they crashed.

"Yes, Midnight. You were so wet for me, but I was trying my damndest to . . ." He frowned and the slashes of his eyebrows drew together. "You're a virgin and the Cause is so much more than this."

He'd just said that this "Cause" of his was so much more important to him than being wand deep in her, but the way he'd said it almost made up for the blow to her pride. Dred leaned close to her, his hard body pressing her into the mattress, his breath sweet and minty on her lips. The duvet was between them, but she was hyperaware of her nakedness beneath.

"Tell me more," she demanded as her eyes fluttered closed with desire.

"What do you want to hear, Midnight? That I wanted to fuck you? That I've imagined the sweet heat of you tight around my cock? Or do you want to know what I was doing while I was imagining your body? That I was touching my cock, sliding my hand back and forth trying to come, all the while knowing it was nothing compared to what it would like to be deep inside of you?"

Middy arched up into him, his words a caress as potent and real as his hands over her body.

"And I couldn't come, because it wasn't what I wanted. I wanted you. So, I kept stroking, touching. . . ."

Middy could see everything that he described to her. His strong hands wrapped around his cock, his head tilted back in pleasure, even a bead of sweat forming on his upper lip as he worked his cock to images of her.

His words gave her a heady power.

"Now please, Middy. It took forever to come and I'm so sore."

She was already sore from her multiple missed orgasms, so she supposed it would be a good idea to quit taunting him. And herself.

"Okay, but I'm going to hold you to that."

Dred rolled onto his back, his eyes closed, and his hand

making a protective cup near his groin, though he wasn't quite touching it.

He pulled out his Witchberry and tossed it to her. "Call yourself. Then you'll have my number. Look at my last text from Godrickle and you'll understand why you have to help me. Our mission is to stop the person behind the murders of the hatchling gargoyles. There are photos of one of the crime scenes." Dred tried to sit up. "Where's the kitchen? I need some ice."

"I could just—"

He interrupted. "I'll get it the old-fashioned way, thanks. And for the love of Merlin, please be dressed when I get back."

Middy was surprised that he just tossed her his Witchberry. Most magickal folk carried around their whole lives in these things and he'd just tossed it to her like a dirty sock.

It felt kind of naughty to be cruising through his personal files. She had to say that she liked it. She paused on a picture of someone named Karla. A pretty witch, but too skinny for Dred. In Middy's opinion, anyway. Then she saw the text from Chancellor Godrickle.

Well, rocky road fudge! Dred had been telling the truth. He was a spy.

That little nugget of clarity caused her to debate opening the attachment. A lead weight dropped from her throat into her gut. It told her, no, it screamed, that if she looked at whatever was in that file, it was going to change everything. For a moment, she thought maybe that was a little overdramatic.

Until she opened the file.

Middy dropped the device in horror as image after image of brutality appeared on the screen. Fledgling gargoyles, mutilated and murdered. It wasn't so much the blood— she'd seen that before. It was look of terror on those little faces, the eyes wide, and the bow mouths open, pleading for their mothers.

It was a wanton destruction of innocence.

She felt completely helpless as the images flashed before her, helpless to get away from them because those scenes had been tattooed into her awareness, and helpless to do anything but sit there and damn a world where something like this could happen.

But no, she wasn't helpless. Dred was going to find out who'd done this. He was going to stop them from doing it again. She could help him. Little Midnight Cherrywood had a chance to change the world.

Now, she understood. Her bit of inconvenient flesh really didn't matter in the face of something like this. She felt a warmth spark inside of her and she realized that it was for Dred Shadowins.

It wasn't the blatant lust that usually colored every single thing that had to do with him, and she still couldn't say that she liked him. He was still a witchinizing bastard, but there was this tiny flame.

Its name was admiration.

There was something else, too. That warmth, that spark—there was hope there. It sparked her magick, like a waterfall of fireworks as if there was something inside of her that could have changed those broken little bodies, could have mended them.

But that was impossible. Wasn't it?

CHAPTER TEN
The Broom Sleigh

Five days later, Dred Shadowins escorted Middy Cherrywood and her bit of luggage to Snow Manor. He was thrilled that she was such a practical witch and managed to cram all of her necessities into one case and a garment bag.

He'd never known a witch who could do that, but Dred thought that it should be a course offered at the Academy: *Magickal Packing for the Smart Witch*. Yes, he'd have to see about talking to the council to get that added as an elective. Middy would be the perfect witch to design the course.

It would also be a way to pay her for her help. He'd already agreed to fund the Gargoyle Masque for the rest of his life, but who knew how long that would be if these bastards had already raised a lamia? A lamia could spell the end of mortal and magickal civilization. Dred knew of only one way to combat something so evil: great sacrifice. And the only thing Dred had that he valued above all else was his life. Still, he'd gladly give it to save his world.

Dred sighed, knowing he had to keep his head in the game. He pushed Spy!Dred down and slipped into his RichPlayboy!Dred persona. He watched as broom after broom arrived, witches and warlocks wrapped in magickal furs, with luggage brooms arriving behind them. Dred always found that to be so pretentious and he knew for a fact, so did Barista Snow.

Her elegance was rooted in her love of simplicity. That was something the social vultures couldn't seem to grasp. Dred knew that she was going to love Middy and that would make it much easier for his fiancée to move about in the circles they needed access to.

Other witches and warlocks continued their procession, but Dred was content to wait in the warm bubble of the broom sleigh. It had four thruster brooms underneath the hood and sailed through the sea of snow like a Cadillac on a Sunday drive.

At least it wasn't one of those pumpkin-shaped monstrosities. He hated those. All of the witches he'd dated always wanted a ride in one around the holidays. Some Cinderella nonsense. He'd rather go face diving in a vat of cranberry sauce. Luckily, his mother never approved of those. Aradia was a staunch supporter of the stepsisters. In her opinion, it took much more dedication and determination to cut off a piece of your own foot than to languish around and wait for some mealy-mouthed fairy to come rescue one from *circumstances.*

He scanned the crowd for his mother, but didn't see her. There was an amazing view of a glitter frosted landscape, the snow making everything fresh and clean. His favorite part of the view was the snowcapped mountains that had looked to him like ice cream-covered breasts when he'd been a young warlock (everything with Dred was about the rack). Middy leaned against his chest. He didn't mind having her there, nestled against him while she took in the sights. She'd confessed with a wide-eyed wonder that she'd never been to the Alps. She'd told him of a favorite childhood snow globe that had looked just like Snow Manor.

She smelled like sugar plums today. Every time she moved, the scent filled the bubble that shielded the sleigh from the elements and he was reminded of Solstice and Yule, of home, of long winter nights reading with his mother while she wove magick pictures into the walls. When the stories and pictures had faded, they always left the scent of sugar plums in their wake.

Dred found it odd in the extreme that this woman he lusted for should smell like his childhood. He couldn't resist wrapping one cherry-chocolate curl from her cascade of hair around his finger.

He'd had his fingers wrist deep in many a witch's hair, but none had ever appealed to him as much as Midnight Cherrywood's, even back at the Academy. That was why he'd turned them into snakes. Dred had dreamt about her hair, dreamt about touching it whenever he wanted. Rather than ask the girl if he could touch her hair, because that had seemed icky to a warlock of his age, he'd tried to destroy it so that it couldn't taunt him.

Snakes weren't shiny, after all. They didn't feel like silk and the sheen of them didn't dance in the light like Middy's hair. His fingers didn't itch to touch them.

She seemed not to notice the familiarity with which he touched her and he was thankful for that. Just because he wanted to touch her hair, it didn't mean anything. He'd have to stop before she noticed. Witches took things like hair touching to be something more than it was.

Unfortunately, his cock was getting hard, too. Touching her hair made him remember what it looked like spread out behind her on a pillow, her legs splayed for the image of him, and the sound of her voice as she called out his name. He hadn't been able to help himself, tasting her. She'd been so sweet; he'd had to delve further.

Her mortification had been intriguing as well. He hadn't known how much the little witch had lusted after him until that moment. Sure, he knew that she wanted him. Most witches did . . . Yeah, he knew that sounded pompous, but it was the truth. If not for his looks or the tales of his legendary cock, it was for his money. He was a commodity.

Though, Middy was the first witch he'd caught doing the nasty with his centerfold. He'd considered simply watching. There had been something so stimulating about watching his own image pleasure her. If he'd joined it, it would have been the ultimate in narcissistic pleasure. He'd be able to fuck himself, while fucking a hot little piece of witch. Dred was sure it didn't get any better.

Then he'd heard her frustration and he couldn't resist. After all, he didn't want it to get around that his centerfold wasn't a good lay. If he was honest, he'd admit that it was more than that. Dred wanted to bring her pleasure. It all went back to that shade of pink that matched her mouth. Her nipples. And her . . .

As he pushed the thought from his head, he realized everyone had arrived. It was time to land the sleigh and put his head in the lion's mouth. He could see from the smug look on Barista's face that she thought she'd finally gotten one over on him.

His Aunt Barista was what one would call a piece of work.

As the valet came to take the sleigh, Dred guided Middy into the reception line and stood behind her. He was looking at Middy when he realized a vital part of their charade was missing. The engagement tattoos.

Double damn. He'd have to do them as soon as they were taken to their room. Dred had to keep himself and Middy from showing their wrists until then. It shouldn't be too much of a problem for Middy since she was wrapped from head to toe in Chimerean fur.

Barista's face warmed as they approached and she smiled as she took Middy's hand. "I'm so glad you could come, Midnight. Mordred has told me absolutely nothing about you."

"Thank you for the invitation, Madame Snow," Middy said with her own smile.

Her manners were impeccable. Dred couldn't have chosen a better partner for this façade if he'd held auditions. Who was he kidding? If he'd held auditions, the casting couch would've been replaced twice from all the shagging and he still wouldn't have found his perfect, virginal Middy.

"You must call me Barista. Or Aunt Bari, if you like. I'm simply dying to hear all about you." She kissed the air next to Middy's cheek and motioned for a servant to come guide them to their room. "And Mordred, darling. Your mother is here. I would advise that you take your bride-to-be directly to her room. She told me that even she hasn't been introduced to Midnight yet, you horrible boy."

Barista turned her attention back to Middy. "We forgive him though because we never thought he'd find the right witch, did we, Roderick?"

The stern man behind her with the aquiline nose and rough-hewn features smiled. "No, my dear. We'd lost faith that we'd ever find the one."

That sounded odd to Dred. He couldn't put his finger on why, but he filed it away to contemplate later after he had Middy safely ensconced and bearing his mark on her wrist.

Middy followed the servant to their room, and Dred found the fellow to be completely unpalatable. He admitted to himself that he might be just a bit paranoid. Something about the man set all of his warning bells to ringing like a tornado siren in Kansas in the spring.

He had an unpleasant smell that wasn't the stench of unwashed bodies, but something else. Something that reminded him of the dark. The creature, for he seemed to be more creature than man, shuffled through the halls at a lethargic pace and Dred had the distinct and overwhelming sense that he didn't want this thing to know where his room was.

That was ridiculous, of course. There was bound to be an organizational chart somewhere so Barista could keep track of her guests. It would be easy for anyone to figure out where they slept, even if he clubbed this thing over the head with a dose of Lethe's Tears.

Nevertheless, he was going to work some serious warding when they reached their rooms. It was going to be an energy sucking bitch of a night. He'd have to do the entire room because in a castle as old as Snow Manor, there were secret passages that had to be warded as well. It was a veritable bitch to work effective wards when one didn't know where all of the entrances were located.

The creature turned and bared his teeth in a smile as he stopped in front of an unfamiliar door. Dred had hoped against hope that Barista would have put them in the quarters he'd used when he'd come to visit in summers as a child. He knew every nook and cranny of those rooms.

He couldn't help wondering if they'd been moved for that very reason.

Dred couldn't explain why he was seeing monsters in every shadow, but he knew from experience they were real.

CHAPTER ELEVEN
Midnight

As soon as they were in their room, with the door secured against unwanted entry, Dred mobilized. He paced around their room, scanning for listening devices, magickal and mortal; he warded the windows, the doors, and even the closets. In fact, she was pretty damn sure he was warding the entire room. She thought that might be a little extreme.

Middy continued to watch him with curiosity as she pulled her Chimerean fur from around her shoulders and dropped it casually on the chair.

"Uh, Dred?"

"Can't talk, warding."

"I know. I have an insta-ward pack." Middy said as she pulled the small sachet out of her purse. "I never travel without it."

Dred flashed her a lopsided grin and after he activated the pack he asked, "Are you sure you haven't done this before?"

"I'm just organized."

Three of the lightbulbs in the chandelier sparked and shot from their sockets, but when they hit the floor, they did not break. Instead, they took on batlike shapes as wings quickly emerged from the white bulb form. Heads popped out with long antennae that were still twitching.

Middy was a gasp away from a scream, but Dred was across the room and had his fingers to her lips. He shook his head, indicating that she shouldn't make a sound. From the way that the antennae were still moving, the bugs were still transmitting. If any of those things opened their eyes, Middy knew that she would scream like a *bean sidhe*. She could feel a slight bit of hysteria welling up in her.

Dred's strong arms were more of a comfort than they should have been. She hid her face in his chest, so she didn't have to look at those Merlin-cursed things. Middy was irritated with herself for being such a . . . such a . . . *pussy*. There was no other word for it in her book. This doubled her irritation because not only was she embarrassed, but she hated that word.

If she'd been with one of her brothers, she would have poked the damn thing in the eye if it had dared to look at her. She stole another peek at it around Dred's very large Viking frame.

The thing snapped its eye shut just as it caught her movement. The fuckers were watching them. She could do this. Really. Middy had a grip on her initial hysteria. They were on a secret mission, for Morrigan's sake. A little bug shouldn't have—she broke off her thought. It really wasn't that little. It was just a bug, though. Middy could go over and stomp on it. Not without ruining her shoes, but still, she could do it if she was so motivated.

It was just a bug. Just a creepy, crawly, slimy bit of dark that had been pulled from the Abyss to . . .

She'd been twelve when her mother had let her go to the magick market by herself. Middy had a pocket full of money she'd saved from her summer of flea-dipping familiars and she wanted to buy a cape. A red one. Her idiot brothers told her a red velvet cape would do nothing more for her than attract werewolves, but Middy hadn't cared. She'd seen the one she wanted in the *Bell, Book and Candle*.

Middy had been ready to pay for her beloved cape, but could find no one to take her money. She'd wandered to the back of the store, down the stairs, and into a secret room. The walls had been covered with bugs; they'd swarmed around her, over her skin, tangled in her hair, and they'd all been seeking entry. Her ears, her nose, her mouth, her eyes, and they'd begun to bite her skin to get inside of her that way. She didn't remember how she'd gotten home, her red cape wrapped in a parcel and all of her money still in her pocket.

None of those bat bugs had been near the size of the ones that now lay on the floor.

"I'm sorry, Dred." Her voice was still shaky. "I think I'm overtired from the trip," she said for whoever happened to be listening through the batbug.

"I'll just get us some refreshment and I think you'll feel better." And with one swift movement, he swept the bugs into the fire.

When he was sure they were ash, he asked, "Are you okay?"

Middy nodded. "I'm not usually so . . . that way."

"You're made of sterner stuff than you realize, Midnight. I wonder if that is why we were put in this room?" he said, still thinking about the bugs. "I also wonder if someone knows why we're here."

"Maybe. Or maybe someone on Barista's staff just wants to see what they can find out? With all of the highborns here, there are people who would pay lots of money for the intimate information that's just there for the plucking."

"Those bugs were a fuck of a lot of magick for a gossip rag." Dred's mouth thinned into a hard line.

"It's not for the sort of money that some of these warlocks can afford to part with to keep their bastards and scandals in the attic."

"Very true. Speaking of bastards—" Dred turned to her.

"Have you given any thought to what you'll do if there are consequences when I fulfill my end of this contract?"

Middy was amazed at how fast he changed subjects. From batbugs and blackmail to sex. No, not just sex, but illegitimate offspring. He was so casual about it. She supposed it was a valid concern and she was ashamed to say that she hadn't given it any thought at all. Good thing she was already on the potion.

"I'm on the potion."

"Did you know that it's only ninety-percent effective?" Dred offered casually.

"What are you, a walking prophylactic commercial?"

"I'm just saying. There's still the possibility that you could conceive. Warlocks have to be super fertile, because we've been so hunted by mortals." Dred shrugged.

Middy colored. What would she do? She knew for a fact that witches could conceive the first time. If she got pregnant, she'd really have to marry Dred. Her mother would petition the council.

Shit.

It was no wonder she was still a virgin! She was never going to get laid at this rate.

"Ah, I can see your wheels turning, Midnight. Be assured, if you do conceive, I'll take care of my responsibilities."

"That sounds so romantic," she snorted.

"Marriage for our kind is rarely romantic, Midnight. I thought you knew that."

"Lovely. We're talking marriage and babies, and I haven't even gotten any of the good stuff yet."

He laughed. "Middy, you're supposed to think that those things are the 'good stuff'—you're a witch."

"I don't see how. What do I get out of that besides being shackled to a screaming, pooping wad of humanity and a warlock who can't keep his wand sheathed?"

"Hence the conversation. It's good to be prepared. Isn't it better to know what you're getting into up front?"

"You really are an asshole." It was more of an observation than an insult.

"I never said I wasn't, sweetheart," Dred replied coolly.

"That doesn't mean I've changed my mind," Middy warned.

"You know, you could marry a highborn if you keep your virginity."

"I don't want to get married."

Dred peered at her as if she were some strange little bug that he'd never seen before. "Isn't it engraved in the witch psyche to want to get married? Don't they drill that into you with dolls with wedding dresses and stories about charming princes in shining armor who slay dragons?"

"I've found dragons to be kind and wise, shining armor rusts like a bitch, marriage is overrated, and charming princes are usually whoremongers. I can buy myself a pretty dress and I don't have to bind myself to someone to do it."

"That's pretty damn cynical, Midnight. I think I might just have to marry you after all."

"You could ask me right now in front of a cleric and I would say no," Midnight said as she charmed her clothes out of her bags and instructed them to hang themselves up.

"Right now, you have to say yes."

"Oh, and why is that? Did you trip and fall in love?" She snorted like a fat piggy with her head in a particularly lush trough.

"No, we just need the tattoos."

"Oh. Right." Middy had kind of hoped he was serious. Just so she could say no, of course.

"So, Midnight Cherrywood, would you do me the honor of becoming my lawfully wedded witch?"

"You're not even on one knee! And where is my ring?" Middy put a hand on her hip.

"You're getting tattoos—why do you need a ring?" Dred asked with disgust.

"It's a good thing that you're not doing this for real. Any witch worth her salt would tell you exactly what you are free to do with your tattoos and your proposal."

He was still standing. There was no knee dropping in sight. Midnight decided that if she kicked him in the knee, he'd have to bend down on the other one. Now, did she want him on the right or the left? She wasn't going to say yes until he did it the right way.

Suddenly, she found herself in his arms on the receiving end of a panty-shredding kiss. With one hand tangled in her hair and the other at the base of her spine, he bent her backwards, bracing her with his forearm. He was so focused on her mouth, it felt as if time had stopped and her whole world swirled with colors like a Monet canvas.

Middy was aware of nothing but the heat between them, the way she fit against his large body, his expert touch causing a symphony of sensation that drowned out anything that wasn't Dred. Even her breath was his and the beating of her heart was like a stampede in her ears.

He wrapped up the kiss gently as if the lack of contact would break her. She clung to him, unwilling for the moment to end.

"Marry me, Midnight." Dred's whisper was harsh and ragged in her ear. The warmth of his breath sent shivers down her spine and curled in her belly before reaching the core of her.

"Yes." The words tumbled out of her mouth unbidden and she tilted her head up to meet his lips again.

She realized there was something soft beneath her now, the bed. Dred kissed her again and Middy cried out. Even the mindless desire he ignited with his kiss couldn't drown out the pain of what felt like a sewing needle jamming into the skin of her wrist.

They both watched as the mark that branded her as his slowly bloomed to life there. Tangled vines and blooms erupted on the canvas of her flesh and curled around the Shadowins crest that became visible on the sensitive side of her wrist. Middy had to admit that even though it burned like hell, it was beautiful.

Dred's wrist was dark with larger vines and foliage, but no blooms. They twined around the scrolling letters of her name which encircled his wrist. Blood welled in places and smeared before disappearing as if it had never been.

"This is completely unfair," Middy muttered as soon as the pain ebbed.

"Oh, how is that?" Dred asked, still inspecting his wrist as if it belonged to some aberration from the Abyss rather than himself.

"I get pricked twice. Once by the needle and once by you."

"It will be more than twice, Midnight, I promise you," he said as he ghosted his fingers over her cheek and down to the hollow of her throat. "And it will be well worth it."

"Don't make promises that you can't keep, Shadowins," Middy challenged him.

"I never break my promises, Midnight." Dred continued to stroke her flushed skin and trailed down to the valley between her breasts.

"Well, you certainly won't be putting out right now, will you?"

"Alas, no." He didn't sound as if he meant it. "There are many . . . pressing matters."

Midnight shifted and arched into his touch, the heat from his hand burning awareness into the sensitive flesh of her breast.

"You could tempt an angel to sin," he said as he edged her blouse open.

"You're no angel, Mordred Shadowins."

"No, I'm certainly not," he said, the pad of his finger tracing farther down toward her belly, but then back up again to her lips. "You're making it awfully hard to not be a bastard."

"How's that?" Middy looked up at him.

"It's the way you look at me, your eyes soft and wanting. The way you arch your body to my touch, the way your lips part when you think about our kisses and"—he leaned in next to her, the weight of him pushing her down into the mattress—"the way you flush that shade of pink when you think about fucking me."

He brushed his lips against hers before he continued. "All I can think about is what it would be like to feel your heat around me, how tight you'll be, and the rapture on your face when you come for me." Dred touched his lips to hers again, hard this time, but it still wasn't a kiss. It wasn't enough. "I could be inside you right now, but there's not enough time to make it good. Not enough time to push you to the edge so that when I take you, it will be a plea-sure-pain instead of only the tearing of your flesh."

Middy felt the evidence of his words pressing hard into her thigh and she wanted more of it. His words, titillating though they were, made sense. She confessed to knowing nothing of sex except what she'd heard from Tally and the perversions she'd inflicted on a centerfold.

She didn't want to stop taunting him, though. Not only did it turn her on to see his desire, but it was a rush like no other she'd had before to be in command of his complete and utter attention. No one had ever made her feel that way.

Middy knew that it wasn't love and it wasn't going to be, but this was enough for her. She wasn't looking for love. She wanted passion, adventure, excitement, and Dred was all of those things. Just these last few days had been filled with more of all that than she'd had in the whole of her quiet lifetime.

"What if I give you permission to be a bastard?" Middy said and kissed the corner of his mouth.

A low sound came from the back of his throat, almost like a growl. "That would be a sin. You should know only pleasure."

"How can I know the beauty of the pleasure without the pain?"

"Indeed, you are a devil. I've never wanted another witch the way I want you." Dred met her eyes and pushed a curl behind her ear. "Perhaps once I've had you, I will never feel that again."

Middy didn't think the word *feel* should have anything to do with Dred Shadowins. He was a bastard extraordinaire. He wasn't supposed to have feelings. She saw an out and latched on to it. "Perhaps. Or you could just wait for ten years until the next generation of witches is ready for your attentions."

"You're heartless," he sighed dramatically. "We haven't even had our mad affair and you've already moved on." He whispered a grooming charm and was immaculate again.

Middy liked it when he looked rumpled and well-used. She wondered if warlocks liked that look on a witch, too.

"We should talk about that," Middy said, veering back to the subject.

"Talk about what?" He scowled.

"I don't want you to see anyone else during our little charade."

"You either."

"What?"

"It's fair. No sneaking around with Belledare."

"Tristan is a douche bag."

"He seems to have reason to think that your feelings are of a more tender nature."

"Like hell," Middy said as she used her own grooming charm.

"Are you ready to put on your happy bride face?" Dred smirked.

"Not until I get my ring."

"Merlin's Blue Balls! You're still stuck on that? Fine." Dred pulled something off a chain around his neck and jammed it on her finger rather unceremoniously. "That was my grandmother's. When this is over, I get it back."

Middy looked down at the simple band and took it off so she could inspect it. There was an inscription. *"Altig Mig Hjerte."* The scrolling letters were beautiful and she felt a warm pulse coming from them when she slid the ring back on her finger. Then she felt the letters on the ring burn into her wrist, tangling in the vines of the engagement tattoo.

Sweet Circe's Tampon!

What if they didn't come off? She'd heard stories of witches who'd lost their warlocks to death or other witches, which amounted to the same thing in Middy's mind, but the tattoos had never faded.

"Uh, Dred? What does the inscription mean?"

"It's Danish. It means 'Forever, My Heart.'"

She stole a glance at Dred and put the ring back on. The scowl on his hard features told her that maybe she shouldn't tell him that the words had become part of the marriage tattoo.

CHAPTER TWELVE

Chancellor Snow, in the Library, with the Candlestick

Three days at the house party and he still hadn't fucked her.

It wasn't as if this was some revelation that had hit him like the hammy fists of an angry troll. No, Dred had spent three agonizing, horrible nights with his cock posing as an alert and anxious soldier—ready to go to war. The thing seemed to be under the impression that it was auditioning to be a cannon.

There had never been any question of sleeping arrangements. Not that he would have offered to take the floor. He'd been fully prepared to demand that they share the bed since she was in such a hurry to engage in certain activities. He'd expected her to demure, but she hadn't even asked about arrangements when she'd seen the bed. In fact, he was sure she hadn't given it a second thought. Middy had smiled her innocent smile, donned her pink, *sheer* night-gown, and gone along her merry way, which included dragging him down the primrose path to Hell behind her.

Things were completely fucked. He was the cad, the millionaire playboy who, wait, make that *billionaire* playboy, who didn't give a shit about anything. Especially not what happened to witches after he'd made them scream in tongues unknown to gods or warlocks.

So, he'd let a little of his devil-may-care attitude slip by spying for the council. A warlock had to care about something. That didn't mean he was going soft.

Maybe he owed Middy something. That was it. Per her demands, he owed her a ride on his wand. So what was the holdup? Why didn't he just fuck her seven shades of blue and call it day? Merlin knew he wanted to. So why wasn't he wand deep right now? This very second he could be enjoying her gasps of pleasure and the tight sheath of her virgin body.

He'd done his part. He'd told her up front what to expect and why this whole thing was a bad idea. He hadn't promised her anything and she hadn't asked for it, at least out loud.

After he'd pulled all of her layers away, she was still a witch. Could she really be that different from the rest of her kind? Her mouth hadn't formed the words, but it was still there in her eyes. Middy wanted to be loved. She deserved nothing less. Dred just didn't have that to give.

He'd tried to reiterate that it would be nothing but a bodily release for him, but she'd given him her carefree Middy smile and told him not to worry, that she didn't have expectations. What bothered him was that he wanted her to have expectations; he wanted her to know that she deserved to have them.

So he'd tried to keep his hands to himself. He'd done his damndest to do the Right Thing. It was easy for his brain to confuse what exactly the right thing was when it was three o'clock in the morning and she was soft and pliant, pushing her rounded curves against his cock, and begging for his touch. Especially with that sweet, feminine scent of hers, the silk of her hair, and the eagerness of her body wrapped around him like a shroud.

Dred argued with himself that he had to fuck her at least once. He'd sworn. A magickal bond bound him to her until he did. And what really pissed him off was the cold chill down his spine when he put fucking and Middy in the same sentence. As if she were too good to be fucked, as if it ought to be called something else.

He had a stray, niggling thought that maybe he was feeling guilt.

This was not a revelation he cared for. Not one damn bit. Not that he even knew what he was feeling guilty for. Fucking was fucking. He didn't see why it had to stop being fucking just because he happened to like the witch he was doing it with. Or not doing it with as the case had come to be.

It was just stupid. She wanted to be fucked. He wanted to fuck her. What was the problem again?

Last night had been the worst; she'd been having some sort of sex dream and it had obviously been about him. She'd been writhing around, pushing her ass up against him, and making small sounds that had become his name. Dred had thought that it couldn't get any worse than that, but it had.

She'd cried out in need, her fingers had moved between her thighs, and she'd been flicking her clit and pleading with him to make her come.

If Dred had been a lesser warlock, he would have given her what she'd begged for so prettily. Instead, he lay beside her, watching her hands travel her body and do all of the things that he wished to do. He remembered the taste of her, how she'd come for him, and only him. Not to some magickally altered version of himself, but him. In the flesh. She'd arched up for his tongue, spread her legs for him and Dred had to admit, he loved hearing his name on her lips. He also loved kissing her afterward, watching her face as she tasted her own pleasure.

That witch was a fantasy made real.

She was the archetype virgin Jezebel that all males, mortal and warlock alike, sought. She was untried flesh, unmarked territory, yet her body was like a Stradivarius violin—he knew it would sing with the touch of a master.

And a master he was. He'd studied the ancient and forbidden tomes of sex magick. With a touch, or a breath, he could ruin her for any other warlock for all time. He could make her believe anything he desired, make her do anything he desired just by playing the right chord within her. With what he had learned, he could invoke a magickal orgasm that was indeed *la petite morte,* the little death. It would stop her heart.

He had all of this power, but when he was around her, it was as if he was still just a warlock trying to get his wand wet.

Dred felt another moment of ball-breaking clarity coming on. He didn't want it. That was the bad thing about being honest with yourself—it was always brutal. Dred wanted to be the good guy. Yeah, that was a revelation that had been a canker on his ass for some time now. He wanted someone to see that there was good in him and that night in Shale Creek hadn't taken what was left of his soul back into the Abyss.

No, not someone. Middy Cherrywood. He felt warm around her and he felt it in places other than his cock. He wasn't sure what that meant, and he wasn't even sure if he liked it, but he didn't want it to stop until he could decide.

He knew when the drunken revelry of the sex magick had faded and the sun was bright on what she'd done, she wouldn't look at him the same way. It was for purely selfish reasons that he didn't want to complete their bargain.

His cock had other ideas. Other ideas that in any other circumstance, with any other witch, would be the right ones.

He'd always had such tight control of his body; it was something he'd learned when he was captured in the war.

Not something he cared to remember now, sitting in his aunt's library waiting for his Uncle Roderick.

Uncle Roderick was the man he believed to be responsible for his capture after Shale Creek. Dred would have been content to disappear into the night with no one ever knowing he'd been there. Roderick had been the only one who'd known his location. Roderick was also the warlock he believed to be smuggling dark objects. If it wasn't him, it was someone in his employ. He'd tracked dark signatures of magick back to Snow Manor. Dred knew for a fact that Barista wasn't involved. She'd lost her first husband to a dark object mishap. So perhaps Roderick had a mistress who was helping him?

Dred drew a copy of Gaston LeRoux's *Phantom of the Opera* down from one of the immaculate shelves. He still had a raging case of wood, cherrywood, to be precise. He opened the leather-bound tome and sat down at the massive desk in the middle of the room.

Roderick had always called it his "reading table." Dred was sure that it was more like his "drilling the maid table." There was no other reason for it to be so large. Unless it was hiding something.

"I wouldn't have thought to see you reading such drivel," Roderick Snow said as he entered the library.

"I've always found the Phantom's plight engaging." Dred leaned back in the chair and dropped his booted feet like two bricks on the surface of the desk.

Roderick eyed his nephew with blatant disapproval. "Really? I've always found it trite. He was a weak man."

"How's that?" Dred let the pages flutter closed as if they held only a passing interest.

Roderick leaned over the desk. "He had everything he wanted, but he let it go. Christine had agreed to be his forever. It was her choice. Not a pleasant one—" Roderick's sharp features bloomed into a smile that was more like a bird of prey opening its beak for a fat mouse. "Still, it was her choice and he let her go."

"I see, but I beg to differ."

"Really? Did you fall for poor little Christine's sob story, too? An innocent ingénue who had enough foresight to move herself from the *corps de ballet* to diva to vicomtessa."

Dred snorted. "Certainly not. But I wonder why he wanted her to start with. A well-schooled whore would be better suited to a man of his depravities."

"Your choice of bride-to-be belies that philosophy."

"Does she?" Dred tossed the question back with little interest. If Middy Cherrywood was to be his bride in truth, he wouldn't have cared less what anyone thought about it. Least of all Roderick Snow.

"Is she another Christine then, forced to the beast?" Roderick made a show of glancing around the library. "Or would that be the Butcher of Shale Creek?"

"The beast? Yes, a beast in Armani." Dred sniffed as if he'd stepped in something unmentionable. "In case it's escaped you, Roderick, your nephew has great magick. Witches seem to find me attractive, regardless of what was done in Shale Creek."

"That's what I thought we'd chat about, Mordred."

"My magick or the Shale Creek Hand of Glory?"

"Why limit ourselves? Both are very interesting topics."

"Are you looking for some pointers then, Roderick? Something to keep the young witches interested in you, Chancellor Snow?" Dred said this last with a knowing sneer.

"Perhaps," he said.

If Roderick was stung by the barb, it didn't show. Dred watched him carefully and decided that this was further proof that Roderick had a mistress and that she was much younger than Barista.

"What is it you really want, Uncle? It's not as if we've ever been close. You don't have to make a show of it now because you want something."

"Straight to the point. I admire that in a warlock. But don't you like the game?"

"I prefer a different sort of game." Dred smirked.

"Ah, but this has a darker quarry." Roderick's mouth twisted into his own smirk. "I want the Shale Creek Hand of Glory."

Dred smiled then. "I'm afraid that's impossible."

"Nothing is impossible." Roderick's features hardened. "I know what you went through to acquire it. I expect it to be pricey."

It would be interesting to know just how far Roderick would go for the Shale Creek Hand, as it had come to be known after the war.

"Now what would Roderick Snow consider pricey, hmm? What can you give me that I don't already have?"

"All of Snow holdings. Snow Manor. All yours."

"And?" Dred rolled his eyes.

"You can't tell me that you don't want the Manor. There are magicks hidden throughout, some dating back to the Crusades, some to before the Christians and their Christ. There are many more caches like the one you found here as a boy, Mordred."

"How many?" Dred asked, showing a bit of interest now.

"It's unknown, but there is a map." A dark twinkle lit up Roderick's eyes as he felt the conversation turning his way.

If Roderick gave up his holdings, what would he have to offer his little mistress? Dred wondered. This was proving to be more enlightening that he'd first thought. Roderick must have some side investments.

What was he going to do with the Hand if he was willing to trade Snow Manor? It had been the first stronghold for the Snow family all of those years ago. It was said the first Snow bride had been a frost fairy, and all Snows would always have great magick, as long as Snow Manor remained in their keeping.

"Uncle, all of your holdings revert to me upon your death anyway. I'm the only heir."

"Can't bribe you with your own money, can I, boy?" Roderick was fairly jovial and leaned into the space between them. "What about a seat on the council? You could be Chancellor Shadowins."

"What makes you think I want a seat on the Warlock's Council?"

"Because you don't have one. And you can't buy it."

"Who says I can't? It's for sale by your own admission. How do you know I still have the Hand?"

"I suppose I don't. Then again, what could anyone else offer you that you don't have or can't buy?" Roderick threw his own words back at him.

"I don't know, perhaps I should think on it." The corner of Dred's mouth curved up in the beginning of a malicious smile.

Roderick sighed. "Play coy if you like, dearest nephew. I'm in no hurry. In the end, you'll give me what I want. One way or another."

"Now it's threats as well as promises. You're in more of a hurry than you'd like me to believe."

"I just know what I want."

Dred stood now and he towered over Roderick. "Want in one hand, *dearest uncle.*" He shrugged as if Roderick's response meant nothing.

"Yes, Mordred. Want in one hand and take with the other. I'll give you a week." Roderick turned on his finely cobbled heel to leave.

"I thought you said you had time? A week is hardly reasonable, even at a dark table."

"One week, Mordred. Just one."

"Is that when your lamia walks?" Fuck it. Roderick had already threatened him.

Roderick spun around like a loose figure on a carousel. His stone features blanched a brighter white and his brows drew together like two caterpillars. "Is that why you think I want it?"

"What else are you going to do with a Hand of Glory?" Dred demanded. He'd only ever heard of one use for the thing, to tear open a hole to the Abyss and drag the dark things forth with those burning fingers.

"It's for Barista's skin cream."

"Are you shitting me?"

"Dark objects are the best, most effective way to stay young. You don't believe all that drivel she spouts to the witches' magazines, do you? This is the last potion though. With the Hand of Glory, we'll keep our youth until we decide to go through the veil."

"Why didn't Barista just ask me for it?"

"Pride."

Dred felt as bright as a gaggle of water-headed goblins flinging their own poo at each other in the display case at Magickal Menagerie. "So, during the war. My capture . . ."

"You thought I did that? Why?" Roderick was aghast.

"Because I stole your dark object stash and—"

"That was you? We fired Barista's beauty consultant. We thought that she did it. She's currently scrubbing floors at Banshee's Bawl. After Barista fired her, no one else would have her."

"Fuck."

"Precisely. Now, about that Hand . . ."

"Show me the rituals for the cream and prepare some for my mother and you can have it."

"I can *have* it?" Roderick's eyes narrowed. "And you don't want anything for it? You will give me the Hand of Glory? Just like that?"

"Why not?"

"You're an odd warlock, Mordred. I think we should really get to know one another after this house party. I can't believe you'd think I would betray you."

"Look at the facts. They all point to you."

"All the facts say that you're the Butcher of Shale Creek and I don't believe that for a second."

"Okay, so I'm an asshole." Dred shrugged.

"That I *can* believe." Roderick rolled his eyes.

"I still want proof of the rituals."

"I wouldn't expect anything less." Roderick shook his head and left.

Dred was only alone for a few moments when he heard the irritating baritone of Tristan Belledare and the sweet tones of Dred's own lovely "intended."

The door was pushed open and Middy was shoved through like some unwanted sack of meal. "You need to listen to me, Midnight."

"I would listen to you, if you'd stop putting your hands on me."

"You don't seem to listen otherwise."

"Look, Belledare. You lay hands on me once more and I'll—"

"You'll what? Tattle to your dark warlock? I thought we were past all that? I remember back at the Academy, you hated him. He hated you. What was the problem with the status quo?"

Middy made a face like she'd licked the wrong end of a swamp frog. "We fell in love. That changes the status quo. It's not like you were doing anything about your"—she made air quotes with her fingers—"feelings." This last came out with a sneer.

"Middy, I told you at the Masque, but—"

"But? What's done is done, Tristan. You've got to stop this."

"Me?" Tristan whirled on her in a feminine sort of fury.

At least, that's how Dred would have described it, eyes flashing, face flushed, his fists clenched. . . . Dred had to bite his lip not to laugh out loud. So far, they hadn't noticed him. He was sure that the dragon muck would hit the fan when they did, but how was it his fault that they hadn't checked to see if the room was occupied before allowing their little drama to ensue?

He was tempted to slip beneath the desk, but was sure that any movement would alert them to his presence. Ah, but not if he used an invisibility charm. Dred didn't feel the least bit guilty about it either.

Dred suspected that his affianced was not safe in Tristan's company; therefore, the only chivalrous thing to do was to observe. For Middy's protection, of course. At least that was what he was going to tell her when she found out he was there and turned that intriguing shade of pink. Of course, it might be more like red, depending on what happened next.

Tristan produced a copy of *Weekly Warlock* and flung it to the table in disgust. "I have to stop? What about you? What is this?"

"Where did you get this?" Midnight demanded, that sweet pink infusing her pale skin as her temper bloomed.

"Your living room."

Middy let out a high-pitched sound that could have been a battle cry. She launched herself at him like a swarm of angry bees. She would have proceeded to sting him in places that Tristan didn't know he had if the magazine hadn't fallen open to the Warlock of the Month.

The program activated.

CHAPTER THIRTEEN
Bookgasm

It was no surprise that the Warlock of the Month was Dred Shadowins. The surprise was when the centerfold Dred appeared wearing nothing but a white loincloth and angel wings. His platinum hair was more of a honey color and he was bearing a flaming sword.

Centerfold Dred raised a pale brow in blatant displeasure. "Are you serious?"

But he wasn't talking to Middy.

He was talking to Tristan.

It was *his* fantasy that had activated the centerfold.

The Dred-toy turned and looked at Middy. "I would have expected this from you. But him? Really?"

Tristan stuttered, "I— it's not me!"

"Let's get this over with," the centerfold said.

"What over with?" Tristan was horrified.

"What do you think?" The Dred rolled his eyes.

"I'll leave you two alone." Middy tried to squeeze past Tristan and the Dred-toy to make it to the door.

She didn't dare let the centerfold get too close to her. She'd have an orgasm with Tristan looking right at her. Of course, from the look of things, it seemed as if he'd be having his own. She smirked. Then she frowned. Middy had no desire to have that sort of knowledge of Tristan Belledare.

Technically, it could be considered breaking her agreement with Dred. The real, in the flesh Dred. They'd both promised no one else and Middy was pretty damn sure that sharing an orgasm, even if it wasn't . . . well, like that . . . had to count.

"Don't leave me alone with this thing!" Tristan demanded.

"Why not, it's yours, isn't it?"

"No, it's . . . I was trying to make a point."

"Well, you've made it with that flaming sword." Middy gestured to the magazine.

"No! Something saved me at Shale Creek. It was an angel. I can't stop thinking about it. She's always on my mind."

"Then why does it look like my fiancé?" Middy shot back as she pushed past him.

Tristan grabbed her and held her between himself and the centerfold.

"I don't know. I never saw its face. But it couldn't be Dred. I have no thoughts of . . ." Tristan shifted to the left, and when the Dred shifted to the left as well, Tristan pulled Middy with them.

This continued for a few minutes until Middy put her hand on the centerfold's chest. "Hold on."

"To what, darling?"

"Me," she said, taking pity on Belledare. The Dred-bot put his hands on Middy's hips and Middy turned to face Tristan.

"Maybe you did see its face and it was Dred that saved you."

"No, he tried to push me into the vortex. He would have sacrificed me like everyone else at Shale Creek for that Hand of Glory." He darted to the side again and the Dred-bot laughed.

"Which would be the more comfortable answer, Tristan?

That Dred saved you and so his image has been burned into your brain, or that you want him to ride you like Pegasus?"

"Why are you so sure I'd be the catcher, Middy?" Tristan whined.

"Because he's Dred Shadowins," Middy replied as if Tristan were the slowest bipedal creature she'd ever encountered.

"And I'm just the hero. Nice warlocks always finish last."

"You got that right, boy-o!" Dred-bot offered.

"How would you know, Tristan? You're not a nice guy," Middy snapped.

"I'm trying to save you—"

"I don't want to be saved! I've made my choice. Why is that so hard for you to understand?"

"Because I *don't* understand it," Tristan snapped back.

"Neither do I, really." The centerfold shrugged.

"No one was talking to you!" Tristan growled.

"Your mouth might not be, but the rest of you is saying something. Why else would I be standing here looking like a horny cherub?"

"I thought you wouldn't do anything that Dred wouldn't do?" Middy demanded. "I'm pretty sure Dred wouldn't prance around in that getup for Tristan Belledare."

"He might if it amused him," the centerfold replied.

"Close the magazine," Middy commanded.

"I can't reach it."

"For Morrigan's sake, Tristan!" Tally shrieked as she barreled through the door.

"What are you doing here?" Middy squealed. What was Tally doing there? She hadn't said anything about coming with Martin after the shopping expedition. Not even when she'd helped bundle her off in Dred's broom sleigh. Very strange.

It was almost as if she'd been outside the door listening, but that would be creepy and not like Tally at all. Although,

Tally had been doing a lot of things that weren't like her lately.

"Getting this douche bag out of your way is what I'm doing. You owe me." Tally grabbed hold of Tristan's sleeve. "Dred Shadowins would roast you alive if he knew you were chasing his fiancée like a bitch in heat."

"You're the one chasing me!" Tristan tried to pull away from her.

"No, I'm here as someone's guest. Someone who is not you. How did I get in otherwise?" Tally turned to Middy. "Look, it was a last-minute thing, with you know who. I'll tell you about it later."

Seeing her friend smile so happily made her regret her earlier thoughts. Of course, she was acting differently. Tally was happy. She'd never been this happy before.

"There aren't any reporters to save your ass here like there were at the Masque," Middy snapped at Tristan. Maybe if she acted like a harpy, he'd leave her alone.

"And I don't see your doting affianced anywhere, do you?" Tristan asked snidely.

Tally growled and jerked Tristan so hard, he practically flew out of the room with her. She must have been taking out her frustration at the gym because Tristan was not a small warlock. In fact, he was almost Dred-sized. Nowhere near as intriguing, but large and muscle-bound nonetheless.

"I guess that just leaves us, hot stuff."

"You're not my program. My centerfold would never refer to me as 'hot stuff.' " Middy chided.

"Then he doesn't know what he's doing. Because you are definitely hot stuff." The Dred-bot winked at her.

"So, are you Tristan's?"

"Not a chance, sweetheart. He stole me from your house." He edged closer to her and she stepped back.

"You don't act like any of the editions I have at my house."

"That's because I was a gift. Someone left me for you."

"Why would they do that?" Middy asked, suddenly breathless. She had to keep distance between them. This wasn't Dred and it wasn't her safe little program.

"Why would you think that Dred saved Tristan at Shale Creek?" The handsome features hardened and his eyes narrowed.

"Why do you care? You're a centerfold. Shut up and be objectified as you're told." That always worked with hers; hopefully, they were all wired like that.

She felt a touch on her cheek. "That's not my programming. Good thing that the real Dred would be mortally opposed to harm befalling you."

"Why is that?" Dred asked, casting off his invisibility charm.

The Dred-bot paled, its reality fading in the presence of the real thing.

"Were you programmed to kill her?" Dred demanded of his double.

"How is that possible?" Middy asked, both irritated he'd been watching the exchange, but thankful he was there. She knew that whatever he was, whether his magick was white, black, or gray, he wouldn't let anything happen to her.

"We'll discuss that later." Dred closed the distance between them.

Middy decided, in that moment, with two Dreds touching her at once, that the centerfold didn't have to kill her. The overload of sensation might just do her in. Dred's fingers were warm and real on the side of her cheek and the Dred-bot was touching her, too. He'd moved behind her and she could feel the unearthly sensation of a ghostly touch.

She'd seen someone write in to *Cauldron Forum* about this fantasy. Middy would have to remember the user name later when she could think. Right now, thinking was not a high priority, not while being sandwiched between two Dreds.

"Answer me," Dred demanded of the bot.

"Yes, I was programmed to kill her. To close my fingers around her neck just as she came for us."

Both of their hands were still moving over her body. What this had to do with questioning the bot, she had no idea. She was just going to go with it.

She wasn't afraid. Dred wouldn't let anything happen to her. Middy knew that she should be afraid, and the rational part of her mind was screaming for her to run, to break free from this madness. Her muffin was louder. It seemed to have taken the wheel and she wasn't going anywhere.

"Us?" Dred questioned as Middy leaned into him.

"Oh, yes, this is what you are supposed to do." The Dred put his hand on Dred's arm. "My master said you'd love to fuck yourself."

"Master or mistress?" Dred questioned.

"I can't tell you that."

"I see," Dred said, trying to move Middy away from his lookalike.

"So, would you, Dred? Would you like to fuck your-self?" The bot asked.

Middy decided that this might be the pair of stilettos that broke the stripper's back—seeing all of that hot male Dred-ness together. . . . It was definitely a witch who'd set this scheme in motion. No warlock would envision Dred-on-Dred scenarios. Well, he might, but he wouldn't say things about fucking himself. No, that was a very witchy thing to say.

Dred's lips were on her ears now. "Close the magazine, Middy."

She didn't want to! She wanted to be shrouded in Dred . . .

"Do it now!"

Damn. She reached back and flipped the magazine shut and the Dred-bot sputtered to a pitiful nonexistence.

Middy was still left pressed up against a dusty bookshelf with one Dred. The real, in the flesh Dred. She supposed that asking for two would be unreasonably greedy. And really, if she thought about it, her virginal self only had a vague idea of what to do with one Dred. Midnight doubted that she'd be able to do anything with two, at least not comfortably. For a moment though, she'd been damn sure that she wanted to try.

"Are you afraid?" Dred asked as his fingers cupped her chin and tilted her face to his.

"No, should I be?" She was drowning in him, falling into his magick, the way his very presence seemed to steal the air.

"Yes, very afraid. That centerfold was sent to kill you." The pressure of his fingers changed and now, his hand was on her throat and his thumb caressed the delicate line of her jaw. "Those sensations of pleasure felt real, and so would those of death. Your brain would read it as such and shut down accordingly."

"You wouldn't have let that happen," Middy said breathlessly and turned into his touch.

"You shouldn't trust me."

"I don't. I know you need me though. At least until the end of this charade. " She touched her lips to his fingers in a ghost of a kiss.

"You're still under the spell. That thing was infused with Sex Magick," Dred said coolly, though he made no move to put any distance between them.

"That's your superpower, isn't it, Mordred? Sex Magick," she said as her tongue darted out to taste his skin.

"I suppose here is where I should tell you that you don't

know what you're doing to me, that you don't want to lose your virginity with your dress up around your thighs, and your back pressed into a musty library shelf, but I think you do." His hand slipped to her hip and then between her thighs.

She wasn't wearing any knickers. Middy had found that she quite liked how naughty she felt, with only a wisp of fabric between her body and Dred Shadowins. Being in such close proximity to him, it made her feel powerful in a very primal sense.

"You're wet for me. Or are you wet for 'us'?" he asked with a knowing smirk.

"Both," she whispered as Dred slipped a finger inside of her.

She dug her fingers into his shoulders and he hefted her easily, propping her against the bookshelves with his forearm as he guided one leg around his waist.

Middy's eyelids were heavy with desire and she had trouble keeping them open. She had trouble processing anything that wasn't Dred between her thighs. She forced her eyes open to look at him.

There was a dark intensity on his face and she could feel the magick pulsing through them both. She knew he wanted her. This was it; there was no turning back now. It frightened her and thrilled her at the same time. She knew that it would be nothing like what she imagined, nothing like her ideals of courtly perfection, but she knew that it would change her forever.

She wasn't so blind as to think that it would change him and yet, she had a feeling that it would. This was a precipice for them both.

"Kiss me," she demanded.

His mouth crashed into hers, claiming and conquering. Just as if she were really a village girl and he was the pillaging Viking. He dwarfed her and Middy wasn't a small witch. Dred was so strong, he held her up as if she weighed less than a feather.

These were all things she'd dreamt about, fantasized about, all things she'd programmed into her own Dred. She still couldn't believe it was real.

"Do you want the magick, Middy?" he asked raggedly in her ear after he broke the kiss.

"Isn't *this* magick?" she replied and kissed the corner of his jaw.

"So there's no pain." His mouth was on her neck, his fingers still pushing in and out of her sheath, just to the barrier of her virginity, and his thumb working her clit. "Isn't the Sex Magick what you want?"

She surprised herself. "No, Dred. I want you. Not your magick."

And she did. She wanted the whole experience; she wanted to feel something real. She could play games with the centerfold when he was gone, when this charade was over. So much wasn't real and Middy wanted something solid, if only to know that later, it had actually happened.

A sound that might have been a growl started low in the back of his throat and he carried her to the large desk where he'd been seated before. Dred splayed her before him like a rare delicacy, positioning her heels and her bottom just at the edge of the desk.

Then he knelt before her like a supplicant and his lips touched her labia, his tongue slid inside her and then up to her clit. Middy had to grab the desk with both hands to keep from crying out.

She wanted to push against his mouth, but if she moved, she'd fall. Middy was at his mercy and she knew that Dred Shadowins had none.

He laved the swollen flesh until she felt her body tense and then he stopped. He stopped!

"Please!" she begged and propped herself up on her elbows to watch him.

His hands were unbearably slow, yet somehow beautiful as they moved to reveal his body to her. First, it was the gradual slide of his black shirt as it inched up his flesh and revealed his hard abs.

Everything about the warlock was hard. His broad chest, his wide shoulders, his biceps . . . He could be an artistic study in the beauty of the male form, more divine than Adonis.

Because he wasn't perfect.

The otherwise flawless expanse of his skin was branded by what she assumed to be his ordeal at Shale Creek. Five long, angry scars marred each side of his body and ran in jagged gashes from his shoulder blades down around to his hips. As if something with claws had tried to drag him down to Hell.

"Do you still want this without magick?" There was no shame on his face, but he knew what his scars looked like.

Middy realized then that those scars were a secret part of him, something that he usually glamoured. She'd said no magick and he was willing to give her what she wanted. Even if it meant showing her this part of him, this secret.

That slight admiration she held for Dred, the person, bloomed a little bit more. She was even more desperate to have his hands on her now. Middy knew that he'd given of himself when he'd gotten those and there was no doubt in her mind that he was a hero. There were whispers that he'd been marked by his dark master, but Middy knew otherwise. She could feel it in the way he touched her.

"No magick, Dred."

"Don't dress me up in shining armor, Middy. I'm the same person I was an hour ago. Just because I can make you scream my name, with or without magick, doesn't change what it means to me when it's over."

"No magick, Dred," she repeated.

He pulled her legs around his waist and she realized that he'd finished disrobing magickally. Which was too bad; she really wanted more of a show. Middy was startled to feel the tip of his cock pushing against her slit.

Suddenly, a paralyzing fear gripped her. Maybe she should have let him use the magick. Just his finger pushing against her barrier had hurt like chewing on aluminum foil. She knew the dimensions of his cock, she knew them intimately. Logically, she knew her body was made to stretch to accommodate him. Logically.

The primal part of her brain screamed at her to run. That mating with him was a mistake and . . . He rubbed the tip against her, moving from her entrance to her clit, stroking her like he had with his fingers.

This was what she wanted, what she needed. Middy had thought there would be more kissing; maybe there would have been a bed, instead of being flat on her back on a desk in a library. She had to admit it was original.

Her body burned for him, so she arched her hips. Pain shot through her.

Middy prayed that he wouldn't move—begged the universe and two pantheons of gods to hold him still.

Tally had assured her that she'd waited so long that her hymen was probably more like a spiderweb than an actual barrier. Well, that had been a big fat lie.

Then something else happened. Something unexpected.

She felt warmth curl in her belly and it spiraled out like an electric current. It was pleasure, but it wasn't hers. Middy was feeling what Dred felt, the tight heat of her body sheathing him, the instinct to move, to thrust, to claim. It was a whirlwind of intensity, of need and it was all for her.

Yet, still he held himself stoically, waiting for some sign from her that she was ready for more.

The pain had abated some and she moved against him experimentally. Sensation flooded her and it was like a hurricane. She felt everything he felt, but she felt her own pleasure now, too.

It was almost too much, but she couldn't stop. She had a tight grip on his forearms and Middy tried to pull him closer. Instead, he moved an arm beneath her to position her for deeper penetration, that closeness she desired.

He knew her every need, every fantasy that was in her head and she knew his. She knew his every thought for each touch. She knew that her skin felt like silk, that he loved her pink. She saw visions of herself splayed naked on the black marble tiles of his penthouse. She saw herself in ways that she'd never imagined herself to look, but it was how she looked to Dred. Middy knew that he was ready to come, but that he wanted her to come first. He wanted this to be good for her. That made her body clench and feeling Dred's response sent a shudder through her.

This was more intimate than either of them had bargained for, she knew that, too. But it was all secondary to the pulsing ache in her body and the need that sang a siren song in her veins.

Dred thrust again and she cried out, but rolled her hips to meet his next thrust. Each movement struck the core of her, inflicting a pleasure/pain that caused stars to burst behind her eyes. This was just like the books she'd read. That was unexpected. And it was real.

Middy wrapped her legs around him and gave herself over to the pleasure, the rhythm of his cock drilling into her softness, the feel of his corded muscles beneath her hands as they contracted and flexed to play her body in a way she'd never known.

What pushed her over the edge wasn't his fingers between them on her clit. It wasn't the way his body already seemed to know hers. It was feeling his pleasure. It was knowing that his orgasm, this sensation that was so much like the birth of a nova, had come from her.

Her walls tightened around his cock again and as she was crying out his name, Dred spilled his seed inside of her. He gave a last thrust as if that act alone had marked her as his, then withdrew abruptly.

Her eyes were still heavy with the aftershocks of her orgasm, but she opened them to look at him. She was still splayed out like the most wanton of creatures, but he was already casting his grooming charms and was dressed as if these moments had never happened.

Now she understood why he'd warned her. Now she understood why he'd thought he'd be doing her a favor by not taking her virginity. He'd imprinted himself on her indelibly; no matter who came after, there would always be Dred.

This meant nothing to him. Even though it was a first for her, she knew from Tally and even from the snippets she'd heard from Hawk and Falcon that what had happened between them . . . it wasn't always like that.

Her body, her flesh, maybe even her soul, was meant for Dred Shadowins.

It occurred to Middy that this revelation was what one would call an absolute bitch. She didn't even like the bastard and now, some soft part of her was struck dumb, like a calf on its way to the slaughter. She realized how very apt that description was as it applied to her. She was just another stupid cow batting her eyelashes at the butcher, one in a long line of stupid cows. Yes, that was her. Right now.

How many witches had come before and believed themselves to be made for this warlock right here? Hundreds? Maybe a thousand. The thought turned her stomach. She should have asked for the magick. Then it would be something that she could put away and bring out to play whenever it moved her. No, this now, whatever it was, this thing was in control.

She couldn't believe how stupid she'd been, how naïve. He'd tried to warn her, so she couldn't blame him. Middy couldn't even be angry with him, not when he was smiling at her like that, the corner of that sinful mouth curled up in a mischievous grin.

Damn him right to the Abyss for being Dred Shadowins. That's all it was, and it was her own fault. He'd warned her.

Middy didn't want to move because when she moved, she'd have to have a reaction. Did she say thank you? Did she just act as if nothing had happened between them, that this cataclysm of intimacy had never happened?

"I thought you said you didn't want the magick." Dred's smile bent into a smirk.

"I didn't," Middy said as she pulled down her dress.

"Then what the fuck just happened?"

Yes, she decided she should thank him after all. He'd brought up the subject and answered her questions all at once. He needed a cookie. Middy would rather have bitten off her own tongue than raise the question herself. Especially if everything she'd heard was wrong. Then his ego would probably have to follow along behind him because they'd never be able to get through any door at the same time.

"You mean it's not like that for everyone?"

"No, Midnight." Dred shook his head, his hair escaped its charm and a lock fell across his forehead. "If I didn't know better, I'd swear you used Sex Magick."

"How would I know Sex Magick?" she snorted and set about the business of grooming herself.

"I don't know, Middy. That's what scares the hell out of me."

His quiet admission sparked a light within her that maybe she wasn't alone in what she was feeling.

"I didn't think anything scared you, Dred. You're dark warlock extraordinaire, after all," she said lightly, trying to break the tension.

"Middy . . ." He sat on the desk next to her. "Here's the problem. No matter what this is, it can't change anything. I need you to understand that."

"I understand what you're saying, but why can't it change anything?" At the stern look on his face, she knew she'd said the wrong thing. Why couldn't her cake hole ever just stay shut like it was supposed to?

"You know what I do. The face I have to wear, the bargains I have to make. Consider the one you made with me." He gave her a reproachful look. "And I can't worry about how someone else is going to feel about it."

"You know, if I liked you, I'd tell you that you don't get to make my choices for me. That I will decide what my feelings are on the matter. But I don't. So, don't worry on either account."

"Middy, you like me more than you want to admit. I like you." He raised a brow.

Her body tightened again at the thought of him liking her, but now was not the time.

"You like fucking me. That doesn't mean you like *me*," she shot back.

"It's good that you know there's a difference, but in all honesty, I do like you, Midnight."

"Well"—she scooted off of the desk—"stop it."

"I can honestly say that no witch has ever demanded that before."

"Look, treat me like you would any other witch. You wouldn't want me getting any ideas, right?" Middy knew that sounded like she was still flirting, but in all honesty, for him to be a total ass was probably what she needed.

He laughed. "No, Middy. That I can't do."

"See, you're treating me like I'm special. Next thing you know, I'll be picking out Old Country Roses service for twelve and deciding that the wedding should be in Paris at Beltane with a dress that could either be called 'blush' or 'bashful,' though it must be done in a sweet Southern accent, and my brothers trying to corral weather fairies with rosewater cookies. . . . It's already started." Middy shrugged helplessly.

"Midnight, you're brilliant." Dred pulled her to him and planted one on her mouth.

She promptly melted against him like butter in a microwave and he broke the kiss.

"This is perfect. Go ahead and plan that wedding, *darling*. I'm sure you'll need to enlist my aunt and my mother, and in turn the Witch's Auxilliary. The bigger the affair, the better. It will be the perfect cover. They'd start to wonder if there weren't plans in the works anyway."

"What if we don't figure this out by Beltane?" Middy asked.

"Then you'll just have to go through with it." Dred returned her cavalier shrug.

"I'm not having this conversation." Middy shook her head in denial and threw up her hands to push Dred away.

"We can get it dissolved easily enough."

"You have truly lost your mind." Middy knew that she was the one who'd lost her mind. This wasn't playing dress up anymore. The Fuck Me Ken doll was a real person.

"So Paris is out?" Dred asked, totally missing her point.

Middy wanted to shriek at him that it was all out, but she'd given her witch's word. She couldn't go back on it. Could she? A cold prickle went up her spine at the thought. No, she couldn't. She wondered for a moment that if she slapped him really hard, whether that would rattle the sense back into his head. Hell, maybe she should slap herself.

"Paris is fine. What witch could ever say no to Paris? By Morrigan, while we're at it, why don't we have the ceremony in front of the Eiffel Tower? I'm thinking evening, white candles, rose petals. . . ." she said sarcastically.

"Yes! Indulge your every whim. Just not the Cinderella carriage. I hate those damn things."

"You don't have the sense Merlin gave a zephyr." Middy sighed and turned away from him.

"What did I do?" he asked her retreating form.

CHAPTER FOURTEEN
Cock Talk

Dred Shadowins was to find out exactly what he'd done that had Middy in a snit. It came to him in a dream. He knew he was dreaming because when he became aware of himself, he was skipping. Dark warlocks, master spies, and Dred Shadowins in particular, did not skip. Nor did they take the time to notice that everything smelled like honey.

He was sure that honey did not have a scent, but here, in this fucked-up version of the world that had been rotting in his subconscious, it did. Dred knew it was honey, but it was Midnight Cherrywood, too. It was what her pink petals had tasted like. He was smelling tastes, so yes, this was definitely a dream.

After gaining control of his traitorous limbs, he stalked down the path that had been set before him. He wondered briefly if this was a magickal dream, a trap of some sort that he could never escape from like Chaldonean Hall.

He thought he saw Middy, her dark cascade of hair brushing the tops of her naked thighs and he heard her laughter, sweet and pure. Dred was given visions of a waterfall, of Middy waiting for him, wet and pliant.

Leaves fell like rain all around him; golden coins that crunched beneath his feet, reds that burned like the early hours of dawn, sharp and bright against the dark browns that were the color of death and shadow. Dred felt as if he'd moved through miles of forest when the swirling, misty cover receded.

It was almost like he was on some sort of pilgrimage and Dred wondered what dark things he might find at the end of this dream sequence or if he'd wake up in time to escape them.

He was plotting how to escape, to wake up, to leave the darkness. Dred was very aware that back in the physical realm, Middy was sleeping next to him and trusting that he would protect her.

"There is no escape. Not for you. Not for her," a voice whispered from the shadows.

"Show yourself."

"You know me," the voice said.

"Then show me."

The sight that greeted him when the waves of darkness retreated like the tide was nothing short of a bad acid trip. Dred was now certain that his scotch had been laced with some hallucinogen.

It was the biggest specimen he'd ever seen; there was no doubt about that. Then, of course, it would be. It was as tall as he was, but its girth was enormous. Again, that should have been expected, given the proportionate size ratio. What topped it off was the head. It was purple and he could have sworn that it throbbed.

Then, there was a face. A face that he knew and loved dearly.

It was his own.

But this doppelganger was indeed a fright. What was wearing his face was his very own penis.

"I know, I know. Don't freak out."

"I'm standing here in the middle of fucking nowhere talking to my own cock. I'd say I was already past freaked out and maybe a couple of eggs short of a meringue."

"Sorry I had to resort to such drastic measures; nothing else would have made an impression." It shrugged.

Dred found himself nodding along and then shook himself out of it. "So, uh, what do you want?"

"I know tings, they've been tough lately." It shrugged again.

He said "tings." Was that a Brooklyn accent? What, was his cock the godfather cock of all cocks?

Dred was sure he'd just gone snap, crackle, and fuck you. He was right out to lunch. With his cock, apparently. Middy had been right, he'd lost his mind. Utterly.

"Yeah, with the broad. That's what we's gotta get straight."

"Midnight?"

"That's the one." His cock exhaled a huge breath and it seemed to shrivel a bit and then perk back up. "Get me?"

"Uh, no."

"The one, genius. She's it for us. That's the only entree we'll be eatin' for breakfast, lunch, and dinner here on out."

Dred was sure he hadn't heard it correctly. That was tantamount to saying that he'd never fuck another witch so long as he lived. That knowledge settled like dirt on a gravel road. It wasn't heavy, but damn, it dusted everything.

"Merlin's balls!" he swore.

"Look here, buddy!" a voice interrupted what had promised to be a most satisfying stream of profanity.

Dred turned to see the source of the new voice that had entered his Sybil-scape. Because that's what it was, it was certainly not a dreamscape. He had two different things talking to him and one was his cock. Oh, yes, he was definitely what they called fucked up. A split personality would be a welcome and classifiable bit of insanity. But this? Now he thought he was seeing Merlin, which was just stupid. The next thing he knew, he'd be sitting in a double-wide broom on blocks watching selkies and mermaids talking about interracial dating. Those people were always the first to admit they saw Merlin and Elvis. Usually at a Waffle House for the all-you-can-eat special.

Dred decided that yes, he might have just reached his breaking point.

"Hey, man." This was from his cock.

He wanted to reach down and grab for it, to see if it was still there, but he had a feeling that when he realized it wasn't, there'd be no surfacing from the deep end for him.

"You know him?" Dred asked.

"Yeah, and you do, too."

"Mordred Arthur Shadowins," the man with the long, white beard pronounced.

"Who wants to know?" Dred smirked, unable to do anything at this point, but rely on his attitude to get him through.

"My balls! I'm sick unto death of being startled out of my daily activity every time something doesn't go your way."

"And how do I have anything to do with that?"

"My name, boy! Stop taking it vain. I think you're the worst culprit in the warlockian world. If it was just, 'by Merlin' or 'Merlin bless' or whatever else, it wouldn't bother me. But always, it's about my balls. I've had enough. And they're not blue, thank you very much. I've pounded the backside out of Nimue three times today," the old man said, looking very proud of himself.

Yet another visual that Dred Shadowins could have gone the rest of his life without having plastered behind his eyeballs.

Balls.

Merlin. Merlin's hairy, old, shriveled, but not blue . . .

"Watch it! Don't even think it!" Merlin corrected him. "And why do you always make me look old? Magickal folk should know better."

"Um, while I've got you here . . ."

"Your damned mission? Me on a horse! You're a stubborn one, aren't you? We give you the one, and all you can worry about is—" Merlin broke off, a little confused. He seemed to be talking to someone that Dred couldn't see. "Oh, well that guy's a douche bag. Yes, I'll tell him. In a minute. No. Really? Damn it."

"Looks like the two of yous have some business to handle, so I'll be leaving. But remember what I said, Dred. Don't park me in any other garage because the engine ain't gonna start, if you get my drift." It winked at him.

Dred would have been more comfortable if the thing had just disappeared, but no, it had to skip merrily along the path that led out of the clearing. So Dred was treated to the lovely, unforgettable image of the backside of his cock skipping down a path. If only it had a cape, it would have given a whole new definition to Red Riding Hood.

"Okay, boy. Looks like I'm going to give you a break. I didn't want to, but here it is. You and your witch need to leave the house party and get to Loudun."

"France?" Dred asked. "She said something about Paris in the spring. . . ."

"Yes, yes. Stick to that. But for now, Loudun."

"Dare I even ask what waits for me in Loudun?"

Merlin looked at him, the lines around his eyes crinkling with amusement. "You shouldn't, but you will anyway. So I'll save you the trouble. In the 1600s, Loudun was the site of a huge clusterfuck."

Dred's chi was irretrievably porked. Merlin was supposed to be a holy man. He wasn't supposed to say "fuck." Of course, he wasn't supposed to be hanging around in the ether "pounding the backside out of Nimue" either. Or so he'd always been taught.

"The possessions at Loudun, right? That was all just a power grab: Cardinal Richelieu wanted to oust Father Grandier because he opposed him politically. The cardinal convinced the nuns to say they were possessed, but it may well have been born from sexual frustration on their part. Or so some scholars say. Grandier was said to be hand-some. . . ."

"Blah, blah, whatever, Dred. It doesn't matter that it was all unicorn piss to start with. You of all people, should know that when you fart around with powers unknown, even in jest, Bad Things ensue."

"What do I want with the evil that's there then? I'd do better to stay home."

"Yes, you would at that, my boy. You would at that, but you won't because Loudon is where you will find clues to the lamia you're hunting. As trite as it sounds, only you and Middy can stop this. Make no mistake, you must!"

"Why can't you do it? I thought you were all powerful or some rot?"

"I am all powerful, the gods' god. The Bigger Boss. But I can't interfere." Merlin shrugged. "All this cross-pantheon nonsense has our hands tied with red tape. You know how it is. Warlock's Council, Gods' Council . . . the bureaucracy never ends."

"Aren't you interfering now?"

"Not really. This is a dream. You could have made this up yourself." Merlin leaned in. "But if you did make this up, you'd be a little wrong in the head if you ask me."

"I didn't ask you."

"That's the beauty of it." Merlin looked very pleased with himself. "Anyway, you're going to wake up in about five seconds. Take Middy to Loudun by way of the broom. You should stop and enjoy the sights on your way, if you know what I'm saying." Merlin winked and nudged him so hard, Dred was sure he'd broken a rib. He was still rubbing the spot when he woke up. He turned to Middy, but her place in the bed was empty.

Dred found he didn't care for that empty spot. It was

bullshit. He was the one who crawled out of bed in the early dawn, and it was the witches who woke up alone. In fact, this had never happened to him before.

Ever.

He wrinkled his nose with displeasure and decided that he'd have to make her come twice to keep her in bed until he was ready to get up. That was the only solution. At least until they no longer had to share a bed.

Dred thought of his cock again. That seemed to be all that he could think about lately. Middy's fault, of course. He supposed it would be the gentlemanly thing to do if he checked on it. Just to make sure it didn't have anything else to do today. Or perhaps Middy had been correct in her assumption that he was barking mad.

He lifted the blanket, but his eyes were closed. Dred didn't know if he could take it if his long-time carousing companion really did say something to him in the here and now.

It was standing tall and proud, jutting even. He eyed it carefully. Then he poked it. Finally, he grasped it firmly and still found it had no input of any kind.

That was more like it!

He gave it a few strokes for good measure and found it to be the same pleasant sensation as always. Now that he'd started, he might as well finish. Dred was sure after the previous night's activity that Middy wouldn't be up for another round of polish the wand.

Dred gave over to the tried and true fantasy that he often fell into when he was looking for a quick one-off with himself. His cock went limper than an overcooked green bean. When he peeked at it under the sheet, it looked just as sad.

This was unacceptable.

And yet, before he tried anything else, he knew what was

wrong with him. Still, he tried imagining his weekend on the yacht with the Pearcy twins. Merlin, but were they ever hot little witches. They'd done things that . . .

Nothing.

Perhaps he just wasn't remembering correctly. The one had sat on his face while the other had—if it was possible, the skulking flesh shrank farther.

He went through the seven stages of grief there in the span of about ten minutes. First, he couldn't believe it. No, a more apt description would be that he refused to believe it. It just couldn't be true. That had been a dream. His penis didn't have any choice in the matter. It went where he told it to. It was the bitch, not him. NO!

A vague voice in the back of his head told him that he'd already reached the anger stage, but he'd never been very good at punishing himself, so that one passed quickly.

He thought about Middy and the thing sprang to life like a fork shot from a toaster. Okay, fine. Middy was hot. That wasn't really a compromise. He thought about her *with* the Pearcy twins.

It was like letting the air out of a balloon.

Then he felt guilty that he'd had such crass thoughts about her. One wasn't supposed to objectify someone one liked. Right? Dred didn't know. He'd never really liked a witch as a person before. Sure, he'd liked Karla well enough, but . . . He really hadn't. She had just been filler, like frosting in those tea cakes he liked so much.

Damn it, but Dred still hated these epiphany moments. They were balls. All of them.

What the fuck was he going to do? It wasn't right lusting after just one witch. It wasn't how things were done in the world of Dred. He released his rebellious cock and if he'd been a witch, he might have shoved both of those chocolates that had been on the nightstand right into his mouth. He might anyway.

Barista had been thoughtful of her guests' comfort and provided each one with a small box of Godiva chocolates on each nightstand. Dred's were all in his mouth. As the chocolate divinity, not to be confused with the old spinster witch candy, melted across his tongue he was momentarily soothed. There was one answer to this conundrum.

That answer being to knock the backside out of her, as Merlin had seemed so pleased to put it. He'd drill her like an oil field until she ran dry. He'd been looking at the situation all wrong. It wasn't less he needed, but more. Lots more. Then perhaps, he could get on with the business of being Dred Shadowins, cavalier and contented playboy. He liked that much better than this new girl creature she'd turned him into. His cock didn't work because he had sand in his vagina. That was the only possible explanation. The sooner he got rid of that, the sooner all of this would go away.

But he was beginning to wonder why everything about this mission had to have something to do with his cock.

CHAPTER FIFTEEN

Harpy Breakfast Tea

"Why me?" Ginger Butterbean whined.

Midnight Cherrywood had come to the quick and painful realization that she would much rather be in her warm bed next to Dred than sitting there, at butt-thirty in the morning listening to Ginger Butterbean waxing poetic about her sad state of affairs. Or more correctly, her husband's state of many affairs.

Her voice was like that of a songbird that'd been sucking on helium. It wasn't a sound that she found compatible with breathing. Middy sipped her tea and waited patiently to die. She wasn't sure what she could learn from this inanity, but sat dutifully through the thing. The lace edge of her napkin had become fascinating. She was afraid that if she looked any of these women in the face, they'd speak to her directly.

"Well, I'm still concerned about that empty cell in Chaldonean Hall," Aradia Shadowins said, changing the subject from poor, victimized Ginger.

Finally, something interesting!

Ginger gasped. "Aradia! Can't you see I'm still upset and I need the support of my friends?"

Aradia looked as if she was hard put not to roll her eyes like bowling balls. "Well, I suppose I should thank you. Some good has come from your tragedy."

"Oh, and what is that?" Ginger asked unhappily.

"My son fell in love," Aradia said and turned her attention, along with that of the rest of the flock, to Middy.

They all looked as if they expected her to say something. "It's true. If you hadn't cut off Gavin's donation"—she almost tripped over the chancellor's first name—"then I never would have had to go see Dred."

"Well, I for one am glad that you did. Although shame on him for not bringing you home to meet me. Our first meeting shouldn't have been at a witches' tea at my sister's house party. I should have liked to fuss over you in private first." Aradia smiled warmly.

Middy had thought for sure Aradia would have hated her. Would have seen her as some gold-digging schemer because Middy didn't run in the same social circles they did. Her family was comfortable, but they didn't have any of the money or prestige that the Shadowins did. And everything had happened so fast. Although, she wondered if it was telling that Barista hadn't come to the tea. She'd pleaded a headache. It made Middy wonder if what Tally said about her had been true.

Middy had called Tally right after the library incident to rhapsodize about Dred and ask her friend why she hadn't told her she was coming to the party, but all Tally had said was that she didn't have time to talk, but to watch out for Barista Snow. She was still chewing on that when Ginger Butterbean decided to add her two cents.

"Yes, well, the sun shines on a closet gnome's ass some days," Ginger said with a smile.

"Ginger!" Aradia admonished.

The old Middy would have wilted like a sick flower, but this was the new Middy and she knew she had the social support of Aradia Shadowins. So, she could damn well say whatever she liked. Not that it would stop her if she didn't.

No, she was never going to let anyone treat her like that again.

"So true, Ginger. So true." She smiled at her with a big flash of teeth. "And since I have you here, where should I put you on my seating chart for the reception?"

"Whatever do you mean, dear?" Ginger practically growled.

"Well, Chancellor Butterbean is bringing someone. So, you won't be seated at the chancellor's table. I mean, I wouldn't think that you'd want to sit next to Aloe Hugginfroth, but . . ." Middy shrugged as if it made no never mind to her either way.

Ginger turned a distinct shade that seemed to match her name. "How could you allow that? I see Aradia must take you under her wing, because you don't know how things are done."

"Me? Dred's uncle is a chancellor. So, they are all invited and they may bring whomever they wish. Just as you may," Middy said with that same plastic smile burning her face.

"How's your mother, Midnight? Is she thrilled you've captured the most eligible bachelor of the warlockian world?" Lila Applelever asked kindly to change the topic of conversation.

"She's well. I haven't actually had him over for the formal meet-and-greet yet. You know Dred's been so busy and this is truly all so sudden."

"Your brothers haven't . . ." Lila was shaking her head as she gasped.

"No, but they'll be on their best behavior. I promise you," Middy said with grim finality.

Lila blushed. "I was kind of hoping for some bad behavior."

Oh. My. God. Lila Applelever was her mother's age and lusting after . . . The bile bubbled in her throat like an angry volcano. She kept looking around the table, trying to decide where she was going to toss cookies if she couldn't hold down the bile.

She'd like to do it into Ginger Butterbean's tea for being such a self-righteous snot.

"Oh, don't you know it? Raven was our pool warlock one summer and . . ." Ginger shrugged.

"I had *all* three of them working on my pool," Aradia said, smirking.

Middy's head snapped around like it had been dangling off the end of a rubber band to gape at Aradia.

"Sorry, Midnight." She was still smirking. "But those brothers of yours are Cougar Bait."

Cougar Bait? Midnight was sure she'd just been struck dead and was lunching in the innermost circle of Hell.

"Do you think that maybe we could have them for entertainment at your wedding instead of a band?" Lila chewed her lip thoughtfully.

Middy took a steadying breath. "No, I don't think my mother would much care for that type of entertainment. Aradia, would you want Dred—" She cut herself off. She knew better.

"Honey, all of my friends have those issues of *Weekly Warlock*. He gets his looks from me, anyway, so I'm flattered."

That smirk on her face was the same one that Dred wore daily. They were so much alike it was frightening. Middy was terribly afraid the next time she and Dred were intimate, she'd see Aradia's face.

Not that Aradia wasn't drop-dead gorgeous; she was, but she was his mom! Aradia could obviously read the distress on her face and knew what she was thinking because she laughed even harder.

"Now that we're all having a good time," Ginger interrupted. "I trust that you're going to fix that little seating snafu?"

"Certainly not. It's her wedding. She can do as she likes. You know, Ginger, you don't have to come," Aradia offered.

Ginger narrowed her eyes at both of them and shoved her teacup up to her mouth, presumably before anything else could escape that would put her on the outs with Aradia.

Middy decided that having tea with these witches was like navigating a minefield, only she wasn't granted the mercy of a quick death before something exploded. She needed to get back to the discussion about Chaldonean Hall.

"So, what were you saying, Aradia?"

The elegant woman turned, her delicate fingers posed just so as she raised her teacup to her red lips. "About Cougar Bait?"

Middy didn't even try to fight the smirk that curled her lip. "Not quite. About Chaldonean Hall?"

"Oh, well, there's an occupant missing from one of the paintings. First time in a thousand years that anyone has ever escaped. He's been free for a good forty years. I think it's unlikely that we'll ever catch him."

"Him, who?" Lila asked.

"You don't know?" Aradia gasped as if it were the juiciest morsel of prime rib or, better yet, gossip. "A dark warlock, Tagrin Larmvill, was imprisoned for crimes against warlockian society. Not only did he commit mass murder, but he plotted to destroy our way of life."

"Why am I just hearing this?" Ginger gasped.

"Because you don't listen to the news? I don't know. I thought everyone knew. Anyway, he was your average evil genius with short warlock syndrome. Tagrin wanted to make everyone pay for whatever. Not too sure on the details. He managed to kill quite a few of our kind before he was captured. He was sentenced to an eternity in Chaldonean Hall, but he found a way to escape."

"My father knew him," Lila said quietly.

"What was he like?" Middy couldn't resist asking.

"Let's not talk about it. We should get to the good stuff!" Lila said, her heart-shaped face breaking into a large grin.

"Oh!" Aradia snapped her fingers and bared perfectly straight, white and, not to mention, sharp teeth in a wolfish grin.

"Finally," Ginger sighed.

Jennifer Cinder, a quiet, yet vicious witch in her own right, spoke up. "That's the only reason I came."

With the snap of Aradia's fingers, the room was transformed. No longer were they taking tea in a snowbound castle high in the Alps; instead, they were poolside. Each witch was positioned on a bamboo chaise longue with her feet tucked into some kind of divine pedi-wrap. The water seemed to glitter and Middy could smell the chlorine. Just beyond the pool was an ocean view and white sands. The sun was hot and the veritable army of cabana boys were even hotter.

Upon closer inspection, they weren't warlocks, but gargoyles. They all had tanned skin that was like living marble. Everything about them was hard, from their pectorals, to their abs, to their . . . They weren't wearing anything but loincloths and each was bearing a silver platter.

Middy could only watch as they moved, their wings splayed behind them like avenging angels, their bodies seeming to flow through the space they occupied like water, every motion intoxicating.

Her mouth was suddenly dry and she reached for the icy, pink drink on the table next to her and gave a couple pulls on the straw. She noticed Ginger Butterbean sucking on her own straw like whatever was in that glass had come right from Merlin's own cup. Or she was slobbing a knob.

This last, Middy realized, was unkind. She knew that she shouldn't be so judgmental, but Goddess, she hated that witch. It wasn't the sharp little comments or the— Middy interrupted her own thought as she realized that Ginger Butterbean was indeed slobbing a knob.

It was a cock straw.

The last three inches of the straw was shaped like a little plastic penis.

She squeaked as she pulled the thing out of her mouth and looked at it in abject horror. The other witches were all sucking happily on their frozen concoct— Drinks. Drinks. No more cock.

Well, today anyway. Middy thought of Dred lying asleep in their bed.

Oh, that was bad. *Their* bed. No. It was just *a* bed that they'd both happened to sleep in at the same time, after he'd fucked her silly in the library. That didn't make it their bed.

She was suddenly thankful for the Harpy Tea, as she'd come to call it. Otherwise, she'd have to look Dred in the face. As handsome as it was, Middy didn't want to see it first thing in the morning. Not when it had last been somewhere in the vicinity of her nethers and had surfaced looking like a glazed donut.

Somehow, the bed was terrifying now that she knew what he was capable of while he was in it. Or out of it, for that matter.

Yes, this was definitely better.

Or not.

Middy quickly changed her mind as she looked down at the platter that one of the gargoyles was holding out for her approval.

"That one is from me, dear. It may surprise you to know, but I'm aware of my son's"—she paused as she looked around the room, seemingly for the right word—"conquests. Hopefully, this will keep him in line." Aradia grinned.

Middy didn't want to look at it, much less touch it, but there it was. It was a wicked-looking instrument made from the hide of a minotaur and it had nine spiked tails. It was a whip.

Aradia giggled like a girl still in Academy when she saw the look on Middy's face. "Okay, look beneath it. Go on."

Middy blushed as she picked up the thing, almost choking on her trepidation. Beneath it was a froth of lavender fabric that appeared to be a corset and matching knickers.

"I want grandchildren as soon as possible." Aradia winked at her.

Middy decided in that moment she was going to seat Aradia at the table with all of her brothers at the wedding.

"Oh, that's gorgeous! Try it on!" Lila demanded.

"Uh," Middy stuttered.

Next thing Middy knew, she was lounging in just the lavender corset and knickers. Her bosoms were perched neatly under her chin and she balanced her frozen drink on top.

"Happy?" Middy said. "I don't think I can get up."

"No. I remember when mine used to do that." Jennifer sighed.

"Why do you need to get up? We've got more presents and then cake. Just wait until you have the cake," Ginger said.

"Presents? I don't need—"

"Yes, you do. My son is only getting married once and we are going to do this up right."

"Most marriages don't make it past the first two years," Middy offered.

"True. But most men aren't Dred Shadowins. Plus, it's written in the family charter. If he marries, he's stuck until one of you dies or he'll lose his magick."

Middy coughed, sending her cock straw flying, but luckily it didn't hit anyone in the eye. It did, however, land at the feet of the gargoyle who was serving her. He looked from her mouth to the straw, then back to her mouth again.

He reached down to the waist of his loincloth.

Every single witch present leaned forward, eyes as wide as saucers. The gargoyle flashed fang and tugged the band of the cloth just low enough so all of the witches could see the triumvirate of masculinity where his hips met corded muscle, drawing their eyes down to . . . where he produced another cock straw.

He winked at Middy and dropped it in her drink.

"That's mine!" Ginger growled and snatched the straw out of Middy's glass, sloshing her own into the frozen drink to replace it.

He flashed more fang. "Now that was naughty."

The gargoyle hauled Ginger up into his arms and swatted her firmly on the backside before depositing her gently back onto her chaise longue.

"Don't do that, Valerian. Or you'll have a whole pack of naughty witches on your hands." Aradia winked at him.

"I think I could handle it."

Each witch was currently occupied with exactly what the handling of said things would entail. He slipped a card to Ginger and she tucked a wad of cash into his loincloth, but the bulge that was already there was still bigger.

The next gargoyle came and knelt before her. His platter was vibrating.

Sweet Circe's Tampon! They'd given her a vibrator.

"Sorry about that," the gargoyle said and whipped out a remote to turn the power off.

"It's so you can hold your ground when you and the warlock fight. Because you will," Ginger promised.

"Hold my ground? Why would that be a problem?"

She rolled her eyes in a most put-upon manner. "Dred Shadowins is a Master of Sex Magick. He can make you forget your name with his—" She paused and looked at Aradia. "He's got skills, okay? To hold out, to use your snatch like the weapon it is, you'll need some sort of fortification. This has the extra setting so you can experience that 3-D *Weekly Warlock* goodness with any warlock you choose. All you need is a bit of DNA. Hair, something from a wineglass, whatever."

Middy was truly impressed. Too bad she'd still probably use it for Dred. She wondered if she could keep all of this stuff even if she didn't marry him; she was starting to like the silky smooth fabric of the corset up against her skin and she definitely liked this last present.

"So, since you got my gift, I'm ready for cake," Ginger demanded.

"Are you always this abrupt?" Middy asked.

"Is that a problem?"

"It takes some getting used to, that's for sure," Middy said, trying to be kind. She thought maybe that Ginger wasn't as much of a super bitch as she'd first judged. She was just misunderstood.

"Ginger, you know very well there is no cake until after presents."

"We could do cake now," Middy interjected.

"Aradia, we all came for the cake," Lila said.

"How right you are," Ginger quipped.

"Midnight, this is a special cake that bakers only make available when there's going to be a wedding. It's like nothing you've ever had. It's called *La Morte Chocolat*."

"Sounds ominous," Jennifer added. "But it's to die for, really."

Middy found a large piece being shoved into her mouth by rough gargoyle fingers. It tasted like chocolate. So far, it was nothing special.

Until the warmth started to spread from her tongue to her throat, to her limbs; it was like molten gold through her veins. The sensation may have started up around her lips, but it centered in her clit. Middy could feel great pulses shuddering through her body and she was pretty sure that she was going to stick to the bamboo like she had a suction cup between her thighs.

It wasn't quite as intense as her orgasm with Dred, so it surprised her when she hit that peak and she had to grasp the side of the chaise as if she were holding on for dear life. The body quakes ran from her fingertips to her muffin.

She loved it!

Middy opened her mouth for another bite and she was promptly indulged. Then she thought about Dred taking food from another witch's fingers. Her eyes narrowed and she opened her mouth to say something, but yet another bite was crammed unceremoniously into her chops.

Lila gave her a knowing look. "The cake is only for witches."

"But what if some other witch . . ." Middy began around her mouthful of sin.

Ginger wrinkled her nose. "Merlin, Middy. Close your mouth when you chew."

"Sorry," she mumbled.

"Midnight, my son is marrying you. Do you know what that means? No matter what he does, he will always belong to you. So, who gives an orc's nut what some other witch does?"

Middy nodded and finished chewing. She was being stupid. It wasn't like they were actually committed to one another. She'd forgotten for just a moment that they were only playing. She looked at the tattoo on her wrist and sighed.

"You're not having second thoughts are you?" Aradia gasped. "Quick, here." She shoved another piece of cake in Middy's mouth after dipping it in a bit of drizzle that she had nearby.

Middy noticed that no one else had the chocolate drizzle and she wondered what the hell her new witch-in-law was shoving into her mouth. It tasted fine, so it couldn't be a potion, could it? She saw the intensity on the other woman's face and had a feeling that not only was she screwed, but that *fucked* would be a better word for it.

The warmth kept spreading and she felt a euphoric joy at the thought of her warlock to be.

Yeah, she was fucked like Aloe Hugginfroth at a stag party.

"It helps with the wedding jitters, dear."

"But I love him!" she blurted out.

Aradia took a hand and patted it soothingly. "I know. That's why you're marrying him. All Shadowins brides drink the potion, honey. Too much power at stake. If you're marrying him for money, or any other reason than love, that will all pale in the light of what you'll feel for him now. I promise, if you just give in to it, you'll be incredibly happy."

CHAPTER SIXTEEN

A Dark and Somehow Divine Comedy

Merlin frowned as he sauntered into the living room of the Big Boss's house. He hadn't bothered to knock, Merlin was the Bigger Boss. He could go where he liked. Nimue said he had a god complex, but he'd told her that didn't signify since he was God. At least, for this millennia. It was kind of like being president. He'd been elected.

Although the process for the Big Boss was a little different. It was more about who could hold the power. Caspian got to be a dictator as the Devil, whereas Merlin had to count votes. Caspian had been recently promoted from Crown Prince of Hell to Big Boss when Hades had retired to a cattle ranch in Texas with his new wife. It was a big job for a guy who was new to fatherhood and husbandhood. So one would assume he'd be working rather than sitting on the couch and watching a movie with his wife and father-in-law.

Merlin was disappointed to see that no one had turned to watch his grand entrance. Maybe he should start smiting? He cleared his throat to see if any of the heads would turn and sure enough, not one did.

"This is bullshit. Come on!" he demanded.

They were all watching some snarky teeny-bopper flick called *Heathers*. Merlin was all about the snark; it was his life's blood most days. It just shouldn't take precedence over his entrance. He was the Bigger Boss after all.

Winona Ryder's image turned to look at him from the screen and stuck its head out through the plasma television.

"That stunt you pulled in the caf' was pretty severe," she said quoting her own lines. Obviously, someone was manipulating the image.

"You're not funny, Grace."

"It wasn't me," the witch said, fluttering her lashes at him.

"You then?" he directed his attention to the resident Crown Prince of Heaven who happened to be looking at his feet.

Raphael snickered. "Nope, but it's sure funny."

"You?" he demanded of the Big Boss. (Who was of a lesser rank than the Bigger Boss.)

"Come on, Merlin. You made the poor bastard have a conversation with his own cock. When I think of all the dark scary places that I put mine, I wouldn't want to have a conversation with it," Caspian offered.

"Are you trying to say something?" Grace narrowed her eyes at Caspian.

"No. I'm not *trying* to say anything. I just said it," the former Crown Prince of Hell and current Adversary tossed back.

"Look, I'm cool with the relationship and all, but must you refer to your parts and my daughter's dark places within my earshot? Really. Just wait until Sera Ann comes home with some sketchy demon in tow and see how you feel about it." Raphael slugged Caspian in the shoulder.

Speak of the devil spawn, Sera Ann peered from around the other side of the plasma TV. Her horns were little pink nubs on the top of her head and her tail flipped off the television.

"Sera Ann, where are you supposed to be?" Grace asked.

The little imp grinned until her mother narrowed her eyes at her further and then she wilted like an unhappy flower.

"And what have I told you about wearing your horns and tail in front of company, hmm?"

"Pappy Merlin doesn't care. And he *is* the boss of you." She stuck out her tongue.

"If you fork that tongue at me . . ." Grace let the words hang.

Sera Ann giggled and stuck out her tongue again and it forked in the middle. Grace's lavender wings exploded out of her back and that was when Sera Ann decided there were lots of things to do outside that needed her immediate attention.

"So, now that my darling monster is out of the way, you were all saying?"

"Your husband doesn't like that I sent the man's own cock to explain things to him in a dream," Merlin said.

"He should just count his lucky stars that it wasn't in real life." Grace smirked.

"You don't think that's wrong, to make a man face his own cock?" Caspian asked as if he couldn't quite believe the words that were coming out of his darling wife's mouth.

"He shouldn't have stuck it where he did. And really, at least it warned the guy. I mean, he could have been trying to get . . . what's that terminology you use, husband? Yes, 'balls' deep, and then have it fail on him. I think it was pretty damned considerate."

"What if your . . ." Caspian paused to look at Raphael and thought better of the terminology. "What if your *parts* decided to have a conversation with you?"

"They don't need to. They talk all the time. It's called PMS."

"I don't know, Aurora and I never had to deal with that. It's all you, bro. I'm out." Raphael leaned back in the chair.

"Look, I just think it was a shitty thing to do," Caspian reiterated.

"Oh, unlike your idea to send the demon crabs to tell him? I think I'd prefer the cock myself." Merlin snorted.

Grace giggled. So did Raphael.

"Of course, you do." Caspian grinned and waited for realization to set in. "Sorry, you left yourself wide open on that one."

"Why did I take this job again?" Merlin rolled his eyes. "I don't know if anything could be worse than the sentient demon crabs." Merlin was referring to Caspian's last gig as a Crown Prince where he'd met his wife. The man had been tormenting Grace and she'd summoned a demon to deal with him. It had been a last resort, but Caspian had taken great pleasure in harrying the man with demon crabs.

"You seem to be stuck on that." Caspian smirked.

"The guy totally deserved it, but it was still disturbing to watch. Anyway, did you see this latest round of fuckwaddery?" Merlin asked.

"Oh, the love potion? Poor Midnight. She would have fallen in love with him anyway, but now she'll never know if it's her own feelings or if it's the potion." Grace sighed for Middy's plight.

"We really shouldn't be meddling," Merlin said, pursing his lips.

"Nope, we shouldn't. But I'm the Devil. *Shouldn't* isn't in my vocabulary, you know?"

"That's one of your qualities that's a strike in the plus column." Grace smiled and twined her fingers with her husband's.

"There's a minus column?" Caspian smirked again and then continued. "Well, this lamia thing is going to be a bitch to clean up if Middy and Dred don't handle it directly. I'm talking making an appearance sort of thing. I really don't want to do the whole Armageddon-Destroyer of

Worlds, but I think that's all we'll be left with after this last douche move from the Pantheon." Caspian's brow furrowed with displeasure. "Nothing is ever accomplished by committee. I don't see why the other gods get a say. Their time has come and gone. The mortals don't believe in them anymore. Most of them, anyway. But instead, they get to sit in judgment and tie our hands with all their votes and bullshit."

"I thought being the Bigger Boss would eliminate all the red tape. Not by a long shot." Merlin sighed.

"Tagrin should still be in Chaldonean Hall. How did he escape?" Raphael growled.

"Sold his soul," Merlin said blandly.

"Middy doesn't know who he is, does she?" Grace's mouth was set in a thin line.

"No, but she will," Merlin promised, though it sounded more ominous than hopeful.

"I like her, just so you know. She's a good person." Grace nodded as she spoke. "It's hard watching people live their lives and only interfering when it suits Fate."

"We'll figure this out, Gracie, I promise," Caspian assured her.

And if you can't trust the Devil, Grace thought, who can you trust?

CHAPTER SEVENTEEN
Stuck in Old Loudun Again

Midnight was damned uncomfortable. The Harpy Tea had been worse than shopping for her first bra with her brothers in tow. It didn't stop there, no. That would have been too simple. It had been her mistake to assume her life couldn't get any worse than shooting Dred in the eye with a cranberry. It was a mistake still to think that having him walk in on her in a mad masturbatory session with his likeness was the deepest pit of humiliation in which she could immerse herself.

Because as soon as she'd opened the door to their room after slinking back from the Harpy Tea, she'd found herself face to face with Dred in the glorious and magnificent flesh. The words had just jumped out of her mouth like a kamikaze F-16.

"I love . . ." She'd been able to hear the words coming, but she couldn't actually feel her mouth making them, or her tongue, which should have been moving against her teeth to make those sounds. Instead, the damn thing felt like it was wearing chenille.

She loved what? It was like that cheesy horror movie where the tramp trips in her tacky heels that were a poor fashion choice anyway, since she was gallivanting in the middle of the woods and—no, don't say it!

She loved what? Ham? But she didn't. Chocolate?

Cheesecake? Grooming charms? Her hair after a Biolage deep conditioning treatment? Burt's Bees lip stain? Puppies?

Her mouth was opening and she could feel it moving, but it was like she'd crammed a whole donut in her mouth: the powdered kind that had been rolled in peanut butter. She wanted to run before the words could come out. Middy's conscious mind didn't know what they were, but it had an inkling.

"You." Middy could hear her own voice and she sounded like a toddler who'd been dropped on her head too many times. Each part of the word was slow like sap running from a mandrake root in the middle of January.

Dred's eyes widened and then the bastard had the gall to laugh. It wasn't just a little giggle, or a smirk, it was an all-out belly laugh. As if that weren't enough, it was a deep sound that curled somewhere in her nethers and made her feel all warm inside. Middy found that to be a particularly inappropriate feeling.

She'd made her Grand Confession and he'd laughed and patted her on the head as if she were a favorite puppy who'd been caught chewing on his shoe. "Mother gave you the potion, didn't she?"

What pissed her off further was that he didn't sound surprised. He could have warned her not to eat or drink anything. Unless he wanted her to be in love with him? That notion was completely unacceptable. Alice had definitely fallen down the rabbit hole; she was still careening through the dark and she had no idea where she would land or if she would land at all, while Dred was like the Cheshire Cat. He was grinning like . . . well, that. Not to mention looking very pleased with himself.

Now this morning, she was pressed intimately against him on a broom riding hell-bent for bristle on the way to France of all places. Some hidden, picturesque version of a town that embodied Martha Stewart's idea of Country

French because a nun had a hard-on for a priest and accused him of being a sex demon.

She refused to look at the parallels there because Dred really was a sex demon, sex god, whatever.

"Are you still mad at me because I laughed?"

Middy didn't say anything. She was actually trying to keep her parts as far away from his parts as possible and she was having shit for luck. Traveling by broom was definitely more intimate than teleporting. She didn't know why they couldn't have used the broom carriage. More conspicuous, probably. It would leave a more obvious trace of magick to conceal something that large.

Or Dred was just being perverse and that was just as likely.

Yes, it was definitely a chore to keep from relaxing against his hard chest, allowing those strong arms to keep her secured on the broom, or grinding her ass against him because being cradled between his powerful thighs made her brutally aware of all of the other things that those thighs were capable of, what they felt like while he was inside of her.

"Are you going to answer?" Dred's breath was warm and tickled her ear.

She still had nothing to say.

His hand drifted to her hip and he pulled her flush against him. Weak, weak, wanton creature that she was, she let him. Midnight was starting to see why Ginger had gifted her with mechanical fortification.

Dred's other hand slid up her arm with a feather-light touch.

"Stop that! You can't steer without your hands."

"Ah, she speaks. Thank you, Goddess, for granting me the sweet sounds of your melodic voice."

"Don't be a dick."

"Okay, so I'm a dick if I laugh and I'm a dick if I compliment you. What is it that I'm allowed to do besides fuck you seven shades of blue?"

"Nothing!" Middy snapped before she realized what she'd said.

"Have it your way."

Middy could almost feel his smirk.

Dred fastened his mouth on the creamy expanse of skin between her shoulder and her throat. The hand on her hip snaked forward between her thighs and quickly found its way beneath her skirt.

Why had she worn a skirt again?

Oh, yes. To punish Dred, to entice him with the way the material gathered around the tops of her thighs, showing her long legs. She'd hoped he'd remember what it was like to have them wrapped around his waist.

The problem with this was *she* remembered it all too clearly: every second of every day, every night, her body against his.

Damn traitorous thing that it was! She'd left the thing to its own devices for five seconds to examine her own thoughts and suddenly, his erection was pressing into her backside and she had arched her back to rest her head on his shoulder and give him better access to anything he would have of her. Right now, that included having his other hand on her left breast and his mouth lingering on the tender part of her neck.

Dred's touch was better than chocolate, better than the chocolate orgasm cake, better than anything she'd ever imagined. Middy leaned forward now, pushing her ass harder against him and he growled.

She was vaguely aware that they were cruising at thirty-thousand feet, but that was a thrill, too. It had to be the potion! The threat of certain death had never been a turn-on before.

Dred raised her up, both hands on her hips to guide her to a better position. He'd freed his cock from his slacks with an incantation and as he tried to settle her, he used the motion to push her skirt up around her hips.

The initial contact wasn't what she expected.

In her haste to be anchored safely to him, she sat down before he was ready for her. She didn't much care to be dangling away from his strong arms and looking down at the scenery that was going by so fast it looked like it had been drawn by a toddler with a tantrum and a paintbrush.

This also meant that Dred didn't have time to aim like the world-renowned snatch hunter that he was. Though he didn't breach the perimeter, having the head of his weapon knocking on the back door of her stronghold was a startling sensation.

If they'd been on solid ground, like sane people, she'd have leapt from his lap with a high-pitched squeal of protest and he could have made it up to her with his tongue. Even though it was her fault for plopping her goods back down before he was ready. If she'd trusted him, Middy would have also been able to trust his grip on her hips.

But since they were mid-flight, her high-pitched squeal of protest was now at a glass-shattering decibel as she recoiled from his grip and plummeted like a walrus that had been unceremoniously dumped out of the cargo hold of a 747.

Dred tightened his thighs around the broom and leaned forward, taking the broom into a dive. He careened face-first toward the ground, but it wasn't fast enough. There was no way that he was going to be able to catch Midnight before she hit the ground. The built-in safety features on the broom wouldn't allow him to match her speed.

His decision was made before he had time to process it

as a conscious thought. He dove from the broom into the empty sea of ether below. Dred sped toward the ground at an inhuman speed and he wasn't thinking about what he was going to do after he caught her, only that he must reach her.

The land beneath him, the endless sky above, it was all a wet canvas, the colors swirling together. Nothing was real except Midnight. She was the one thing he was focused on and he knew that their time was quickly running out, even though it seemed as if the freefall had pulled them out of space and time—that velocity and gravity didn't apply to them.

Spell after spell was running through his fevered brain, but nothing that would save her.

When their fingers touched, threads of Fate snapped; time and space returned to the status quo. It was the motivation he needed and Dred recited the incantation that would pluck them from the freefall. Too bad he misjudged the distance. They materialized two feet above what would have been a safe and perhaps even graceful landing on a grassy hillside, then fell unceremoniously to the ground.

"Uh, Dred?" Middy asked tentatively.

"You can thank me later."

"Yeah, we'll get to that 'my hero' stuff in a minute."

"What could be more important than that?" Dred said, trying not to sound winded, even though that quick introduction to the ground had knocked the air out of him.

Middy just looked down to where his trousers were still open. "Ask him."

"I know he seems sentient sometimes, but he's not," Dred said with a certain finality.

She put her hand on his to stop him when he would have secured himself; her fingertips softly brushed the head of his still hard cock. "Don't you want your hero's thank-you?"

"We both almost died because you thought I was trying to break down your back door and you still want to—"

"Look, I was startled. And I heard stories from Tally," Middy interrupted.

"It's a wonder that you ever had sex at all living with that witch." Dred shook his head.

"She saved me from Tristan in the library."

"I saved you! That centerfold was trying to kill you. Tristan just wanted a piece of ass."

"Isn't that what *you're* after?"

"The pot and the kettle, love. You're the one with your hand on my cock." He closed his fingers around hers as they moved over him.

"Oh? I'm not the one who decided to initiate broom sex." Middy leaned closer to her work and licked her lips.

"No, but you are the one who wore a mini-skirt and straddled the broom like a cowboy on the rodeo circuit."

"You're the one who threw me off the broom." She stroked the shaft harder and closed her mouth over the tip, velvet on velvet as her tongue drew lazy circles over the swollen flesh.

"Is this my punishment?" Dred asked, his gaze intent on her every movement. He didn't even argue that it was Middy who'd jumped from the broom.

She replaced her tongue with her fingers and spoke, "No, your punishment is in our luggage at Snow Manor. Your mother gave me a whip before I drank that Merlin-awful potion."

"Don't take Merlin's name in vain!"

Middy stopped what she was doing. "Okay, I'm jerking you off and you're telling me not take some warlock's name in vain? Seriously?"

"You're the one who mentioned my mom."

"This blame game isn't fun anymore." Middy pouted.

"It rarely is."

"The mood is just gone." Middy flopped on her back in the grass.

"I was kind of surprised that you wanted to do it out here in the open. Most witches are shy."

"What do I have to be shy about? You've already seen everything. If someone happens along, you have that handy invisibility spell. What could—" Then she closed her mouth. She really did know better than to ask what could possibly go wrong.

Damn it! She'd decided that she was going to seduce Dred and that's what was going to happen here. Midnight was tired of being put off, tired of being interrupted, and tired of not getting what she'd paid for.

She'd signed on for this mission, not to get thrown off of brooms, but to use Dred Shadowins like a sex toy. That and support the Gargoyle Masque: She wasn't totally selfish.

He was still hard.

How did the warlock manage it? He always seemed ready to go at a moment's notice. Were all warlocks like that? Middy didn't think so. She wondered what it would be like to really be married to him.

Would he be a faithful husband? Or would that cock do his thinking for him? She pitied the witch who actually married him. Of course, she envied her, too, but she chalked that up to some nasty side effect from the potion that his evil mother had disguised as chocolate drizzle. That woman would have been a talented assassin.

Middy noticed Dred hadn't made a move to get up. Perhaps he knew what she was going to do and was waiting for her to get on with it. She wasn't sure which would be more humiliating, if he knew or if he didn't. If he didn't, that meant he was just content to lie there with a raging erection and a willing witch and . . . She had said that she was out of the mood, though.

Well, he should be expected to read her mind. It was that simple.

They'd had some mind-meld Sex Magick the first time; where was that shit when she wanted it? The closet gnome had probably stolen that for his hidey hole, too. It was probably making out with Aloe Hugginfroth's broom.

Midnight straddled him. "So you want to be my broom?"

"I thought I was punished?"

"You are."

"Whatever you say, *Mistress*." He raised a brow.

She narrowed her eyes at him. He couldn't possibly know about the time that she'd tried to get the Dred-bot to lick her boot heel. Could he? *Don't tell him, this time!*

Middy felt the head of his cock rubbing against her slit. She imagined herself wanton there in the bright light of day where anyone could see them, even though she was still clothed. She'd have to thank Tally later for convincing her to go sans knickers.

She felt powerful, too.

Dred's cock strained for entry, but she refused him, instead rolling her hips so that it made contact with her clit. She moved his hands so they were under her shins.

Midnight had to admit that she loved feeling like she was in control, that this strong warlock was at her mercy—and he was at her mercy. He could do nothing unless she allowed it.

"Let me touch you," he pleaded.

"You are touching me," Middy said as she rocked forward.

"Let me taste you."

Did she dare? It was something that she'd fantasized about for so long. Yes, he'd tasted her before, but not when she was the one in control. Not like this.

Middy slid up his body and positioned herself with her slit next to his mouth, her knees on the ground on each side of him. He seemed to know what she wanted to do and moved his hands so that she could link her fingers with his when she leaned back.

Her body arched into an impossible position and made her feel all the more exposed. The first touch of his tongue sent shockwaves though her and she cried out. She felt his pleasure again and saw what he wanted of her, watched them in her mind's eye as he licked her.

She caught a glimpse of her and two other women, but that was quickly replaced by something else, as if he didn't want her to see it. Again, her nakedness was against the black marble tile of some room that was familiar to him. Midnight knew that these were his fantasies about her. Midnight wasn't into girls, but seeing herself as he saw her brought another rush of power and another wave of desire.

She felt the same things he was feeling as he pushed his tongue past her labia minora and inside of her. Middy was tempted to release his hands so he could use his fingers, too, but that wasn't part of the fantasy.

Dred sucked her clit into his mouth and tugged lightly with his teeth. She strained to arch her back farther to push herself down onto his mouth and he raised their linked hands to give her the leverage she needed.

"More!" she demanded.

Dred complied and he increased the speed and strength of the friction he created with his tongue. He would vary between the slow, languorous motion of pushing his tongue inside of her and then licking from her slit up to her clit and just focusing on that distended bud of flesh that brought her such intense pleasure.

Middy felt a rush of fluid and instead of slowing his attentions, Dred sucked and licked with more pressure. She could feel his intention and it wasn't just to get her off: He was enjoying her pleasure.

Her fingers tightened around his just as her passage tight-

ened and she came against his lips, the evidence of her orgasm ambrosia on his tongue.

Dred's hands were somehow free; she was digging her
fingers into the soft earth beside them as her body shook
with her release. He was guiding her where he wanted, but
she wasn't fighting him, she couldn't.

Middy was on top of him, but he was in control again.
He positioned her as she had been before, the head of his
cock against her slit and his fingers anchored to her hips.
She was slick and ready for him, but he didn't enter her. Instead he slid his cock just to the entrance of her channel and
then back up against her already sensitive clit.

Middy wanted him inside of her, but when she shifted,
he did as well. It was an erotic one-upmanship that he was
winning by a landslide. She didn't care anymore; she just
wanted him inside of her. Middy didn't understand how, after she'd already gotten off, she still needed his cock.

Perhaps because he hadn't gotten off? It had to be the Sex
Magick.

"Give me your mouth," Dred demanded.

He hadn't asked for a kiss, he'd asked for her mouth. That
made her shudder in expectation.

Middy complied and leaned in to him. One hand snaked
through her hair and angled her just as he wanted and he
took her mouth. It couldn't be called a kiss, but perhaps a
taking.

He tasted her lips, crushing her down to him. Midnight
could taste herself on his lips; she was sweet and a bit salty,
just like her favorite treats. She'd tasted herself before, on
her own fingers, but tasting herself on his mouth was better, more decadent.

They both cried out when he pushed inside of her and
he didn't move. Middy was sure that she was going to die
either way. If he moved, she'd shatter; if he didn't, the anticipation would break her apart.

"You're still so tight." His whisper was ragged and he pushed himself into an upright position without forcing Middy to move.

Dred wrapped his arm around her and braced himself on the ground with his other hand and thrust his hips. Middy kissed him this time and it was a kiss in truth, soft and sweet. He grazed her bottom lip with his teeth, but then returned the kiss with a softness that she hadn't known he possessed.

She knew it didn't mean anything, that he changed his response according to what got her off, but that didn't matter. What mattered was that he was inside of her, that they belonged to each other this way for a little while.

Midnight locked her legs around his waist and moved to meet his thrusts. He changed his hold on her, curving his arms under hers to grasp her shoulders, and he buried his face in her neck.

She ran her fingers through his hair, traced them over the line of his jaw, his cheek. Their lips met again and he spilled inside of her.

After a moment, he spoke, "You only got off once, didn't you?" Like it was a crime.

"That's okay. I came before."

"It sure as hell is *not* okay! I must be sick." Dred sounded panicked.

"Why must you be sick?"

"I don't know, but it won't be tolerated."

"No, why do you think you're sick?" She smoothed his hair.

"I never come first. I'm a good lover."

"I never said you weren't," Middy replied.

"You don't have to. You only came once."

"Yeah, but it was really hard."

"Don't console me." He pouted.

"Really, I usually only get off once. Even with myself.

Though I've tried like Merlin to be one of those multiple orgasm witches."

"The gauntlet has been thrown." Dred's already hard jaw looked as if it had been carved from stone and his eyes narrowed like he'd just acquired a line of sight on his prey.

"It wasn't a gauntlet!" Dear saints and goddesses above, she'd just challenged a sex god to a battle of the orgasms.

"Oh, but it was, my dear. It was." Dred looked as if he were already plotting.

She was terrified and thrilled all at once.

CHAPTER EIGHTEEN

Coming In Out of the Rain

How long were they going to be at it? Shit! The "villagers" were coming. Well, not like her star-crossed lovers were, but they were venturing forward with pitchforks and torches.

Grace didn't understand how she was supposed to play fairy godmother to two people who were too stupid not to come in out of the rain.

Why did she keep coming back to *come*? She couldn't even think that word and not find herself hot and bothered.

She had sex on the brain and of course, it was all Caspian's fault. At least until Sera Ann tugged on her hand. Thoughts of going to the Caspian Rodeo were washed away by the decidedly frigid shower of her daughter's presence.

"Whatcha doin?"

"What am *I* doing? What are you doing?" She was tempted to demand that Sera not look, but that would be the fastest way to ensuring that her daughter got two big peepers full of Dred and Middy goodness.

"I'm trying to help a hero defeat the evil monster."

"Aren't *we* the evil monsters?" Sera Ann asked in a serious tone.

"No, darling. Who's been feeding you that crap again?"

"Grandpa Raphael. He keeps calling me a little imp. All

of the books say imps are devious, evil monsters from Hell bent on destruction and mayhem."

"Those are mortal books, sweetie. Remember that Hell is subjective."

"But we live in Hell."

"Yes, but isn't Grandpa Raphael a Crown Prince of Heaven?" Grace returned. Talking with her daughter was almost as much of a verbal spar as it was with her husband. She was a smart cookie, maybe too smart.

"I guess." Sera Ann seemed to chew on this for a moment. Then she pointed to the clearing where thankfully, Middy and Dred had finished their activity, before the child got an eyeful. "Those guys with the torches look like something out of that last book I read."

"Which one was that?" Grace asked her daughter.

"Frankenstein."

"I was trying to get them to stop what they were doing and get them to safety, but it's like herding cats."

"I know what you mean." The little girl nodded, still serious.

Grace was wondering how best to approach them when her daughter, with full horn and tail regalia, decided to do it for her.

Sweet Bleeding Hell.

"So you're the Butcher of Shale Creek, huh?" A little girl popped out of nowhere just as Middy pulled down her skirt.

"And you are?" Dred asked casually after Middy let out a startled yelp.

"Saving your ass?" The girl shrugged and pointed to a grassy hilltop where an angry mob had gathered.

"Don't say ass!" A great, thunderous voice boomed across the clearing. It sounded like an angry goddess.

"Yes, Mama." The little girl's tail popped out from behind her and it flicked the ground sulkily.

Middy wanted to ask the child where her parents were, but that bellow pretty much answered the question. She wasn't sure if she wanted to know *who* the girl's parents were at this point, especially with that pointy little tail.

Or the horns that were peeking out of her curls.

"You two don't have the sense that Morrigan gave a stone. I swear!" A voluptuous woman emerged from seemingly nowhere.

Middy had to admit, she was a little jealous. The woman had an ethereal presence that made her look like a goddess. For all Middy knew, she might be.

Or a demon.

"Okay, people, do we see the angry horde?" Her lavender wings sparkled in the sunlight, making it hard to look directly at her. "What possessed you to land so close to Shale Creek?"

Middy pointed at Dred and he scowled.

"Of course! It's always the man's fault." She smiled. "Let's get you to the church on time!"

Grace began chanting and noticed that in the second she'd looked away, Sera Ann had wandered out of her circle of transport and was currently taunting the fairies inside the Loudun/Shale Creek fairy ring. Sera Ann was tossing them oatmeal raisin cookies that she'd smuggled in her pockets.

Raisins gave fairies the runs, but they loved cookies. So, she was just being cruel.

It would serve her right if they left their displeasure in her shoe. Not that she wished anything bad on her child, but it might teach her a lesson.

Grace huffed in mid-incantation through her teeth and it was a sound that Sera Ann recognized. It was what she always heard before her mama popped her on the rump, or made her clean out the hellhound cage. She scurried into the circle that Grace's magick had wrought and they disappeared.

CHAPTER NINETEEN

Things to Do in Loudun When You're Dead

Dred was off his game. Probably because he'd died and gone to Hell. They were currently in the dark ruins of a seventeenth-century convent, but all he could think about was the fact that he'd only gotten his witch to come once. Of course, they'd been interrupted by an angry mob of villagers intent on beating them both to death with various vegetables and farming equipment, but that was neither here nor there.

"You're so pretty," Middy said to Grace as she reached out a hand to touch her wings.

Grace promptly retracted her wings, but took Middy's hand in her own. "Sorry, only my husband gets to touch my wings. It's one of those things." She smiled again. "And you're pretty, too."

Dred was watching this display intently. They were holding hands. They were talking about how pretty the other one was. Yeah, baby. The seventeen-year-old warlock that was always present in the back of his mind was jumping up and down like a cheerleader on Red Bull. *Dude, they are so going to make out. Don't miss this action!* He was almost ashamed to admit that the grown-up part of his consciousness just shrugged and nodded his head, hoping to catch the action, too. Yes, there was a tiny, rational part of his brain that wanted to bitch-slap him for being so juvenile, but it was kind of intrigued as well.

"Not happening, Dred," Middy warned.

"I didn't say anything."

"No, but I was in your head an hour ago and I know exactly what you're thinking. Of course, I did grow up with the Trifecta of Doom. So, what's dancing through that devious brain of yours is no surprise to anyone."

"It would be hot."

"I know she's smokin', but no fantasizing about my wife. At least, not without me," a dark-haired man said as he stepped from the shadows.

"What are you doing? You were supposed to be watching Sera Ann!" Grace scolded.

"Oh, like I can keep her anywhere she doesn't want to be."

"Why not? You're the Devil, for fuck's sake." Grace sighed.

"The Devil?" Middy and Dred exclaimed at the same time.

"First Merlin, now the Devil. It keeps getting better," Dred growled.

"You saw Merlin?" Middy asked.

"That's not something you want to hear about, girly." Caspian cut the unspoken question off at the knees and nodded sympathetically to Dred. "I thought that was just wrong. But he's the Bigger Boss, so what can I do? And call me Caspian."

"Thanks," Dred said and genuinely appreciated the sentiment. "Sorry about ogling your wife."

"It happens." Caspian grinned and shrugged.

"Now that you two are done jerking each other off, can we get down to business? And I'm Grace, by the way."

"Wait, so Merlin is like the Boss of Bosses?" Middy asked.

Dred cringed at the reference. Caspian did, too. What

made it worse was that Caspian and perhaps all of them had been privy to his cock talk.

"Boss of Bosses. God. Whatever. Anyway, we can dicuss semantics later. We're of the all things to all peoples sort of philosophy." Grace looked around. "Where the hell is that child?"

Dred imagined that she was much like all children, and finding that the adults were not paying her any mind, she'd run off to find some fun of her own. Even though she was the daughter of the Devil, he hoped that she didn't run into any trouble. She was kind of cute and a little bit like what he imagined his own spawn would be like.

"I can see the path of your thoughts. If you'd like to baby-sit, we'd like a date night next week." Caspian grinned.

"What are you talking about?" Grace asked.

"Man talk. Mind your business, woman!" Caspian demanded playfully. Then he said in a softer voice, "She wears the tail in this family, but I'm good with that."

"You certainly wear the horns," Grace shot back and then blushed. "I'm still not seeing Sera Ann."

"So, where are we?" Middy asked.

"This is the ruin of an Ursuline convent that was the scene of mass possessions in the 1600s. It's not visible to anyone outside of the magickal realms. There was so much pain and suffering here, greed and just general evil, it slipped from the world of men."

"Ugh, then why are we here?" Midnight frowned.

"This is where Merlin told me to go. He said we'd find a clue to the lamia and how to stop it here," Dred said.

"A clue? Is this a treasure hunt? Why are you ruling types always so damned cryptic?" Middy huffed.

"There are certain rules; we're not even supposed to be here now," Grace said.

"Oh. Well, thanks?" Middy seemed to be at a loss for words.

"Yeah, well, seriously, guys. This lamia thing is on the apocalyptic scale of doom, just so you know. You have to stop it or everyone is screwed. Yeah, no pressure, right?" Grace rolled her eyes.

Sera Ann poked her head around the corner. Dred saw her horns before he saw her very large, violet eyes.

"Daddy?" she asked softly.

"No," Grace answered for him. "Whatever you found, you can't keep it."

"What is it?" Caspian asked her.

She emerged with a baby gargoyle in her arms. It wasn't old enough to have developed its humanoid features and was still almost birdlike, but its eyes were huge, blue, and obviously sentient. It blinked with long lashes and let out a pitiful wail and snuggled deeper into the child's arms.

It wasn't plump like a baby should be, but thin and undernourished. It also had stumps sticking out of its back where its wings should have been. They were caked with dried blood and oozing with infection.

The effect that the sound had on Middy was instantaneous. Her eyes filled with tears and Dred felt as if something had stabbed him in the chest. He realized it was her pain at seeing the creature suffer. Damn that bond! He thought he was only supposed to share her feelings when they were fucking. That he could deal with. This was shit of another color. Perhaps it was during any extreme sensation?

He didn't want to know that about her. It would make what they had to do all the more difficult, unless he really did marry her. His mother had given Middy the potion; it wasn't really a question of "if" anymore. It was when.

Dred knew she deserved better than what he had to offer her. That realization in itself was something new for him. He'd always thought any witch should be pleased to have him, down on her knees thanking Merlin for her good luck. Not Midnight Cherrywood. She deserved to be loved.

He kept saying that to himself, but why, he wasn't sure. Perhaps he should try to love her. It wasn't as if she was unlovable; it was just that Dred didn't want to be in love. Love was a weakness he couldn't afford. If he was really going to give Middy what she needed, he'd have to give up spying for Godrickle, and that just wasn't something he could do.

Dred watched her as she held out her arms for the baby gargoyle. Sera Ann squinted at her for a moment as if judging her worth, but something about Middy earned her approval and she carefully handed the hatchling over to Middy's waiting arms.

Midnight held the child close to her heart as the tears rolled down her cheeks in a caravan of sadness. She sank to the floor, rocking back and forth, and words Dred couldn't understand poured from her mouth in a kind of litany.

He realized it had a cadence to it, but he knew it was no language he'd ever heard spoken.

She rocked faster and the hatchling's tiny claws grasped her shoulders, drawing tiny spots of blood on her shirt. Middy didn't notice. Though he did feel the pain in his chest ebb as Middy's rocking slowed. Those strange words became a hum and when she collapsed against the wall, her arms limp at her sides, the hatchling was still clinging to her.

Its bright blue eyes were bold jewels in a chubby face, humanoid features had replaced the reptilian, and its wings were fully formed and whole, fluttering like twin butterflies on its back.

Dred tried to go to her and it growled at him like a rabid dog. He ignored it and when it nipped at him, he growled back. He took Middy into his arms. "Midnight!"

Her head lolled against his shoulder and her eyes fluttered. "What happened?"

"I don't know." He looked at Grace and Caspian, but they shook their heads in unison.

"Mama," Sera Ann began. "You were right to help them. Look what she can do!"

"Middy is the key," Caspian said decidedly. "Only magick wrought of purity and sacrifice could heal wounds like that. And only the same can stop a lamia."

Merlin stuck his head through the remnants of a window. "You've been here long enough. Time to go. Or Bad Things . . ."

"Coming, coming." Caspian shook his head.

"Did she have some bad seafood?" Merlin said, nodding to Middy.

"No, she healed this baby gargoyle though." Sera Ann plucked him from Middy like a recalcitrant puppy and held him up for Merlin's inspection.

"Give me that. There's still another clue. The portal is closing. Move your"—he paused to look at Sera Ann before he decided on his vocabulary—"bottoms."

Dred was suddenly alone with Middy as the strange crew vanished. That had been weird, but he supposed weird was a relative term. He lived in a magickal world, so logically, nothing should surprise him.

"Midnight, are you okay?"

"My back hurts," she said softly.

This was another one of those brutally honest moments he didn't want. Dred had a feeling that he knew what he was going to find if he looked at her back, specifically, her shoulder blades. He was sure that there would be blood and infection. He had to get her out of here.

"It feels wet," Middy said.

"Lean forward just a bit."

She made a small sound of protest.

"A little more. It's okay. It will be okay." Not that he had any right to promise that, because he didn't know. He couldn't make okay happen either and that irritated the piss out of him.

"I think I'm bleeding. Wait, where's the hatchling?"

"Middy, you don't remember? You healed it."

"Good," she whispered as he pulled the back of her shirt up to reveal the open wounds on her shoulders.

"At what cost to yourself though? Did you know you could do that?"

"Dred, seeing it suffer like that, it just broke my heart."

"I know. But you didn't answer me. Did you know that you could do that?"

"No. I don't know if I could do it again either. All I could think about was how it had suffered and my magick was suddenly hot in my veins like lava." Midnight was quiet for a moment. "Is it bad?"

"There's no infection, thank Merlin for that at least," Dred said. He knew a pitiful healing spell that was good for skinned knees and bar fights, but nothing else.

He did what he could and enchanted her shirt to act as a bandage until he could get her to a Magick Medic.

"Do you think maybe I could have an aspirin spell, too?"

He pulled her to him gently and rested his chin on the top of her head as he spoke the words that would ease her pain. That at least was something he could do.

"Hey, if you keep holding me and petting me, I might start to think that you like me."

"Never said I *didn't* like you, Middy."

"So, dipping my hair in potions and causing my yogurt to sour—that was all you liking me?" Middy asked as she settled against him.

"I was a snot-nosed kid who didn't know what to do with his obsession with a certain witch's silky hair," he admitted.

"You're full of unicorn piss."

"Don't forget vinegar."

Middy laughed. "I love you." She said it quietly and sincerely, unlike her initial unhappy eruption. "I know it's probably the potion talking, but it feels so real."

"What do you want me to say?" Dred asked, his voice equally soft. He didn't know what she wanted from him.

"You shouldn't tell someone that you love them with any expectation they'll say anything. Love is a gift and whether you want it or not, mine belongs to you."

"Thank you." He wanted to give her something in return, he wanted to say it back, but he just couldn't have those feelings. Not for her, not for anyone. He wouldn't lie to her.

That's what he could do for her, he could be honest. "If I could have those feelings for anyone, Midnight, it would be you."

"Now that you've said it, it feels true." She snorted. "That sounds stupid."

Her heart was so big, big enough to love him when he had nothing to give back. Dred knew that even thinking those thoughts was grounds to suspend his man card, but he didn't care.

Because he was a bag of dirty dicks.

Now was as good a time as any to tell her about the wedding.

"I guess it's a good thing that you love me."

"Oh, why is that?"

"You have to marry me now."

"Look, I said I would plan the thing and—"

"Middy." He let his fingers tangle in her hair. "You took the potion. We have to get married in ten days or you'll lose your magick."

"If we get divorced, you'll lose yours," Middy cried.

"Not unless you have the tattoo," Dred said as if he were

teaching a class on the matter. "Those words that were inscribed on the ring you were asking about? It's fine as long those didn't manifest in the tattoos."

"These?" Middy turned her wrist so he could see the words of the ring that were twined in her engagement tattoo.

"Where the fuck did that come from?"

"So, now that you're tied to me as well, I'm a scheming bitch. I can feel what you're thinking." Middy moved away from him.

"I didn't say that."

"You didn't have to. Let's just find whatever it is we're supposed to find and get the hell out of here."

Middy stood up, but it was a slow and painful process. When he tried to help her, she jerked away.

"Middy, what am I supposed to believe? We've got this inexplicable connection and now we're bound together forever. Do you really want to live without your magick?"

She turned to him, her dark eyes like coals. "No, but I will. Just because I love you, that doesn't mean I'll spend my life married to a warlock who *doesn't* love me."

"Then I guess I'd better figure out how to love you. I won't live without my magick. I can't."

He realized then that he'd jammed a sharp object into a tender place. "I didn't mean it like that."

"But you did."

"Middy, you can't live that way either. Look what you did for that hatchling. There's great power in you and it would be selfish of you to give that up, not when there are so many you could save."

Her eyes were pools of despair, deep and endless as his words cut into her further. Oh, he was worse than a bag of dirty dicks. He was a bastard, the same bastard that he'd promised himself he wouldn't be.

"You're right." She nodded her head slowly. "I could do

something for a change. Something real, something tangible. Not just be arm candy on some spy mission. I could be worth something."

"Midnight . . ." he trailed off. He wanted to tell her that she was worth a lot of something. That she was worth it to him, but that was too close to a declaration.

She turned on her heel and left the room to explore the rest of the ruins, but promptly tripped over Tristan Belledare.

He was dead.

CHAPTER TWENTY

The Hero at Rest

The face that had last looked at her with such concern was now frozen in a pale death mask. Those lips that had sought hers were cold and blue. The hands that wanted to touch her could feel nothing. Not even her fingers as they intertwined with his.

Middy hadn't really liked him in life, no. His death hadn't changed that, but she couldn't help feeling that his death was tied to her somehow. She wondered where he'd gone with Tally and if she'd been the last witch to see him alive.

There was something in his hand. Something firm, like cardboard was tucked into his palm. She let go of his hand and found a matchbook. It was black and highly processed, with a satin finish. The gilded imprint read "Donatien."

What the hell was that?

The cause of death wasn't readily apparent until Dred rolled him over. Tristan's back was nothing short of a horror. It had, at one time, been a bloody mess. Now, it was just gaping flesh and hanging fascia. Bloodless. Middy could see inside of his body and ribs were missing. So were precise sections of vertebrae: the axis bone of his cervical spine, two from the thoracic, and one from the lumbar. It appeared as if another from the lumbar had been chosen, but abandoned. There were score marks that could only have been made by powerful teeth set into even more powerful jaws. Something had drained the blood and the marrow from him.

Something like a lamia.

Tristan hadn't deserved to die like this. He'd been a hero.

She stole a glance at Dred. He was a hero, too, but if he died, his funeral wouldn't be a warlock holiday. His coming and going would be noted with a column in *Magickal Finance* and no one would ever know he'd tried to save the world.

Middy wasn't angry because he didn't love her. She was angry because she'd trusted him enough to confide in him and he didn't trust her the same way. He assumed that because he felt something between them, that she'd done something to manipulate him when he'd been shortening the strings himself all along.

Would she marry him? Probably. He was right about her responsibility to use this new magick she'd found. She couldn't do that without marrying him after Aradia had cheerfully stuck her finger in the pot and stirred.

Dred pulled out his Witchberry and snapped pictures of the crime scene, excruciatingly efficient while she was pondering the unfairness of life. She watched him work and understood why he was the way he was, but that didn't mean she had to like it.

Middy had to turn away. "I can't look anymore, but when I look away, I still see it."

"That never changes, you know."

"How do you keep all of this in your head?"

"Someone has to," he said, taking a last snapshot before he rolled Tristan on what was left of his back.

"Why does it have to be you?"

"Why does it have to be anyone?" Dred shrugged.

"I wonder how he could have been right outside the door all this time without Sera Ann tripping over him when she was exploring."

"Unless he wasn't there for her to trip over. That would mean someone or something dumped the body here for us to find." Dred frowned, his mouth a grim line. "It's no accident that this convent is so close to Shale Creek."

"Do you think Tristan's death has something to do with what happened there?" Middy asked.

"Did you really believe what you said to Belledare in the library?"

"I said a lot of things to him in the library. Which thing do you mean?"

"Let me ask a different question. Do you believe that I tried to kill him for a Hand of Glory?"

"No," Middy said without any hesitation.

"How can you be so sure?"

"I just know."

"Because of the potion?"

"I knew that before the potion. For a spy, who is supposed to be aware of all things at all times, you're awfully thick in the head."

"No one else has ever believed me innocent. Even Hubert."

"A Hand of Glory is powerful magick."

"I still have it. Does that change what you think of me?" Dred asked carefully.

"No, but why does it matter?"

"I'm going to need you to trust me for what happens next. And you jumped from a broom at thirty-some-odd thousand feet in the air because you thought I was going to hurt you."

"You startled me."

"Midnight Cherrywood, you thought I was trying to

hitch a ride on the Hershey Highway without so much as a 'Do you like gladiator movies?' "

Midnight blushed and turned away. "Well, what would you do if you tried to sit down and found your chocolate cherry about to be snatched from you either by unhappy accident or devious device?"

"Devious device?" Dred snorted.

"You sound like a pig."

Dred looked around for a moment as if considering. "Yeah, kind of. I'll own that. Sure. Why not?"

"So, you were saying something about trust? This isn't your perfunctory 'Do you like gladiator movies?' is it? Tally has told me some stories about the trust conversation and for some reason, it always comes back to the chocolate cherry. Or an orgy."

"Midnight, I will try anything that turns you on or gets you off, but I've had my share of chocolate cherries, orgies, and pretty much anything that you can think of. Which brings us back to the trust."

"See, Tally told me the trust conversation always comes back to some strange sex act. Well, hit me with it. Goddess, if this what being married to you is going to be like, I don't know if I can take it. And you're certainly not going to have anything on the side because I—"

"That matchbook you found in Belledare's hand, it was stamped with a name. Donatien."

"How did you know that? I didn't even show you the stamp."

"Because I've been there. I recognized the box. It's a sex club not too far from here."

"We're going to a sex club?" Middy's voice hit a rather high pitch.

Dred laughed.

The bastard.

"Not just any sex club, my sweet. Donatien caters to a specific sort of kink. It's named for Donatien Alphonse François, the Marquis de Sade."

"The guy who liked to write dirty stories with his finger up his ass?"

"I see you've watched *Quills*."

"And you want me to go to this club? Have you lost your mind?" Middy asked him in all seriousness.

"No, Midnight, I have not. In fact, I think you'll rather enjoy it."

"Why would you think that?"

"I suppose since I'm asking you to trust me, I should be honest." Dred looked a bit bashful. "Whenever someone tries to access a function that I've not okayed for my centerfold, it sends feedback to the company. Which just happens to be part of my financial portfolio."

"So, you've been spying on me?"

He looked as if he was going to say no and maybe rationalize, but instead he answered with a simple nod of his head and a shrug.

Middy held her temper. It was only by a thread, but she was clinging to that thing for dear life. He wanted to play master and slave? Okay. She could do that. She was going to make him lick her toes. It didn't matter that she thought that was gross, it didn't matter that she'd tickle herself into unconsciousness by demanding that he do it. All that mattered was that she was going to make him pay for spying on her like that. Her and Cerridwyn knew how many other women. That was how he knew about her fantasies.

He'd known all along that she wanted to fuck him six deviant ways from Sunday brunch.

"Yes, Dred. I'll go."

"Great!" His eyes sparkled and he looked like a little boy who'd been turned loose in a candy shop with a hundred-dollar bill and no parental supervision.

"I've got a condition," Middy added.

"Witches always do."

"You're the slave."

"I wouldn't have it any other way. *Mistress*."

Son of a blue-furred goblin! Even when she was in the dominant position, he could still play her body any way he chose. She was wet for him again, and even after all of the horrors they'd seen, all it had taken had been the one word out of his devil-sculpted mouth.

Middy did her best to act unimpressed. "I think we should explore the rest of the convent before we go traipsing off to Salon Hell, or whatever it is."

"I think we've seen all that we need to see. Every minute we spend here is dangerous."

"What do you mean?"

"This is where I opened the portal. This is where the gargoyles conjured that thing from the Abyss that decimated a good number of our troops at the beginning of the war. The veil here is thinner because of all of the blood spilled and the fake exorcisms. It tears easily."

CHAPTER TWENTY-ONE

The Lady and the Tiger

Aradia Salome Du Lac-Shadowins stood before the War-lock's Council to present her son's wedding for council approval. She knew that it should have been done before Dred had asked the witch for her hand and certainly before the potion had been administered, but it was merely a formality. The Shadowins family had married as they pleased for generations. No marriage had ever been denied. Aradia was confident that Dred's would be approved, too.

Until she saw the unhappy frown on Hubert Godrickle's aged face.

What was this fuckery?

Aradia never let her icy veneer slip, at least not on her face. Her lips twisted into a hard smile that didn't quite reach her eyes. She appraised each of the council members coolly, watching for the one who wouldn't meet her gaze.

"Lady Shadowins, I regret to inform you that the council has denied your petition." Hubert's mouth was turned down in a grim frown.

"On what grounds, High Chancellor Godrickle?" Aradia wrinkled her nose as if it were an insult that she was forced to breathe the same air as the rest of them.

She wore her status and position like armor and, usually, it was enough to get her by. Aradia wondered just how much this was going to cost her and began to mentally list her assets, both monetary and organic.

Yes, organic. She'd take whatever steps were required to secure this marriage for her son. He wanted Midnight Cherrywood, then by Merlin, he would have her.

"The bride in question isn't highborn," Godrickle answered, but it was obvious that the words were sour on his tongue.

"If it doesn't matter to me or my son, how does that concern the council?" Aradia raised a brow and met each chancellor's gaze with the hard stare of a witch used to getting her way.

"It's for his own good," Vargill interrupted the High Chancellor.

"Indeed, and how is that, *Martin*?" Aradia said his name with a sneer as if it were a dirty thing. Further, it demonstrated to the council that she did not respect his position or his family line.

"The Shadowins bloodline must be continued with only highborn blood."

"My son will have no woman if he cannot have Midnight Cherrywood. Is the end of the Shadowins line preferable?" Aradia said softly.

"The council can order him to marry." Vargill shrugged.

Aradia knew it was this man who had blocked the vote. This tiny, insignificant troll of a warlock who thought it was his duty to decide her son's future.

Like hell he would.

She bit her tongue. Literally. Aradia could taste blood. It was either that or threaten the warlock's life in front of witnesses. How dare he!

"I would think, Martin, that you of all warlocks would be for the integration of, what are we calling it now?—oh, yes, less than highborn stock. After all, highborns have almost bred out of existence. Soon, our children will have webbed feet and two heads."

"I've seen the error of my philosophy, *Aradia*." He sneered. "Highborns are something separate and I'm thankful to have been shown the way."

"I will thank you to remember, *Martin,* that you may address me as Lady Shadowins. Chancellor though you are, a highborn or intimate you are not." Aradia had nothing against lowborns, but she knew it was one of Martin's buttons. He'd pursued her relentlessly at Academy, but all he'd wanted from her was to say he'd been with a highborn. He didn't see her or any of them as a people, only status symbols.

She was pleased to see the mottling begin underneath his jowls; it was as if their jiggling was like a pepper shaker, spreading the color up to the rest of his face and then down his hairy neck.

There was no smart retort for that. The council's charter had been set in stone and she was due her proper title.

He could kiss her *Wii-Fit* ass and do it twice on Tuesday.

"Still, with a fortune of that size and highborn rank at stake, I cannot give my consent to the marriage."

She had to admit she was impressed that he managed the pronouncement without stuttering, the fat fuck. She also had to admit he had her ass over a barrel and was about to shove something in it that she didn't care for.

"Well, you simply must change your mind. The girl has already taken the Shadowins potion." Aradia shrugged.

"Lady Shadowins, I regret to inform you that I don't care." Vargill shrugged back.

"She will lose her magick if she doesn't marry him!" Godrickle spoke up. "The girl works in your office. Could you really sentence her to that?"

"Choices for the greater good are often difficult," Martin offered.

Where had Aradia heard those words before? They were

familiar and the way he said them, it was as if he were getting more than just a perverse joy out of blocking her machinations. It was almost as if this scene had been something he'd imagined. Something he liked more than cake.

Something that was pretty damn satisfying, from the look of him.

"Well, I suppose there might be in a bit of trouble then." Aradia broke her cool façade with a smirk that bloomed into a mischievous grin.

"What do you mean?" Vargill growled, leaning over his place at the council table like a hungry wolf ready to pounce.

"The Shadowins family has been left to its own devices for generations, as I've mentioned previously. As it happens, Dred and Middy are already married."

An animalistic roar echoed throughout the hall and the air crackled with gathering power. A mad fire blazed in Vargill's eyes and Aradia rose to the challenge.

The very foundations of the hall shook with her power and ice suddenly covered every inert surface. Snowflakes fell from the ceiling and a blast of frigid wind lifted Aradia into the air, her long, white hair swirling in the storm behind her.

"Do you challenge me, Vargill?" Her voice echoed with an otherworldly influence, as if there were something else that filled the flesh of Aradia Shadowins.

"You had no right, Aradia," Godrickle whispered softly.

"I am the Lady of the Lake and my blood can be traced back to Arthur. To Merlin himself and you dare tell me of my rights with my own son?"

"See, they have no respect for the law of the land. No respect for the council! She's dangerous, High Chancellor. She must be imprisoned in Chaldonean Hall for the greater good." Vargill's temper had calmed some, or he'd figured out that his rage was getting him on the train to nowhere fast.

Aradia realized she had overstepped herself, but it was getting hard to care. Indeed, who did these red-tape licking, parchment-sucking bureaucrats think they were to dictate to her?

She pulled in her power and was pleased to know her new grooming charm had held up to her fit of pique. Aradia smiled at the council, using her magick to send calming thoughts to each of them. In five minutes, they'd forget that she'd just pulled out her Bitch Goddess of Doom heels and stomped all over Vargill. She'd bet he hadn't expected that.

Aradia knew that she'd have to be more careful around him from now on. She also knew that he didn't give a rusted-out damn about the Shadowins fortune or their line. He was plotting something else and she was going to find out what it was.

She needed to talk to Dred, but she couldn't do it via Witchberry or spelltop because all of those communications were too easily monitored. She'd have to dream walk, which made her really uncomfortable.

A woman just didn't need to know what went on in her grown son's mind. Or perhaps her hesitation was because she already had such a clear idea? But this was more important than any motherly discomfort. Aradia had a feeling that Martin was out to get Middy Cherrywood, among other things. She just needed to figure out why.

And then crush him like the disgusting troll-dung beetle that he was.

Chancellor Godrickle gave her a smile; the rest of the council was smiling as well. All but Vargill, of course. The others had already forgotten, but not Vargill. She wondered what sort of talismans he had that could protect him from magick as old and as powerful as her own.

Godrickle's power was no secret. As High Chancellor, he could not be bespelled, cursed, charmed, or generally fucked with in any way in which he did not approve or consent.

"Aradia, you were saying?"

"The ring that Dred gave to his bride, it's the traditional ring of our family. When the bride accepts, the engagement tattoos become wedding tattoos. They are for always and unbreakable. Please don't blame the children, they didn't know." And they didn't. Dred knew he'd have to marry her after she took the potion, but she'd never gotten around to telling him about the ring. After seeing it on the girl's finger, she'd decided it was just as well.

"How did you manage that?" Gavin Butterbean asked, but not unkindly.

"You know that Mordred was never interested in marriage, so he never bothered to learn all the traditions."

"It was an accident of Fate, Vargill," Butterbean offered.

"Indeed, and we cannot punish them for that," High Chancellor Godrickle said. "I have made it a policy never to overturn the council's findings. I'd never want to silence a chancellor. But this vote was only a nay by one and I believe that it is in the interest of the greater good that Midnight Cherrywood's and Dred Shadowins's marriage be sanctified by this council. The Cherrywoods have always held great magick in their blood and could do nothing but enrich the Shadowins line. Your petition is approved."

Aradia waited for the council to be dismissed before she left the hall. She almost slipped on a stray bit of ice on her way out. She knew it was what she deserved for having a Change moment, as the mortals called it. If anyone ever mentioned it, she'd say she was having a hot flash. Warlocks tended to leave witches alone after a comment like that.

Vargill narrowed his eyes at her as he left and there was a promise of retribution there. Fuck him and the dragon balls he rode in on. Her dick was bigger; he'd just have to accept that.

Godrickle came from around a corner and jerked her abruptly through a secret passage that led beneath the hall.

"Aradia Salome!" he said by way of admonishment.

"I know. I couldn't help it."

"You're lucky you have that neat little trick in your arsenal or you'd be in Chaldonean Hall right now and there would be nothing I could do about it or I'd be hanging right next to you."

"I know that, too. A mother's love. What can I say?"

"Dred has been working for me."

"He *what?*" Her liquid silver eyes hardened.

"Before you go all ice bitch on me again, you should know he has been doing it for years. It was his choice not to tell you." Godrickle held up his hands as if that act of submission would cool her rage.

"So why are you telling me now?"

"He's in Loudun."

"Sweet Merlin in Chains! Are you trying to kill me, Hubert? Really? Because one more surprise like that and my heart is just going to stop." Aradia fanned herself.

"How you do carry on. I don't know how you got this reputation for being so calm and controlled. You're a drama queen."

"Guilty." She was totally unapologetic. "So, finish tearing out my heart. Why is he in Loudun?"

"He's investigating the ruins of the Ursuline convent and it's fairly close to Shale Creek." Godrickle waited for a moment to see if more than her eye would twitch. The right one was a little wider than the left and the left one blinked a few more times independent of the other. "Shale Creek, it wasn't—"

"I don't care about that. How do I get him safe?"

"That's just the thing. Tristan Belledare was there, too."

"He was just at my sister's house party. What's he doing in Loudun?"

"Dying," Godrickle informed her.

CHAPTER TWENTY-TWO

Cauldron Burn, Boil, and Bake

Whore!

He was going to kill her. It was that simple. Aradia Shadowins had interfered with his plans for the last time. She'd dared to insult him in front of his peers! *Lady Shadowins.*

Indeed, Lady Shadowins only by the grace of Merlin. In his eager second-youth after escaping the painting, he'd attempted to kill her before, but he'd gotten sloppy. Dred's father's death had been attributed to a dark object—that much was true.

But it had been Martin's own hand that had wielded the dark object. Such delicious wickedness. It had been intended for Aradia.

He'd asked to hold her hand, there under the stars on a warm summer night at Academy. She'd laughed at him then and she was laughing at him now. She'd burn like he burned and then he'd keep her forever in a painting in Chaldonean Hall. He could look at her frigid beauty all he liked, he could touch as he liked. If he wanted to hold her hand, if he wanted to break it with a hammer, he would do it.

She wasn't good enough for him anyway. He'd thought she was smart, brilliant, really. He'd expected her of all people to have figured out that Martin Vargill was an anagram of Tagrin Larmville. He'd wanted her to figure it out, to see the horror in her eyes, the thudding of her heartbeat in her pale swan throat as she realized just how powerful he was. But no, she'd been too arrogant to see farther than the end of her own nose.

Vargill decided he needed to check on his little project. He teleported himself to that room in the Banshee's Bawl. He didn't bother with the stairs; he didn't bother with the cape. None of it gave him any sense of power anymore. All he wanted was Aradia Shadowins and this.

He pulled out the handcrafted whip that had been made of selkie hide. It gave a vicious snap to the thighs of the creature that was chained to the wall. It didn't cry out or mewl, but its black eyes glittered with pain. Its mouth opened as its breathing quickened and it sighed as the whip struck again.

Martin threw a still squirming gnome to the thing and watched with a sense of contentment as it ate.

"Martin, I need more."

"You must wait."

"I'm starving, Martin. Innocent flesh, it must be innocent." It growled and threw a bloody bone. "I want Middy Cherrywood!"

"Well, she's not going to do you any good. She's married Dred Shadowins. Too bad your taste doesn't run to dirty whores. Shadowins's mother is in our way."

The creature howled and strained at its chains before receding into the petite form of a witch. She hung limply against the wall, her hair greasy and hanging across her forehead. Her mouth was still bloody and she retched all over the floor.

"You will eat what she eats!"

"What have you done me?" the woman cried, her voice hoarse.

"Nothing you didn't do to yourself. Did you really think that anyone would want your used-up body? Thought you could fuck your way into some security, did you? Well, this is it. Soon, you won't even be able to take your own form. It will be only the lamia. All of those lost hours? That was the lamia in control of your body. You are the gateway. And now that you're open, I can't risk you running around free until I don't have to look at your mewling face and the lamia is fully manifested."

"I loved you, Martin," the witch whispered softly.

"You're a lying whore. Just like all of them. Your cunt is a weapon and you use it to hurt and maim."

"You were nice to me. You were kind and I fell in love with you. I did everything you asked of me. I trusted you. I can't believe I was so stupid as to believe you were just looking out for Middy when you asked me to come to the house party and spy on Dred."

"It doesn't matter one way or another, does it? No one knows where you are now and by the time anyone who gives a damn realizes you're gone, there will be nothing left of you and the lamia will be free."

Drusilla Tallow sank against the cold stone of the wall, useless tears marking pale tracks down her dirty and bruised cheeks.

CHAPTER TWENTY-THREE
Dressing for Donatien

Middy was reminded of Tally as she charmed on the outfit that she was going to wear to Donatien. She wished that Tally were here. Tally would charm that leather up her thighs in no time! She missed the other witch and had a horrible feeling that something had happened to her.

She hadn't seen Tally since that night in the library and she wondered where her friend had gotten off to. Middy brushed off the feeling. She was just hurt that Tally hadn't confided in her. She was probably wrapped up with Martin and they were having a wonderful time. For Middy, that was the more acceptable answer than thinking that Tally was in trouble.

Even though, as far as she or Dred could tell, Tally had been the last one to see Tristan Belledare alive.

Merlin damn these vinyl pants! They were stuck on her hips. She knew that they fit, but they were supposed to stretch.

"Stop taking my name in vain," a disembodied voice echoed through the dressing room.

"Then fix these pants!" Middy growled, frustrated.

"Maybe a size bigger—"

"These are my size, damn it."

"Maybe your size isn't your size in *these* pants."

"Look here, if I die tonight, the tag in my pants will not

read the next size up. I am not Chubby Cherrywood anymore. Fix. The. Pants."

"I always thought you had a rather nice figure."

"I do now." Middy continued to tug on the pants.

"A bit on the skinny side for my taste," the voice continued.

"Me? Skinny? I'm insulted."

"Hourglasses are pretty, but I like apples. Pear shapes have
their advantages, too."

"Merlin?"

"Yes?"

"Can we stop debating the shape of my ass and cover it
in vinyl?"

"I guess."

And the pants fit as if they'd been made for her.

"I told you these were my size," Middy grumbled.

She emerged from the dressing room and caught a
glimpse of herself in the mirror. Okay, so it was more than
a glimpse. There were three mirrors and a stage to stand on
to get the full effect of the outfit.

The leather-look pants clung like a second skin to her
every curve. The "fetish boots," as the clerk had called them,
laced up to her knees and the purple-and-black corset left
little to the imagination. Middy was sure that she could
stash a grenade in her cleavage and no one would be the
wiser. If she got tired, her ample breasts were so high under her chin that she could rest her head on them like a
chicken tucking its head under a wing.

She pulled the half mask over her eyes and decided that
she looked like an x-rated superhero. Leaping tall dildos in
a single bound, but she'd look damned good doing it.

Middy reached over and grabbed the tactical belt that
hung on the chair and secured it around her waist. At first
glance, they all looked like sex toys. If anyone saw her on
the street, he might think she was some sort of nymphoma-

niac gunslinger. She could see herself quick on the draw with cocks in each holster.

Her imagination was certainly running wild tonight. She was thankful for the mask so the other patrons wouldn't see her cheeks flame.

Dred's costume did nothing to quiet her fevered brain either.

He stepped from his dressing room, tall and confident, with that devil smirk on his lips. Sweet, sweet, Merlin.

If he answered her, Merlin that is, right at this moment, there would be certain hell to pay.

Dred was wearing leather pants, too. He had what she liked to call pillaging thighs. His build harkened back to his ancestors, those demons of the north that came down from the land of the midnight sun to spread their seed and increase their wealth.

Middy had never seen a man so solidly built, with his hard thighs, sculpted calves, and an ass that was made to be slapped. She was sure that she could bounce a quarter off of his glutes. Her fingers itched to try.

Until the studded belt he wore distracted her. The buckle was made of silver and she couldn't even describe what the shape was because it served as a neon light for his goods. The way the belt hung on his hips, she could see the finely crafted lines of that triumvirate of manhood that drew the eye straight down to his cock.

She forced her eyes up and it was like pulling melted gum off of a brick wall. Her gaze seemed to get stuck in places, like the light sprinkling of golden hair around his navel. Then it was the particular demarcation between his abdominals and his pectorals. Middy was especially entranced by the Atlas-width of his shoulders and that tender place between his shoulder and his bicep. Around his neck was a leather collar that came with a thick nylon leash.

It should be a high crime for that warlock to ever wear a shirt. She found, though, that she was looking for his scars. She needed to see them. They were what made him real to her.

No one would ever know what this man had sacrificed for them. What twisted her insides was that Dred was okay with that. He didn't need a medal or an honor, and he didn't want it. Instead, he bore the whispers and the slander without complaint.

It made her wonder what he thought he needed to atone for.

He placed the leash in her hand and raised a brow. "What is your demand, Mistress?"

"Stop it."

Dred grinned, flashing his charmed teeth. "Stop what?"

"Stop trying to make me wet."

"Is it working?"

"You know perfectly well that it is." Middy scowled.

"Then why are you scowling?"

"My muffin and vinyl don't mix. You won't be putting your chip in this bean dip for at least a week if you make me any hotter."

"We should pick up a miconazole potion on the way, then. I'm nowhere near done enjoying you in that getup." He looked her up and down with a licentious grin. "I know for a fact you'll enjoy this leash play. Won't you, Midnight?"

"I'm the one in charge here," Midnight said as she snapped the leash like a whip.

Of course, she had to cross her legs after she did it, otherwise she'd stick to the next place she sat down like an industrial suction cup.

"Good. You need to stay in character. No matter what happens." He closed the distance between them and knelt in front of her and licked up the calf of her boot. "Even in submission to you, Midnight, I'm still in control. I'll still make you come."

She found herself nodding. He could say that he was the Muffin Overlord from the Great Snatch Revolt of 1763 and she'd have nodded happily.

"I don't want you to forget." Dred's mouth was now on the vinyl that was currently hugging the inside of her thigh.

Right there, in the fetish shop dressing room where anyone could see!

She was tempted to throw her thigh up on his shoulder and demand satisfaction. Sure, there'd be a potion in her future, but wasn't there always?

Midnight jerked on the leash (it was a mistake, letting her have that) to draw him closer. "You can make me come? Do it."

"Midnight, I—"

"I said now!" Middy jerked the leash again.

He bent his blond head and ran his tongue down the seam of the vinyl between her legs. He lifted her right leg to give him better access and balanced it on his shoulder, just as she'd imagined. His fingers were splayed on her thigh to hold her steady.

She turned her head and she could see them both reflected in the mirror. Middy found this to be embarrassing and exciting at the same time. She was entranced by the look on Dred's face as he did as she demanded.

His eyes were closed, his lashes like snowflakes on his cheeks. There was a look of pleasure on his face; this wasn't mechanical for him. For some reason, it surprised her. She'd always thought that his seductions were planned. He always knew what to say, what to do. But tonight he wanted to please her. She didn't know if it was just the challenge of the single orgasm, or something more.

The light sensation of his tongue through the vinyl was a

delicious tease, but it wouldn't make her come. She was torn between telling him what she wanted and challenging him to do more.

"Don't do it!" Merlin's voice interrupted.

Middy shrieked and if not for Dred's hands on her, she would have flown backwards into the mirrors.

"Dirty old man," Dred muttered.

"All Seeing has its rewards, you know. It took forever to charm her adorable ass into those pants—don't you dare charm her out of them."

"I'm never having sex again. He's worse than Santa. Sees me when I'm sleeping. Knows when I'm awake. Knows when I want to ride my husband like a pony."

Oh, what the fuck was that? How had that horrible word escaped her mouth? Not the pony part, though she couldn't quite believe that gem had slipped past her lips un-censored. He *was* the Bigger Boss, after all. No, it had been the word *husband*. As if they were already married.

Maybe Dred wouldn't notice.

Nope. Too late. At least, that was what she gathered from the insanely superior smirk on his face.

"Baby, if he's watching, he deserves what he gets."

"Can I have my leg back?" Middy asked.

"Only if you say 'Now!' "

"Now!"

Dred dropped her leg and was on his feet in one fluid motion. When Middy watched him move, she felt like she was watching *Big Cat Diary* on Animal Planet. She loved how smooth every articulation of muscle and tendon seemed to be—how every movement was silent and like a dance between the man and the space around him.

"I find I quite like this. Perhaps I was wrong to have ex-cluded domination from the centerfold's programming."

"No, you were right to do so. It would give your enemies power to be able to watch you do these things. It would take away much of the awe that your presence inspires."

"Awe? Are you in awe, Midnight, dearest?" he tossed lightly.

"You know I am," she said without looking up.

"Don't forget, you can't break character," he said as he adjusted himself.

Middy's gaze followed the motion of his hands. "That's going to be hard to hide."

"Why bother? It's a sex club."

"You really want an answer to that?" Middy asked.

"Sure, why not?"

"It's going to distract me and we'll get nothing done."

"Is that a threat or a promise?" Dred brushed the pad of his thumb over her lips.

"Just a fact."

"If that's the case, they we'll just have to *keep coming* until we get it right." He traced his index finger down the side of her cheek to the valley of her breasts.

"What are you, fourteen?" Middy tried to sound unimpressed. If she'd managed to get rid of the "fuck me now" breathless quality to her voice, it would have helped considerably.

"If I was fourteen, I sure as hell wouldn't know how to handle you, Middy." His hand was on her ass now, as if to demonstrate exactly what his "handling" skills happened to entail. "We really need to get this act on the road."

"Oh, does depravity have a closing time?"

"No, but I have to check in with my mother. She thinks we're scouting out locations for the ceremony."

"Well, what are you going to tell her?"

"The location? I thought you wanted to do the Eiffel Tower thing."

"I was being facetious." Middy rolled her eyes.

"What *do* you want to do?"

"You're talking like we're really doing this."

Dred palmed his forehead. "Balls, woman! I thought we had this conversation. Yes, you're marrying me. Remember the whole losing our magick clause? Yeah."

"I don't want to." Middy pursed her lips into a pout.

"You just called me your husband not ten minutes ago. You want to."

"No, I really don't. You don't love me."

"Fine, I love you. Can we get on with this?"

Her foot just happened to be on a spring-loaded hinge that had a hair trigger; that trigger being a false declaration that insulted both of them. If he hadn't been paying attention, she would have nailed him right in the stones with her stiletto heel.

"First, you want the Grand Confession. I give it to you and you kick me. I don't understand you."

"You have to mean it."

"I did mean that I don't understand you."

"The love part, asshat."

"Yes, I will wear your ass for a hat. A proper bowler with a feather. Can we get down to business?"

She would have called him a douche, but she was sure he'd find some vulgar comeback that would leave her irritated further. Middy found relief when she realized that she still held the leash in her hand. She snapped it twice.

CHAPTER TWENTY-FOUR

Drudgery in Donatien

For those wishing a discreet experience, Club Donatien was anathema. Middy's thoughts on the subject were a bit less refined. She thought it looked like Hell if they'd gotten the right publicist.

It smelled like a whorehouse.

Not that she'd ever sniffed a whorehouse, but the scent of heavy, cloying perfume wafted from the doors. Perhaps it was incense? Whatever it was, it turned her stomach in three different directions at once.

There were two great, white pillars that marked the doorway and flames shot out of the tops every fifteen minutes. She realized that the pillars looked like cocks. So, the fire was supposed to be . . . Eww.

The bouncers were particularly scary. They were both bald, all over. Not a bit of hair to be seen on either of them. They wore masks with zippers for the mouths and cock corsets that were attached to thin mesh clubbing shirts. It was a strange sight, to be sure.

They opened the doors and revealed the inside of the club as Dred slipped a hundred into one of the bouncers' hands. Where he was going to put it, Middy didn't want to know.

The walls were covered in plush, red velvet and they were led down a long and twisting hallway that opened up into a great room full of sights and sounds that Middy could have gone her whole life without seeing.

It bothered her somewhat that Dred was not only unfazed, but that the waitstaff seemed to know him. There was a woman that Middy was sure she'd seen before. In fact, Midnight was sure it was the same woman that she'd seen making out with Middy herself in Dred's fantasy.

Middy could have gone the rest of her life without seeing—well, that was a lie. Considering all the women he'd been with, she figured there was no way she'd go the rest of her life without seeing *someone* he'd had sex with.

"Hi," the waitress said, addressing Middy in a voice that was way too happy. "We're practically sisters."

"How's that?" Middy gave her a surly look.

"We've both fucked Dred. I do hope we can be close." She smiled and ran her hand down Middy's arm.

"Then you'd have to be close to the entire female population of the world. Perhaps even the universe."

"Oh, I wish," she sighed dreamily.

"I was an experiment." Dred shrugged.

"Would *you* like to experiment?" the woman asked.

"Maybe another time," Middy said, trying not to blush.

"Oh," the waitress pouted. "Can I get you two anything to drink? A dance with the Green Fairy?"

"Does it have real fairies in it?" Middy asked, completely serious.

"She is so cute!" The waitress slapped Dred's arm playfully and sauntered off, shaking her ass as she went.

"Well, does it?" Middy asked again.

"No, it's absinthe. They call it the Green Fairy. That's like asking if they make Girl Scout cookies out of real Girl Scouts."

"Don't they?"

"She seems to like you. Maybe you should 'torture her' to get her to talk." Dred raised a brow.

"What did I tell you?"

"Hey, you can't blame a guy for trying."

"Don't try again," Middy warned.

"Can I think about it?"

"Trying or the . . ."

Dred winked.

He looked like sex on a stick when he did that. "I have no control over what you think about," she said repressively.

If she was being honest with herself, she'd admit that she loved the idea of him fantasizing about her, no matter what he pictured her doing. It was the fact that she occupied his thoughts when she wasn't around.

"Would you like to?" he asked in a silky tone.

For all of her need for control, she didn't want that. "No. If I did, I might as well go back to fucking myself."

"No one said you had to stop. I'd like to watch."

"You did watch!" Middy's voice was a harsh whisper.

"It was beautiful," Dred said as he leaned in against her so that his voice was just in her ear.

She didn't know how he managed it, but this felt intimate. Even though they were here with all of these people, he was talking about something that was just theirs.

"I want to do it again. I want us to watch each other," he said and pressed his lips to the soft pulse at her throat.

"What are you doing? We're supposed to be gathering information," Middy whispered.

"We are. Remember when I asked you about trust? This is where you trust me. People are watching. Some are magickal, some are not. Your arousal must be real."

Dred took the lead, though it looked as if she chose their course as he was still on the leash. They made their way to a divan that was partially surrounded by curtains, but afforded a view to the sexual melee going on around them.

Their absinthe arrived via seemingly invisible hands and

Dred took a drink and rose up on his knees so that he was above Middy on the divan. She was still clutching the leash like it was a lifeline, but she knew that ship had sailed a good hour ago.

He kissed her, careful to keep his hands at his sides, but used his mouth like a chalice to feed her small sips of absinthe. It was an intimate act that went beyond the erotic and sent tremors through her body.

Dred used his tongue to clean a drop of the spirit she missed on her bottom lip and then he held the glass to her lips. She held the burning liquid in her mouth and he kissed her again, sharing the bite of the Green Fairy.

She didn't want anyone to see her doing these things, but yet, when Dred touched her, nothing mattered but that: his hands, the heat of his body, the taste of his lips. Middy still wasn't sure how putting on this display was going to get them anywhere.

He'd said she had to trust him.

So she gave herself over to him, put herself wholly into his keeping and played the game.

Middy was torn between losing herself in Dred and watching everything that was going on around them, from the couple in the alcove next to theirs where the woman had a corset piercing that began in the small of her back and ran up to her shoulder blades to the tangle of limbs and bodies in the alcove across the way.

Dred didn't seem to mind whatever she wanted to do. His hands and his mouth were occupied only with her. With this smorgasbord of sexuality for the taking, he just wanted her.

Middy had an epiphany.

It was a soft whisper against her skin, it was a kiss. It was no more substantial than a drop of water in an endless sea, but it rocked her to her core. This could be as close to love as she'd get with Dred Shadowins.

That wasn't the epiphany.

It was that she could live with the realization. Not only live, but perhaps even thrive. A new peace filled her, but unfortunately, it would have to take a backseat to the urgency that was building in her clit.

"Want some company?"

Hell no, they didn't want company! Middy almost growled audibly. They wanted to— Right. They did want company if they were going to get any information.

She looked up to see a man with two rings in each nipple and chains attached to them that disappeared into his kilt. Middy imagined what it would look like on her real-life, dress-up Dred doll. It would be tasty, just like everything else. The kilt, not the rings. She could only pray that the chains weren't attached to what she was sure they were attached to.

"Yes, we would."

He smiled, the expression softening his appearance and he sat down on the divan. "Is there anything in particular you're looking for this evening?"

"Yes, there's—"

Dred had forgotten the game and had spoken without permission. They didn't want to blow their cover so she jerked on the leash. The look on his face told her that she was going to pay for that later. That and the images of her over his knee that were racing through his mind were a pretty vivid clue.

She thanked Morrigan that their thoughts were only connected when they were engaging in sexual activity.

"Did I give you permission to speak?" Middy watched him for a long moment, as did their guest. "No, and I still haven't. Lick my boot."

Her mistake.

Dred knelt and licked from the ankle of her boot all the way up to the soft place behind her knee. He didn't look down like a true sub would have, but met her eyes during the whole display.

"My mistress would beat me if I looked at her in such a way," the newcomer offered.

"He does as I command. If he has no spirit, what use is he?" Middy asked. "So, as I was saying. A friend of mine was here last night and had a particularly . . . interesting treatment."

"And you'd like the same?"

"Yes, indeed. I want the same room he was in, too, if that's possible."

"The treatment and room?"

"I'm not sure; he wasn't altogether coherent this morning." Middy nodded knowingly.

"His name?"

"Tristan Belledare."

"Hmm, I remember him. He didn't pay for a treatment. Just rented a room. I wish he had though. My mistress would have enjoyed him."

"He must have been with someone," Middy encouraged him.

"I can't really tell you that."

"You will tell me. Right. Now." Middy threw caution to the wind and grabbed hold of the chains that led from his nipples to . . . and tugged.

"As you command," he breathed deeply, obviously enjoying the pain. "A blond woman, petite. She kept calling him hero."

"We'd like that room," Middy said as a sick trepidation rose inside of her like bile. Had he been with Tally?

"I'll be back with the keys." The man left reluctantly after Middy let go of his chains.

"You're a naughty witch," Dred said into the shell of her ear. "He didn't want you to let go."

"Too bad for him."

"Too bad for him, indeed. In all of this bacchanalia, you don't see anything else you want?"

"What kind of question is that?" Middy did her best to look bored and at ease with her environment.

"Besides me, Midnight. I've seen you looking, but it was only a passing glance. You were a virgin. There's no other flesh that intrigues you?"

Middy shook her head and it was an honest answer. She didn't want anything but Dred Shadowins and she had a sneaking suspicion that the potion didn't have anything to do with it.

"I would ask you the same question, but I don't think I want to know the truth. I've decided what I want to believe and I'd like to stick with that, thanks."

"Not even if I could answer the same?"

"Not even then, Dred. It was easy enough for you to lie about loving me earlier. Why should this be any different? Your lust isn't the consolation prize."

Dred's attention was suddenly on something that wasn't her. Well, that had lasted a grand total of twenty minutes. Middy stubbornly shut that voice out of her head. It never said anything that she wanted to hear anyway.

"Middy! Do you remember the servant who showed us to our room at Snow Manor?"

"The stinky one?"

"He's here!"

"Eww! I mean, why?" Middy supposed even the un-washed needed love. She just hoped that they made him bathe before allowing him in a room.

"It looks like he's on staff! He just went through a service door."

They dashed after him, pushing their way through the li-centious crowd. It was as if the creature was waiting for them: He would slip out of sight and then Middy or Dred would catch another glimpse of him.

He turned just as they rounded a corner and then a white light exploded between them. The light took on a familiar shape and Middy cried out. How could Tristan Belledare be standing in front of them?

CHAPTER TWENTY-FIVE

Things to Do in Loudun When You're Still Dead

Tristan Belledare had watched with an unhappy frown as the events unfolded in the world below. He had to say that this was, indeed, bullshit. Yes, it was.

First, he'd been eaten by his ex-girlfriend. That sucked all on its own. It didn't need any help. Second, he was still in love with Midnight Cherrywood. Third, he'd just taken a new job. From hero to Duke of Heaven. It didn't have the nice ring to it that Crown Prince of Heaven did, but he'd have to earn that.

The new job? Babysitting his current love interest. Upon his untimely and rather sucktacular demise, he'd been made her guardian angel. Talk about a selfless act? She was in mad love with another warlock and it was his job to see to it that she was happy. He knew that Dred was the right one for her, but that didn't make Tristan want her any less.

That witch was an accident waiting to happen.

It was damned lucky for her that she had a special gift; otherwise, her ass, as they say, would have been grass when she'd fallen off that broom. Not that Dred wasn't all badass hero, too, but without Tristan's little push, they would both be dead.

Now, where in the name of all that was holy had Dred's angel gotten to? That was another question Tristan wanted the answer to. Merlin knew that the warlock needed one.

Crazy bastard.

Tristan had been shown many things after his death. He'd seen what had happened at Shale Creek. And he was thankful for more reasons than one. The first being that Dred had saved his ass. The second being that the image of Dred that had been forever burned into his mind was there not because Tristan had repressed desires, but because it was a repressed memory.

That made him much more comfortable in his own skin, needless to say. Tristan had been worried because he'd thought that if he had a man crush, he'd know it. It had been disturbing to think that his mind had been going places without him. That was a sure recipe for crazy.

Tristan watched with rising alarm as he noticed that the revenant belonging to Barista Snow turned to wait on the other side of the door for Dred and Midnight. Damn, but he hated that witch. She'd just been irritating on her own, with her mad quest for eternal youth, until she met Vargill and got power hungry.

Tristan continued to watch the scene unfold, sure that Dred would take precautions, but he was just barreling ahead, hell bent for . . .

Damn it.

Tristan had no choice but to manifest himself. A bright, white light blinded the creature, which scurried from it like a roach caught out in the open at high noon.

"Tristan!"

Middy had seen him.

He watched as Dred turned at her cry and abandoned the chase to see to her.

Tristan chortled like a monkey who'd just won King Shit of Turd Mountain. Dred was in love with Middy! His aura was so bright, but the colors ran the gamut from the bit of black where the Abyss had touched him to the searing white spaces that were the goodness in him.

But they were all tinged with pink. A color that Tristan happened to know had become a bit of a compulsion for Dred. Yes, he would take very good care of Middy and they would have a fairy-tale happiness, if only Dred would recognize his feelings.

An old adage about leading a unicorn to virgins came to mind.

Midnight, he could see, was head over arse for him. Her aura bloomed wherever he touched her. When his attention was on her, Middy literally glowed. She could be seen from space.

Tristan could see where the potion had affected her, but it was such a small place. She would have come to this over time on her own.

Dred's hands were on her now as he checked her wound and their auras both changed to a lovely purple. Tristan took that as his cue to go look elsewhere. As much as he still thought of Middy, this was where she was supposed to be. Tristan also knew that this increased need for her was Fate's way of making his job easier. He had to admit, Fate was either one sadistic bitch or had quite the dry sense of humor. Middy would always be out of his league. If she used her gift selflessly, all that light inside of her, she would ascend and become a Crown Princess of Heaven. But Tristan wanted that for her: It was the pinnacle of her journey, what she was meant for.

He wondered briefly how very much trouble he would get into if he eased Tally's pain from the transition just a bit. She didn't deserve this. All she'd done was fall in love with the wrong man after Tristan himself had broken her heart. And her faith. Sure, his death had been horrible, but that wasn't her fault. It was his own. Tristan wondered if he maybe should have been a Duke of Hell instead.

CHAPTER TWENTY-SIX

A Dark, Marbled Affair

"I know that I saw Tristan," Middy said as she followed Dred into the rented flat in Paris.

"Middy, you do know that he's dead, right?"

"I saw him! There was a flash of bright light, almost blinding, and I saw him standing there. He had the most beautiful wings," Middy said as a warm feeling enveloped her.

"You, yourself, just said the light was blinding. Maybe you *wanted* to see him?"

"No! What else could have scared off that thing? Did you see that guy when he turned? He was like a Hollywood zombie."

"I don't know what that was. It looked like the servant we saw at Snow Manor, but up close it was more like that guy after he'd been dead for fifty years."

Middy noticed the black marble floor of Dred's kitchen and she flushed. This was where she'd seen herself in Dred's mind. She'd been naked and . . .

Dred shrugged. "A warlock's brain is never a safe place."

"How many witches have you had on this floor?" She rolled her eyes.

"None."

It was hard not to snort like a pig.

"Seriously, it's marble. It's cold."

"I've been told that some things are better in fantasy than reality," Middy said, smiling shyly.

"Yeah? What do you think about that?" Dred implied that she had reason to offer her expert opinion.

"Stop fishing for compliments. Your head is big enough as it is."

"Let me check your back. If there's no improvement, you are going to the Magick Medic and that's final."

"I liked it better when I was in charge," she said sullenly.

"No, you didn't." He lifted her up on the island counter and turned her to suit him.

"What can I say? I do love an alpha male."

He lifted the back of her shirt and was surprised to find that her wounds had healed. Completely.

"Is there any pain?"

Middy shook her head, trying not to lean in to his touch like a cat begging to be stroked.

Dred's Witchberry was lying at the other end of the counter. So, when it rang, Middy jumped and fell off her perch. Dred had grown accustomed to Middy's penchant for throwing herself off things and was there to catch her. Unfortunately, that meant that he was not there to intercept the call.

Aradia Shadowins's face was drawn and white and she scowled at them.

"So you two flit off to France without even a word to your mother?"

"Aradia," Dred began.

"Don't you Aradia me, Mordred Arthur Shadowins. I was worried sick. Sick! And instead of calling me you two are fiddle-fucking around playing house? You've got some explaining to do, young man!"

Dred eased Middy upright and picked up the Witchberry. "Look, we're a little busy; I promise I will explain everything later."

"The one and only heir to the Shadowins's fortune and magick disappears without a trace and . . . do you know what I've been through? You will explain right now!"

Dred dropped the Witchberry into a drawer, but as soon as he did, there was a knock on his door.

"That would be my mother," Dred sighed and opened the door. Aradia brushed past him with casual irritation.

"So, did you know that the council denied your marriage petition? Good thing you already gave her that ring, Mordred, or we'd be screwed."

"What does the ring have to do with it? Besides that thrice-damned tattoo on the inside of her wrist?"

"It means you're already married." Aradia set her purse and her broom down next to the counter. "Family magick."

"What?" Middy blinked like an owl that had fallen into a vat of coffee—eyes wide and organ failure about to ensue.

"I couldn't very well call you and tell you, now could I? Especially since High Chancellor Godrickle revealed that you were off on some sort of secret mission. I can't believe you didn't tell me." Aradia sniffed delicately.

"Mother, your temper is going to give you age spots."

Aradia gasped. "Ungrateful boy, I had my hair done today, but I still hopped right on the broom to come all the way to Paris and warn my son that his cover might have been blown. And this is the thanks I get?"

"Since all your help comes with a hearty side order of nag, then yes." Dred handed her a bottle of water and she sipped it like a cocktail.

"Really, Dred. A spy?" she huffed. Aradia took a breath before speaking again. "I'm so proud of you."

"We thought it best that no one knew."

Middy saw that he was uncomfortable with his mother's praise. Aradia embraced him and while he returned the gesture, he looked around as if he were checking for an escape route.

"So we're already married? Dred hasn't even met my mother. My brothers are going to make me a widow before I've had a honeymoon."

"It will be fine; you just leave all of that to me. Midnight, have you called your mother? She doesn't know, right? About the spying or anything?"

Middy shook her head.

"First of all, call the witch. She's probably worried sick. I will go smooth things over and she and I will commence with the formal wedding plans. You two know there's no way out of that now."

"Middy, you're going to be on the cover of every magickal newspaper for some time. How you managed to snag Dred Shadowins with no pre-nup." Dred grinned.

"Considering that we'll both lose our magick if we split up, I'd say that's one hell of a pre-nup," Midnight sighed.

"Midnight, Shadowins don't get divorced. They die first."

Aradia said that with such a cheerful smile that Middy was tempted to ask if it was ever of natural causes. She wasn't sure that she wanted to hear the answer.

Dred pulled out a bottle of George Dickel bourbon and poured himself a double. He downed it.

"Is it that bad?" Middy asked, not a little insulted.

"Yes. Have you thought about all of the paperwork?" Dred downed another shot. "It will take days of meetings with lawyers and boards and so on and so forth. I have to add you to my health insurance, the life insurance, shares in the Shadowins's holdings. You have to meet the griffins as an official part of the family so you can travel freely through our holdings. We have to change your name and, yeah, we're going to change it. None of this hyphenated garbage. You can walk me like a dog on a leash and I'll call you mistress all day long and lick your boot heel or whatever the hell else you want, but you'll wear my name."

Middy snatched the glass from him and downed a shot herself. "Don't call me 'mistress' in front of your mother."

"You didn't argue about the name."

"Did you expect me to?" Middy asked.

"Kind of, yeah. I mean, you argued about marrying me to start with." Dred picked up the bottle, then seemed to think better of it and put it back down.

"I'll take care of all of that for you. Middy, I'll have your new IDs, credit cards, and registrations delivered here tonight," Aradia said helpfully.

"I can't believe this is really happening."

"I can't believe that for all the magick we use everyday, someone didn't invent a spell, a charm, or something to eliminate paperwork," Dred added.

"It's universal, I think. Even the Powers That Be have paperwork issues," Middy said.

"Rather than try to demure, I'm going to duck out honestly. I'm sure you want to shag like mad now that it's official." Aradia grinned. "I know when to make an exit. And, Dred?"

"Yes, Mother?"

"Midnight is correct. I know my friends all have naked pictures of you, and that's fine since you get your looks from me. It's actually quite flattering. I even know that you and Midnight have intercourse. You're a grown man. I accept that. I'd just rather not hear about what exactly that entails, m'kay?"

"You're the one who said you were leaving so we could," Dred replied casually.

"Don't underestimate what a mother will do to secure grandchildren," Aradia tossed on the way out the door.

Middy noticed that Aradia always got the last word.

Suddenly, she was very aware that she was alone with Dred. That shouldn't have been anything new or intimidating. But now, they were married.

She was his wife.

He was her husband.

They were a "they."

It did little to reassure her that he seemed uncomfortable, too. Where were they going to live? Were they going to live together? She hadn't even checked out the bathroom in this place to see if there was a spot for her toothbrushing charms.

Would she have to change her Witchberry account?

So much banality was crashing in on her idyll with Dred. All she'd wanted was to lose her virginity. Instead, she was going to spend the rest of her life with this warlock. How had that happened? Well, she knew how it had happened, but it still didn't seem real.

"I didn't know about the ring," Dred offered, breaking the heavy silence.

"I know." Middy bit her lip before she spoke again. "This is stupid. We've been talking about doing this for real anyway. We've been living together, basically. So why is everything suddenly so awkward?"

"I'd like to say I'm sorry, but I'm not. You deserve better than me, Middy. I know that."

"Why do you keep saying that?"

"It's true. If I can own it, you can, too. I'll be a good husband to you though."

"As good as duty and country will allow, I guess."

"We don't have to have it all figured out today, you know. We can keep on as we have been," he suggested.

"Does your mother think I'm a spy, too?"

"I honestly have no idea what goes on in that woman's brain."

Middy looked up at Dred's profile and found she wanted to touch him. So she did. She pushed her fingers through his hair and smiled. "Is this okay?"

"The package is all yours now. Do what you want with it." He raised a brow in invitation.

With a single touch, Middy had shoved him back into a territory that was comfortable for him. She didn't like to see the uncertainty on his face. She wanted him to know that even if he didn't love her, he was a good man and she didn't feel cheated.

Middy didn't think he knew that. Perhaps in his younger days, all he'd had to offer the world was his pretty face, but he was so much more mow. Maybe that was why he couldn't love her, because for all of his show, he didn't love himself.

He'd dived headfirst into a free fall from a perfectly sound broom to save her. Underneath his cynicism, Dred Shadowins had a pure heart. The love she felt for him surged and blossomed with a warmth that spread through her like a kiss from the sun.

Middy pushed her hands up beneath his black T-shirt and scored her nails lightly down his sides.

"I've been in charge enough for a while, I think."

"What if I've decided I like you in charge?" Dred asked as he bent his head to kiss her.

"I think you'll like this better." Middy tilted her face up to meet his kiss and melted against him like many a witch before her. Yet, unlike the witches before her, Middy held the key to his fantasy and she knew it.

She loved the way he kissed. It was so real. Middy supposed that was a stupid thought to have, but after so much fantasy, knowing him, knowing his touch, the reality of his wants and desires fed her own.

His touch was visceral. It cut her in the softest places, but it healed her somehow, too. She wondered if he felt the same sensations as she did. Middy hoped so. It would be a sad thing to experience this wonder alone.

"Middy, you know I'm a warlock, right?" Dred said against the corner of her mouth.

"Oh, yes. Definitely." She nipped at his bottom lip.

"Then you know I'm not a witch and don't need to talk about every feeling we have." Dred laughed as he kissed her again.

He'd said "we!" Middy was elated.

"So what is it that I'll like better than you telling me how you want it?" Dred refocused her attention.

"Me on this floor, in all my *pink*. Isn't that what you wanted, isn't that what you showed me?" Middy slipped her cotton dress off her shoulders and let it fall into a pool at her feet.

Dred snapped his fingers and a fire crackled to life in the great room and bedroom fireplaces; the cold, dark marble of the floor warmed instantly.

"As much as I love the visual, I'd rather have you on the chimerean fur duvet on my bed," Dred said as he swung her up into his arms with ease.

Middy enjoyed the feel of her nakedness against the soft cotton of his shirt, how small she felt wrapped up in his arms. She especially liked feeling his muscles move under her fingers as he carried her to the bedroom.

He smelled of leather and pine; there were undercurrents of another scent that was just him. She breathed him in, trembled with anticipation.

Dred deposited her on the duvet, the fur supple and lush against her bare skin. He watched her for a moment, taking her in. She still blushed under his gaze.

He knelt at the foot of the bed and pressed his lips to the inside of her ankle and moved up to the tender place just at the inside of her knee. He touched his mouth there as well. He kissed farther up her leg to the alabaster smooth skin of her thigh.

Middy's breath caught in her throat and she relaxed her legs to allow him better access. She kept waiting for his mouth to descend to her slit, but it didn't. He kissed the plane of her hip and moved to her belly. Her nipples tightened with desire and expectation. Dred's mouth closed over one rosebud peak, his tongue hot and insistent.

She wanted to touch him, to pleasure him as he pleasured her, but he gripped her wrists and held her hands above her head.

"No, Midnight."

"Why not? Don't you like my touch?" Middy taunted. "What is it you like to say? Be silent and objectified?"

"Are you objectifying me?"

"Be silent and find out," he said before taking her other nipple into his mouth.

"Make me," Middy dared him.

He released her nipple with a sigh. "I've figured out why you're not a multi-orgasmic witch."

"And why is that, Oh, Great Sex God?" Middy smirked back at him.

"Because you won't be quiet long enough to have more than one orgasm. The banter has to stop sometime."

"Why? Isn't that what sex is? It's what comes after the witty exchange, but it's still a give and take. Just with other body parts."

She thought she had something else to say, but Dred kissed her. Middy knew why that always silenced heroines in the books. She couldn't keep a coherent thought in her head with Dred's lips anywhere near hers.

Middy hadn't been sure what to think about their first kiss. It had been so raw, but now his mouth was new and familiar at the same time. She wondered if it would always be like that.

She met his kiss and proved that she was as hot for him

with all of her chattering as she would be without it. Perhaps even more so because the man could think even while his brain's blood supply was otherwise engaged.

That thought alone made her slit clench and sent a small tremor through her. It also made her wonder what she'd have to do to make him lose control. He was always so in command of himself, of his body and hers. What would it take to make him give in to her?

She whispered a quick spell that reversed their positions. He was flat on his back, naked, and she was holding his hands above his head.

"Oh, yeah?" Dred's mouth curled in a satisfied smirk.

"Yeah," Middy said as she let go of his wrists and scored her nails down his chest.

He kept his hands above his head. "Let's see what you've got, sweetheart."

Middy straddled his hips and rose up on her knees. She guided her breast back to his mouth and moved the tight nipple against his lips. He took the rosebud peak and sucked it into the hot cavern of his mouth.

When she felt his hand knead her other breast, she pulled back. It was divine, but she wanted to pleasure him. Middy took his hand from her breast and placed a chaste kiss on the tip of his index finger. She lingered there and kissed the tip again, but much more slowly and with deliberate intent.

His gaze burned her with its intensity and when her pink tongue darted out to swirl over the tip where her lips had been, his cock jerked against her slit, seeking her wet channel.

Middy wondered what he would do if she licked the length. She ran her tongue from the base of his finger to the top before taking the whole of it into her mouth.

She was startled when she felt the effects of the sensation herself and her eyes fluttered closed for a moment as her clit throbbed. She wondered if it would always be like this, if this link was forever.

Still, he was in perfect control of his body.

She caught a flash of an image. It was her. She loved that it was always her now. Dred was fantasizing about what it would be like, the contrast of her pink lips after he'd come for her mouth.

Middy was getting to that.

She moved down his body and grasped the base of his cock in her hand and touched her lips to the head just as she'd done with his finger. Middy said a silent prayer of thanks to Tally and her lessons with the banana when he groaned.

"Midnight—" he said as he tangled his hands in her hair.

She leaned away from her task. "Hands back where they were, please."

"Wicked witch," he said lightly as he obeyed her.

Rather than offering a response, she took the tip of his cock into her mouth. She enjoyed the texture much more than she had the banana. That had made her feel stupid and inadequate, but this, it made her feel powerful and beautiful. Dred's complete attention was on her; she knew she occupied his every thought. She felt like the most feminine of witches and she was pleasuring her warlock in a way that no other witch could.

Middy knew that he was very visual so her every movement wasn't just about the sensation. It was also about what he could see her doing. It was about the show. He was focused on her pink parts. Anything that was pink, her lips, her tongue, her nipples . . .

She wanted him inside of her now, but she kept licking and sucking, stroking her hand up the base of his shaft. Pearlized fluid welled at the tip and she used her tongue to move it over the head. It was salty and sweet at the same time. Middy wanted more of it.

Dred's cock surged as he felt her wonder, and she doubled her efforts.

"Midnight, you have to stop. I'm going to come."

She wanted him to come this way; she wanted to fulfill his fantasies as he'd done for her. Middy kept the images she'd seen in his desire in the forefront of her mind and she moved her mouth and fingers over his cock faster and with more pressure.

He bucked his hips and his hands were in a white-knuckled grip on the duvet, but he was still watching her. His lips were parted and his breath was coming faster. She could see that the corded muscles in his neck were standing out with the exertion.

The throbbing in her body kept time with her ministrations to Dred's cock. When she suckled the head, she felt it in her clit.

Just as he came, an orgasm shook her and she had to fight to keep her attention on him, but she licked the remnants of his seed from her lips as he cried out. The aftershocks of their orgasms were still rocking her body.

When Middy lay down beside him, he pushed her damp curls from her brow and kissed her. They tasted each other on her lips and Dred drew her legs up around his waist.

She was still slick, but his entry was gentle until she'd stretched to accommodate him. His thumb ghosted over her clitoris, so light a touch, but it was so sensitive that just that brush of contact made her burn.

Dred was up on his knees now and he used his other hand to guide her legs straight so that they were resting on his shoulders. With that first thrust, he was so deep inside of her that she was sure she was going to shatter.

But she didn't, though every stroke into her was a mad sort of bliss. He ground his body into her with a fierce need, one that she met with her hips. Her fingers were digging into his thighs and she felt the magick gather between them.

A sudden wave of euphoria hit her and she heard screaming that she realized was her own as Dred continued to drill into her. Stars exploded behind her eyes and she could sense nothing but radiating waves of pleasure, liquid gold that began deep inside of her and moved from her belly throughout her limbs, then to her clit and finally back into that place deep in her body that she'd never sensed before.

Dred relaxed against her, his weight pushing her down into the plush duvet, though he supported most of it on his elbows. He dropped a tender kiss to her forehead and studied her for a moment before he rolled to her side.

Middy expected that he'd drop off to sleep like a stone. He didn't seem like the "afterglow" kind and that was okay; she figured she had enough afterglow for both of them.

He tucked her into his side, with his arm around her and his fingers tangled in her hair.

Even if he never loved her, Middy decided that this would be a good life. Being married to a warlock who could win a gold medal in the Sex Olympics, who looked like he could kick a Greek god's ass, was filthy rich, and a good man to boot? Not a bad deal at all. She could have done a hell of a lot worse.

Middy had hope though. She didn't want to change Dred, but she believed in him and believed that he had room for her in his heart. She just had to be patient.

CHAPTER TWENTY-SEVEN

Brawl at the Banshee's Bawl

"What the fuck?" Dred demanded from the sledge-hammer of a fist that had hammered into his chiseled jaw in triplicate.

"You know what the fuck!" a dark-haired man insisted. Correction. Three dark-haired men insisted in unison.

Guy must have one hell of a right hook that he was seeing and feeling things three times over. He'd buy him a beer or three, once he figured out why the guy had punched him. Maybe there really were three. Middy had triplet brothers. . . . These behemoths were almost as large as Dred himself. There was no way that these Cro-Magnons were related to his sweet Midnight.

"What? Did I fuck your mother, your wife, or your sister?"

Another crack to the jaw. Good thing it was made of solid stuff, or he'd be lying flat on his back wondering why six of these clones were kicking his ass.

"No, really. Just tell me and we can have a few beers, it'll all be good. I'm married now. Nothing to worry about."

"He doesn't even try to deny it," one said and reared back to clobber him again.

Dred was ready for him. He caught the sledgehammer, er, fist in his own and squeezed. Too bad he didn't have another set of arms; then he could have blocked the one that was suddenly behind him and crushing his windpipe like an empty soda can.

"Where's our sister?"

"Which one was your sister?" Dred used his last breath to answer and decided for sure that this must be the Trifecta of Doom.

"That's it, calendar boy. You're carrion bait!" One of them picked up his feet.

Dred was fairly certain that if he used any of his more powerful magicks on the Trifecta, Middy would frown. He wasn't sure yet if frowning included the loss of bedroom privileges, but he wasn't willing to take that chance.

"He's turning blue," the one who seemed to be in charge said and peered in close to his face.

Dred decided that while he shouldn't throw hexes at her brothers, he wasn't averse to the idea of biting one. He had the right to defend himself after all. Barring that, he'd play the pity card. Dred was sure he had a split lip. He'd appeal to her softer tendencies if Midnight got angry that he'd bitten one.

With the next gut punch, Dred had given up the idea of placating Middy, and it was, as they say, on like Donkey Kong.

Dred opened his mouth and closed his chompers on the wrist that was holding him, or rather crushing the life from him like an undesirable bug. His foot shot out and connected with an ear of the one who seemed to be in charge. Dred still had hold of the third guy's fist. When he relaxed his grip for a moment, the warlock tried to free his limb, so Dred helped him along and forced it back into the other man's nose.

A great shot if he did say so himself.

Of course, they promptly dropped him like he was on fire. He was not pleased with the beating his ass was taking lately. First, he landed on it in Loudun after an insane freefall and now this. Good thing he hadn't hit midlife yet, when Middle-Aged Man Spread was all too common. With his solid Viking and English heritage, his was already as plentiful as it needed to be.

He stood up and made a show of brushing bits of this and that off his shirt and sat back down at the bar, where he motioned for three beers. The bartender pointed behind him and he turned just in time to take a hit over the head with a barstool.

A splinter of wood sliced into his cheek.

They'd damaged his face.

Oh, hell no.

Dred gathered his magick and a dark blue halo of crackling light surrounded him. He moved so quickly that the Trifecta didn't have time to block him. The three found themselves plastered to the wall of the bar, as if they'd been bound with plastic wrap and forced to sit under a heat lamp.

"So, I assume that you're my brothers-in-law? Look, I get that you're trying to look out for Midnight, but she's my wife now. I may have deserved a bit of roughing up for marrying her in such a hurry, but you should be happy that she's married instead of knocked up and alone."

"She's pregnant?" The middle one looked like he was going to have apoplexy.

Dred grinned wickedly, but decided that knowing he was banging their sister was enough for them to swallow in a day. Also, it was untrue, as far Dred knew. Oh, what if . . . Best not to tempt Fate. She was one to do things just because one called her chicken. He and Middy were definitely not ready for that.

"No, but like I said, it could always be worse. Anyway, as I was saying, I understand your frustration, but I won't tolerate damage to the face. Middy happens to like my face the way it is."

"You're Dastard Dred! She walked around calling you a 'dastard' because Hawk washed her mouth out with soap for calling you a bastard. There's just no way!"

"Hell, I called her Cherry-Would-If-She-Could."

They started struggling again in earnest.

"If you weren't my lawfully wedded witch's family, you'd already be dead. Don't push it. I'm still debating if this wound to the face is worth however long she'll want to lock me out of the honeypot for kicking your asses."

They seemed to come to some sort of unspoken accord and Dred released them.

"I'm Hawk, this is Falcon, and Raven here is the baby," Hawk said, gesturing to each one of them in turn.

"Ah, yes, the mighty Trifecta of Doom." Dred handed each one of them a beer and picked up his own.

"I see Middy has mentioned us," Falcon said, his chest puffing.

"Yeah, and my mother had some story about one of you being a pool warlock?" Dred smirked.

Raven grinned. "That's me."

"Ginger Butterbean has an opening," Dred said, barely able to contain his laughter. "Or so Middy tells me."

"I guess you're okay, Shadowins," Hawk said.

"So, um, don't drink that beer. I pissed in it when you weren't looking." Raven smiled before taking a drink of his own beer.

"That's okay, man. I switched the glasses when *you* weren't looking." Dred clapped him on the back good-naturedly.

Raven spewed the beer all over the bar and the bartender frowned.

"Hey, if there's really piss in that, I'm not cleaning it up," she said bluntly.

"And we'll never know for sure." Dred sighed dramatically.

"This could be the start of a beautiful friendship, Shad-owins," Hawk said. "I think we like you. Are you sure you want Midnight, because if you fuck up . . ."

"You don't even want to know what happens if I fuck up. Believe me, I've got all the motivation I need," Dred said as he remembered his cock dream.

"We heard that Belledare is dead." Falcon changed the subject.

"I'd heard that." Dred took a heavy breath, wishing he could come right out and say what he knew.

"Let's cut the orc crap. We work for Godrickle," Falcon said. "We saw the crime scene photos you uploaded."

"Merlin on a stripper pole! Does everyone know? How can it be secret if everyone keeps running off at the mouth like a gaggle of damned geese in a knitting circle?"

"Our involvement was need to know." Falcon shrugged.

"Oh, and I didn't need to know?"

"That's why we're telling you," Raven added.

"After you tried to kill me," Dred tossed back.

"We had to make sure you weren't treating Middy badly, or we'd have had to kill you, regardless," Hawk declared.

"Good luck," Dred scoffed.

"I'm not saying it would have been easy, but it would happen," Falcon said.

"For fuck's sake, will you just go to the can and whip out your dicks so you'll know once and for all whose dick is the biggest?" the bartender snapped.

"It's cold." Hawk frowned.

"Shrink factor." Dred shrugged.

The bartender paused for a moment and looked at each warlock carefully. "Then I'll solve it for you. It's that one." She pointed to Dred. "Now, get the hell out of the bar. That guy over there called Warlock Patrol to lock your asses up for disturbing the peace." She grinned at Dred. "I'm sure I don't have to tell *you* where the back door is."

"Let's go." Dred and the Trifecta headed toward the back door and slipped out easily just as the brooms with their sirens wailing pulled up to the front.

"So, that back door thing," Raven began.

"Long time ago," Dred assured him.

"Oh, no. I'm not worried about that anymore. If she let you, I was curious if she'd let me."

"Maybe. I have her Witchberry number somewhere. Hell, you can have my black book. I don't need it." As Dred heard the words coming out of his mouth, he decided that this must have been what Middy had felt like when she'd blurted out she loved him. It had been like a popcorn kernel popping right out of his mouth. The worst part was that he knew it was true: He didn't need his black book.

Not that it meant he was in love with the witch; he was just going to try to be a good husband. Good husbands didn't have black books. At least Middy's idea of a good husband didn't.

"Merlin's cock! That's the holy grail for the single warlock." Raven nodded with appreciation.

Dred nodded. "Don't take Merlin's cock in vain."

"What, like the old bastard is going to show up and tell me not to?" Raven laughed.

"He just might," Dred said seriously.

Hawk snickered and then so did Falcon. "Yeah, Raven. Don't take cock in vain."

"Real mature." Raven rolled his eyes.

Hawk's grin turned into a frown. "We need to find Tally."

"What does she have to do with it?" Dred raised a brow.

Hawk nodded. "You haven't had a chance to talk to Godrickle? She and Vargill were supposed to show up to a dinner party at Godrickle's. They didn't. And with everything that's happened, Hubert is sure that they're tied to this somehow."

"You don't think that maybe they just took a lovers'

weekend and forgot about the dinner?" Dred could understand how that could happen. He'd rather be with Midnight right now than hanging out in a seedy bar getting his ass handed to him by her brothers. Or waiting for a contact that never showed.

"Because Hubert suspected that the perpetrator ran in high society, he did some checking on all of the chancellors' financials. Vargill's don't even begin to balance and there's a paper trail that connects him and some known cursed object dealers."

Dred was thrilled at this possible break in the case, but suddenly worried for Midnight.

"I know, we're worried about Midnight, too." Falcon voiced what they were all feeling at the revelation. "But there's more."

Dred waited, knowing by the look that crossed the triplets' faces in unison that he wasn't going to like what they had to say.

Falcon continued, "There was a witch we connected to the paper trail. Your aunt, Barista Snow."

Relief washed over him. "No, it couldn't be her. She must have had Vargill doing some discreet digging for her. She wanted a dark object for a youth serum. She had my uncle ask me for one."

"We have to look into it all the same, Shadowins."

Dred brushed it off. "That's fine. I understand. But she won't." He smirked.

"Back to Tally. Has Mids been in contact with Tally?" Falcon asked. "I haven't found anyone who has spoken to her or seen her since before the house party at Barista's and she's not answering her Witchberry."

"We actually saw her at the house party. Middy said she came with Martin." What had Tally been doing right outside the door to the library just as the Dred-bot had been trying to kill Midnight? Had she sent it? Dred scowled.

"Good. Just don't let her see Tally until we get this figured out."

"Don't let her . . . you know she does whatever she pleases," Dred said.

"I know." Falcon nodded. "As much as I hate to say it, keep her occupied in any way you can until we get this figured out."

"Good. We'll do aerial surveillance at Belledare's funeral. You've got the ground and Midnight?" Raven asked Dred. Dred nodded.

"Speaking of, where is she?" Falcon scowled.

"Playing World of Warlock on my spelltop."

"Does she know that you're at a bar? At *this* particular bar?" Falcon asked and all three brothers' eyebrows crawled up into their hairlines.

The Banshee's Bawl was well known for its extra services and hourly room rentals.

"Midnight knows I'm here." He'd come to meet an informer who'd never shown.

Dred decided not to tell them about how he and Midnight had come to be married. It would be enough for them to know that their sister would be cared for. They didn't need the gritty details. Dred didn't fancy another sledgehammer to the bridge of his nose.

"She didn't curse cat litter to stuff itself in your mouth?" Raven was incredulous.

"Actually, she was going to join me, but the leather pants from Donatien haven't been spell-cleaned yet. You know how she hates to do that. She stayed home."

"You took her to . . ." Falcon trailed off. "I don't want to know."

"We're good, thanks," Hawk said as he nodded.

Dred waited for them to leave before he teleported back to the flat in Paris.

CHAPTER TWENTY-EIGHT

Doppelganger Dippity Do

Drusilla Tallow knew she was going to die.

She knew it was going to be soon and she also knew that it was going to be agony. If she'd been a stronger witch, she'd have killed herself already. Tally had hoped that when Middy lost her cherry, some of her innocence would fade and whatever made her a delectable buffet to the lamia would be diminished.

It had only served to whet the creature's appetite for more.

She looked at her flesh and wondered just how something so horrible could lurk beneath the surface. Not only that, but how she could have allowed Martin Vargill to do this to her?

Tally had fallen in love and like many a love-struck witch, had been persuaded to do something foolish. She'd trusted everything he told her, believed he was trying to look out for Midnight. He'd even warned her about the Dred-bot that Barista Snow had sent to kill her. Yet she realized now he'd warned her just in time for her to help Middy—to make a suspicious and sudden appearance—but not enough time to warn Middy so she wouldn't be in danger.

She felt as if her insides were being ripped apart, but she

didn't dare scream. She wouldn't give Vargill the satisfaction. Tally knew it was the creature's hunger and it centered her thoughts on Midnight Cherrywood, the succulent sweetness of her flesh, and the goodness inside of her.

Tally could also feel herself slipping away into the darkness; it was a survival mechanism that the lamia used to make it easy to give in to her. Those pictures were how it communicated its needs to the host body, and Tally also knew that they weren't as repugnant to her as they'd once been. It was training her. The pain receded when she allowed those thoughts. It tempted her into believing that if she gave in to it completely, there would be nothing but an eternity of bliss.

She knew better though.

Her body prepared itself for Martin's entry. He liked fucking her more now that she held the lamia within her. Tally could tell that it was like playing with fire for him, flirting with danger.

She wasn't going to tell him about any of the other changes she'd experienced. Like the extra set of jaws she'd grown inside of her mouth and still, the third set of teeth. That last set of teeth had erupted somewhere he'd never expect them.

Let him put his flaccid cock in her then and he could glory in the beauty of his creation.

Tally had told him their first time together that it hadn't mattered if he couldn't keep it up and she'd meant it. He'd taken her for a nice dinner and walked her home. He'd held the door for her. It had been out of simple kindness and respect that she'd invited him in, but he'd been like a fucking vampire. Once she'd invited him in, she'd given him a power over her.

If she could get free, she'd kill this body and the lamia inside of it. Tally's time was over no matter whether the flesh lived or died. She'd tried too hard to protect Middy; she'd dumped her into Dred's lap and instead of tarnishing her goodness, he'd only made it brighter.

Tally figured they were all fucked.

She wanted to cry, but the tears were all gone and she didn't know if they'd dried up because she'd cried them all out or if she was incapable of crying now that the transition had come this far.

And she was so hungry.

The door opened and Vargill entered. He wasn't alone. Behind him was the lady herself, Barista Snow.

She had under her tailored jacket a package wrapped in brown paper. It was the Shale Creek Hand of Glory.

"Look what I've brought you, darling." Barista bared her teeth at Martin in a smile that was more like the maw of a jaguar.

"Did you kill your nephew?" Martin asked slyly.

"I didn't have to. The fool gave the Shale Creek Hand of Glory to Roderick."

"And your doting husband was foolish enough to give it to you?" he said, sneering.

"Of course not. He's in the deepest dungeon in Snow Manor where I put him after I took it."

Tally wished there was a way that she could warn Middy. She'd dropped herself right into a nest of vipers by getting mixed up with Dred Shadowins.

Even if she could escape, there was no way to warn her. Tally wasn't safe for anyone to be around anymore.

She thought of Tristan's blood and that eased her somewhat, until the human part of her flamed to life and burned those thoughts from her brain. Tally didn't know how many of those she had left. Tristan was dead now, so he wouldn't know what she was thinking anyway. If it soothed the beast to think of the sweetness of his marrow, then so be it. Yet, her humanity cried out against it. She'd loved him, too.

All the men she'd loved had hurt her.

Now that she thought about it, his marrow hadn't been that divine after all. He was a cheating bastard who couldn't keep his wand to himself. All those screaming witches who needed a hero were just too much temptation when all he had to come home to was Drusilla Tallow.

Damn him.

Martin's eyes changed to a uric yellow and he appraised her differently now, almost as if he could see inside of her.

"She's ready," he said.

Barista stood the Hand of Glory on a makeshift altar and lit the tips of the fingers on fire as she spoke the ancient Sumerian words that gave her power over the lamia.

Tally felt a new kind of strength surge through her and she pulled at her chains. They came away from the wall with such ease that she wondered why she hadn't done it before. Barista and Martin made no move to stop her, but continued chanting.

Tally had only one thought in her mind as she fled and that was to find Midnight. Her wings splayed and took her into the night sky as she searched for her prey.

CHAPTER TWENTY-NINE

Cock Talk: The Sequel

Dred was dreaming again. He knew this because he was on the same cursed path to that same clearing and he was still skipping. He tried his damndest to get his dream legs to obey him, but he had no luck. He figured he might as well be wearing a dress and pigtails. When a crinoline tried to manifest itself, he cleared his mind and surrendered to the skipping; though undignified, it was better than a flouncy skirt. He wasn't an Alice, after all.

He squeezed his eyes shut when he got to the clearing, but it was like they'd been pried open with a staple gun. It was a very unpleasant sensation. He wondered if he looked like Alex from *A Clockwork Orange*.

Damn thing shouldn't be able to sit up and talk to him. Even the Devil agreed.

Instead of seeing his cock, he saw Tristan Belledare.

"What fresh hell is this?" Dred asked as he stalked their surroundings, searching for cock sign.

"Merlin sent me instead," Tristan answered.

"For what? To tell me who killed you? I figured it was the lamia."

"Yeah, I can't answer any questions about that."

"Then why are you here?" Dred was genuinely confused.

"The birds. The bees. Middy. Unless you'd rather talk to

the cock?" Tristan shrugged as if it made no never-mind to him one way or the other.

"I don't ever need to talk to the cock again," Dred assured him.

"Here's the thing. It's great that you married her. Fantastic. You know she loves you, right?"

"She may have mentioned it."

"It's not just the potion, man. She really loves you. She'd die for you." Tristan said this last as if it were a benediction. "Would you do the same for her?"

"Yes," he answered with no hesitation. "The world is definitely a better place with her in it. So, yeah, I'd trade my spot for hers."

"Still bloody cavalier! I'm trying to tell you something and you're not hearing me."

"Try again?" Dred raised a brow.

"Merlin fuck!" Tristan reached out his hands, presumably to shake some sense into Dred, but seemed to think better of it. "Listen to me very carefully, Shadowins. I'm going to use small words. Tell the witch that you love her."

"I don't."

"Are you sure?" Tristan asked with a grim finality and a disgusted scowl on his face.

"Ye— No."

"Well, which is it? Do you have grits on your tampon? Just say it."

"I can't," Dred said. "Can't I just be a strong and faithful husband? I'll take care of her until I die."

"Until she dies, shithead. You're still not getting the enormity of what I'm telling you."

"She's going to die?" Dred asked in a strangled tone.

"Yes."

"Me for her—" Dred almost cut him off in his hurry to make the trade. The thought of living in a world without Midnight was impossible.

"No, it doesn't work that way," Tristan said sadly.

"Then why in the hell did you ask me if I would die for her if there's nothing I can do?" Dred grabbed hold of Tristan's collar and it became silver armor under his touch.

Shining armor that glittered like all of the things that Dred Shadowins wasn't.

Perhaps Tristan would have been a better choice to save her. He could give her all the things she deserved. He could love— No, Tristan *did* love her.

Dred took a breath. "Me for you, then."

"What?" Tristan almost choked.

"I'll take your death and you can have my life. Would that save her?" Dred looked away for a moment. "Would *you* save her?"

"Do you know how bad my death sucked?" Tristan looked at him meaningfully.

"You didn't answer me."

"You are a fucktard. I just don't know any other way to put it. You love her. Tell her that you love her before she's gone."

"I refuse to accept that as my only answer."

"Dred, sometimes, there's just nothing else," Tristan said quietly.

"I met this Devil guy earlier. How do I summon him?"

"You can't be serious." Tristan raised his eyes skyward. "Really? This is what you give me to work with?"

"If Merlin won't take my life for Middy's, maybe Caspian will take my soul in exchange."

CHAPTER THIRTY

Surprise, Surprise

"I bet you didn't see that one coming," Caspian snorted.

"He's enterprising, I'll give him that." Merlin ran a hand through his hair.

"You'll get a receding hairline if you keep doing that," Caspian said helpfully.

"This is so frustrating. Why can't he say it? If he did, this whole mess could be averted. At least until the lamia catches Middy, but I think we've found a loophole, haven't we?"

"If not, I'm going to do what we talked about. The Pantheon can suck my fat, pointy tail. I know what I went through to get Grace and Dred seems willing to go to the same lengths."

"Get up there and give the man a contract, if he wants one so badly." Merlin lit a cigar. "Nimue hates these things. If I can't smoke in Hell, where can I smoke, really?"

"Actually, um"—Caspian looked around for an escape route, but seeing none, he continued—"Grace hates the smell of that brand."

"What is the world coming to? Even the Pantheon Halls are no smoking now. You'd think I'd get a little consideration since I'm the Bigger Boss. It's not like I'm in charge of the whole world or anything. Assholes," Merlin muttered.

"It sets a bad example. I don't want Sera Ann to smoke. I've sworn I'd shave off her horns if I ever caught her."

"Aren't you supposed to encourage smoking, drinking, cursing, and general bad behavior?"

"Aren't you supposed to work in mysterious ways? So far, you haven't done jack shit but sit on my couch and bitch."

"And you find that very mysterious." Merlin smirked.

"No, it's not a mystery. You're waiting on Grace to invite you to stay for dinner. She's making Shrimp Diablo tonight."

"I thought that was Shrimp Diavlo?" Merlin looked confused.

"Not in my house."

"If I'd met her before you did . . ." Merlin let that sentence hang as he peered around the corner to see Grace moving about the kitchen.

"Nimue would still be kicking your ass," Caspian added cheerfully.

"Are you going to offer that poor, besotted bastard a contract or what?" Merlin asked.

"Let me think about it. It needs to be good. Unbreakable." Caspian grinned. "Infernal."

CHAPTER THIRTY-ONE

Snatch N' Grab

The morning of Tristan's funeral dawned bright and sunny. Dred didn't want to go; it was hard to grieve for a warlock who didn't seem dead. He hadn't really liked the man anyway, but they were expected to put in an appearance.

All he could think about was what Tristan had told him, that Midnight was going to die and that Dred was helpless to save her.

Dred watched Middy dress for the funeral. He took in the way she smoothed her stockings up her long legs, the ease with which she fastened her own pearls behind her slender neck. The way her breasts looked when she leaned over to check her stockings for runs before she slipped into her heels. He watched her fingers move with an elegant precision over the buttons on her black dress.

When she charmed her hair, he liked how there were a few errant curls that just refused to do her bidding and she fussed with it for only a few minutes before she sighed and applied her makeup charm. She was low-maintenance that way.

He even liked seeing her grooming charms next to his on the sink. They were neat and tidy, and rather than dominating the counter, they complemented his. It gave him a sense of security to see those things next to his own. He'd never let witches leave things at his penthouse before. Sure, he'd find an occasional pair of panties, or a bra, or a thigh high. Sometimes, the cleaning witches would leave a pile of buttons on the counter to return to whatever witch he'd ripped them from, but that was it. Or the discarded toothbrushing charm in the trash. He had a whole drawer full of those one-use charms.

She turned to look at him over her shoulder and her eyes softened. He could see how much she loved him. He could see how much more she'd made of him than what he was, and in that moment, he would have done anything for her if only to keep her light shining on him.

Midnight smiled and something curious twisted his insides.

He smiled back because he knew what he had to do. "Go ahead down to the broom and I'll be along in a minute."

"We could teleport," she said shyly. "I've gotten to where I kind of like it."

"That will save us some time."

How had he gotten so dependent on this witch in such a short time? How had her little habits become intrinsic to his well-being?

"I'll wait for you in the kitchen."

"I have to finish up this spell before we go. It'll only take a minute."

Dred waited until she'd gone and then set about making the circle to summon Caspian. The guy didn't seem as bad as his rap sheet; he only hoped that he didn't make a whole to-do about the summoning. He didn't want Middy to know what he was up to.

He worried for a minute that maybe his britches were a size too big, thinking that the Devil had nothing better to do than be bothered with him, but he'd shown up before.

"What's new, pussycat?" Caspian asked as he stepped from the closet. "No smart-ass remarks about the closet either."

"Actually, I was just going to see if you'd take my call," Dred said diplomatically and motioned to the circle.

"You're a very enterprising young warlock to think of such. Pretty ballsy, too." Caspian straightened his jacket. "Grace and I were just out to see *Faust*. I never get tired of that production."

"*Faust* is a good one," Dred said as he debated how to open.

"Interesting themes, which brings me to the point of my visit." Caspian smiled. "I brought a sample contract. Look it over. Let me know what you think and we'll talk again soon."

"How about we hash it out now? What do you want for Midnight's life?"

"That's a tough one. I mean, how long do you want her to live? What quality of life? These are details you need to think about. I hesitate to remind you, but I am the Devil."

"Whatever her life would have been if I hadn't interfered in it. If I hadn't asked her to help me with this mission."

"What if she never would have realized her potential without meeting you? What if she would have been miserable and lonely for all of her days? Would you wish *that* on her? How do you know that this isn't the pinnacle of her soul's journey? Who are you to fuck with The Great Wheel?" Caspian asked seriously.

Dred shrugged. "I'm a selfish bastard and I'll give anything to know that she's safe. She can reach her pinnacle or whatever in another life where I don't have to live without her."

"I understand where you're coming from. So, the question is, what will you trade? Will you live in the body of a leper on your next turn around The Wheel? An AIDS patient? A woman in the Burning Times? Will you die for her? Or the ultimate sacrifice, serve me in Hell for all eternity?"

Dred knew from the many companies he'd bought and absorbed into Shadowins Holdings that it was always wise to get details and have lawyers dissect the contract with a fine-toothed comb, but he didn't care about that right now. Perhaps not the smartest move in the world when dealing with the Devil, but he had his reasons.

"Any of it, all of it. It doesn't matter. I want her to be happy, healthy, and safe. Whatever that entails."

"Hmm, that's going to be a problem. She's not going to be happy without you," Caspian said.

"That's just the potion. It'll wear off soon enough after I'm gone," Dred said.

"Tristan was right." Caspian sighed like an actress in a fit of pique. "You are a fucktard. Do you understand that you're selling your soul for this woman? If you haven't realized by now that you love her . . ."

Dred didn't want to say it, but he had a feeling that the deal wouldn't happen without his admission. "Yeah, okay. Whatever."

Caspian flashed a toothy grin. "I know it sucks when you first figure it out. It's like finding out that your favorite candy is made out of dog shit. I've been there. Anyway, sign here." He produced a very large parchment that unrolled a few feet before landing in a mess on Dred's shoes. "You can read it if you want."

"I don't care about the rest of it." Dred took the sharpened quill and touched it to his finger and marked his blood on the parchment. "So, it's done."

"It's done." Caspian grinned and disappeared in a tower of flame.

Dred waited for something to happen. He waited to feel something different. There was nothing. He was fairly sure that the Devil would keep his end of the deal. He knew that was probably naïve on his part, but it was all that was left for him to believe.

He did notice the faint aroma of sulfur that clung to his clothes. Dred changed quickly and met Middy in the kitchen.

"Who were you talking to?"

"The Devil."

"Caspian was here? What did he want?"

Dred decided to answer honestly. It was a new trend. "To offer me a job."

"Did you take it? What are the benefits like?" Middy asked, obviously operating under the impression that he was joking.

"Spousal coverage is great, so I'd say the benefits are pretty good. I signed the contract. Not sure when I start though."

She laughed.

There was a light inside him that hadn't been there before. Something warm and out of place. He realized it was Middy. It wasn't the Devil calling him a fucktard that made him ready to admit she was inside of him. It had been the clear sound of her laughter.

He grabbed her by the nape of her neck and kissed her hard and she melted against him. Her body was pliant in his embrace, her lips opened beneath his, and just when he would have explored the contours of her mouth, he pulled back.

"I love you, Midnight."

"Dred, you don't have to say that. I already promised I'd stay." She gave him a half-smile that was somehow more devastating than what her tears would have been.

"It's okay, Dred. Really. It's okay," she reiterated and put her hand on his arm before she pressed herself against him to teleport.

He was at a loss for words and Middy didn't seem inclined to want them anyway. Dred hadn't realized how strong she was. It was another thing about her that he admired. Dred hoped that after he was gone, she'd remember that he'd said the words and she'd know that they were true.

Dred closed his eyes and they teleported.

They arrived at the funeral and were immediately led to the front of the staging area where ushers guided them to their seats. They paused at the funeral pyre where Tristan's body was laid out for viewing before the flames would take him.

His body had been washed by the women of his family and ancient sigils had been magickally pressed into his skin. They were to mark his safe journey to the Summer Land where death and sadness would never touch him again.

Dred wondered what his family would say if they knew Tristan had spoken to him. Seeing his dead body, Dred wondered if perhaps the stress of this mission had been a little much and he'd sold his soul on the word of a figment of his imagination.

Then he remembered the first dream. Everything that he'd learned then had been true. Midnight moved closer against him and twined her fingers with his, so he gave Belledare a last look and proceeded to their seats.

Photographers from *Magickal Mayhem* were snapping furiously and Middy kept turning her face into his coat. He shot a fireball at the magickal boundary. Though it didn't hurt them, it would blind their cameras for the next hour.

Barista sat down next to Dred. "Darling boy, will you help me find Roderick? He's wandered off in the crowd, I think. I'm simply lost without him."

Dred didn't want to leave Midnight. He had a sinking feeling in his gut, but Middy smiled up at him and told him to go.

"I'm sure he's around, Aunt Barista. He'll find you," Dred said by way of dismissal.

"I know you don't want to be apart from your lovely wife for even a minute, but please, Dred."

He looked at Middy and she waved him off. Dred didn't see any way to get out of this. He was comforted by the fact that the Trifecta were his eyes in the sky and Middy would be perfectly safe.

Dred followed his aunt to where she'd last seen Roderick. He cast a quick location spell and quickly discovered that his uncle was nowhere in attendance. Barista narrowed her eyes as a certain knowledge filled Dred.

The house filled with dark objects. The zombie in their employ. The paper trail that connected her to dark objects dealers. It hadn't been Roderick he should have suspected, but Barista. She was the one who was behind his capture during the war. She'd traded his life for a dark object.

He was sure that there was no youth potion. Barista had raised the lamia. Now, she'd succeeded in separating him from Middy. A dark shadow fell over the gathering and Dred looked up in time to see one of Middy's brothers crashing to the earth, his body broken and bloody.

Witches were screaming and magick was flying fast and furious, protection spells, fireballs, it was as if the world had caught on fire.

Barista didn't even bother to gloat. As soon as the realization hit him, she smiled, but it was more of a baring of teeth than a real smile. She jammed a ceremonial dagger into his gut before he had time to react. He saw her arm move, but he didn't feel anything. She stepped away from him, still smiling.

Dred put his hands to his wounds and realized that she'd sliced him from navel to breast bone. Blood poured out of him. He could feel the hot, sticky warmth on his hands, and all around him; all he could see was red.

Then he heard Middy scream.

Dred knew he was dying, but he couldn't let go until he he was sure that Middy was safe. He muttered a spell that would hold his gut together long enough for him to get to her, then stumbled through the crowd. He didn't know how he was still on his feet, but he was thankful to Merlin and Caspian both for it.

His magick was failing; sparks spluttered from his fingertips as he tried to use a location spell on Middy. It didn't matter though. As the shadows swallowed his vision, the last thing his brain processed was a lamia wearing Drusilla Tallow's face taking to the skies with his wife in her claws.

CHAPTER THIRTY-TWO
A Lamia, a Witch, and Her Warlock

Middy watched helplessly as Dred's life poured from his body and still he struggled to get to her. She reached out to him, trying to activate the link between them. She'd healed the hatchling gargoyle; maybe she could heal him, too!

She knew she couldn't absorb all of his wounds, but maybe she could take enough to save him. Activating that bond between them had never been voluntary, but it was as if a switch had been flipped.

Middy had felt the dagger pierce his flesh; she'd screamed at the agony. But after that, the connection between them had gone dark and quiet. Dred was gone. She prayed to Merlin that he'd help Dred. If she had to, she'd pray to Caspian, too. Dred couldn't die!

She'd seen Falcon drop from the sky and she prayed that he'd survived, that her brothers had been able to use their magick to break his fall. Unless they were dead, too. What the hell had they been doing circling Tristan's funeral anyway?

Her world was falling apart. It was as if she'd been living in a snow globe and it had been dropped from the top of the Sears Tower. Everything she loved was being taken from her.

That was when the claws pierced the flesh of her middle.

It was as if she'd been wrapped in barbed wire. She looked up and saw what could only be the lamia.

It was a grotesque creature, the wingspan like that of a crop duster. Its body was furry like a bat's, only the wings were feathered. It seemed to be bipedal, but its feet were curled into massive claws that gripped Middy tightly.

Most awful of all was that its large head bore Tally's face. Her mouth had morphed into a sharp beak that gaped open during flight and Middy could see the rings of teeth that were like the mouth of a great white shark.

Middy was afraid; she didn't doubt that this creature would ravage her as it had Tristan. She recalled the viscera and hollow bones that she'd seen and the memory terrified her more.

But she hadn't forgotten that this thing was part Tally now. The woman who had been her constant companion, her confidante, her sister—she was still in there and she was alone in all that darkness.

Midnight knew that she had to try to save her.

She thought briefly about her brothers and her mother; she missed them so much now. Middy had a lead weight on her chest that was a sure knowledge she would never see any of those who were dear to her again.

Midnight recognized their surroundings instantly. They were in Loudun! The lamia could cover ground faster than anything she'd ever seen. The lamia landed in the open ruin of a tower in the old convent. She dropped Middy roughly to the crumbling stone of the parapet.

Every instinct told Middy to get as far away from the creature as possible, to run, to shrink herself into a dark corner where it would never find her, to use her magick— even though she knew all of these options were futile.

She looked the thing in those eyes that were at once both familiar and reptilian. "What are you doing, Tally?" Middy asked softly.

The creature's great strength forced her against the wall and that beak nosed at her throat as if trying to decide where the tastiest bits were, where the marrow and the blood would be the sweetest.

Claws dug into her arms and blood welled at the wounds. A long tongue licked away the precious drops.

"Tally," Middy began again, this time more firmly.

The creature's head jerked and met her gaze. Middy was falling into an endless darkness in those eyes; it was reaching out from the Abyss to swallow her whole.

Middy felt that same, impossible hope inside of her that she'd felt when she'd seen the hatchling, when she'd reached out to Dred. It spiraled inside of her and even though her world was broken, her heart in pieces, and grief was devouring her soul, there was hope. It glittered like a jewel in that sea of black despair and it grew.

It grew until it was a nimbus at the crown of her head and it gathered in warm, soft pools around her fingertips. It blossomed and shrouded Middy in a mantle of light.

The lamia cringed and tried to shield itself from her light, from the goodness that made for tasty meat, but could also be its destruction.

"I'll suck the marrow from your bones, bitch. There is nothing for you to hope for," it growled in a gravelly voice.

Middy felt nothing but peace; there was no fear. She took a step toward the retreating horror.

"Your Tally is dead, your brother, your mate. There is nothing left. Nothing," it said again, but took another step away from her.

"Tally, you have to fight. Come out of the dark," Middy pleaded.

The reptilian eyes blinked and she knew it was Tally looking out of that misshapen body. The mouth opened and closed and Middy could sense the other woman's anguish, the despair that kept her imprisoned.

"I tried to warn you," she gasped. Tally's gaze was drawn to the blood that continued to well on Middy's arms and around her middle. "Run, Midnight. Run," she choked.

"No," Middy said with more confidence. "I'm not going to leave you here." Midnight wasn't sure how she could save Tally; she only knew that she wouldn't leave her. She had faith in the light.

"Then you'll die," the lamia growled.

When it moved to an attack stance, Middy opened her arms and welcomed the tearing claws and gnashing teeth.

The attack never came. The creature watched her with predatory intent evident in its eyes, but still didn't close that distance between them. So Middy did it for them both.

CHAPTER THIRTY-THREE

A Crown Prince of Hell Gets His Wings

Tristan was right. Dying really sucked.

When Dred opened his eyes, the Devil was leering at him with a cheeky grin.

"Why does this scene seem familiar?" Caspian mused. "Oh, yes. I was offered a similar deal while I lay dying and the villain had run off with my lady fair."

"And what did you do about it?" Dred asked as pain knifed through his every nerve ending.

"I traded my Crown Prince status for becoming the Big Boss. Too bad Grace's father got there first. That angelic can of whoop-ass was messy. I got the bad guy in the end though. He lives in Detroit now—a submission slave to one of my more fun-loving employees." Caspian grinned as if he were remembering good times.

"Can you save Middy now?"

"No, that's your job. Here's your crown, your Infernal Handbook, and grooming brush for your wings. Unless you want the bat style, but chicks dig the black feathers, let me tell you," Caspian said as he shoved a burning crown into Dred's hands.

Dred found that the fire didn't burn him, though it did singe his Infernal Handbook.

Caspian frowned. "We're still working on the paper thing."

Dred positioned the crown on his head and he felt something large and heavy hanging from his back like a cloak.

"They're white!" Caspian exclaimed with shock. "Crown Princes of Hell do not have white wings."

"Maybe this one does. Again, details I could give a shit less about. Where's Middy?"

"Sorry, buddy. I can't do any more or the Pantheon will be up my ass with injunctions like a gerbil and a . . . Anyway. I'm sure you have a good idea where she is."

Loudun! Dred didn't even bid Caspian farewell. He figured he had eternity to perfect his workplace etiquette.

The world looked very different to him now. He could see good, evil, and all the gray in between. He could see auras of places, things, and people. There weren't too many that were all one or the other.

He focused on Middy and he could feel her in Loudun. If he concentrated hard enough, he could see her. She was one of those few whose aura burned with purity. But she was with one who burned with an anti-light. It was bleak and hopeless: the lamia.

Dred could see a spark in that black blight and with his new powers, he could sense that was what was left of Drusilla Tallow. He couldn't be too late. He'd struck his deal, eternity for Middy's life. But hope died as in his mind's eye as he saw the darkness and the light merging.

With a blast of demonic strength, he teleported to Loudun.

Middy was embracing the lamia; she held it in her arms with all the tenderness she would a child. Her eyes were closed and she was singing a melody. Tristan suddenly materialized behind her, a flaming sword raised and poised to strike, his white wings splayed behind him. But he hesitated.

The lamia cringed in the embrace, but human fingers

clung to Middy. They morphed between talons and digits, each shift digging into Middy's soft flesh.

"I'm here, Tally. I won't let go."

The lamia growled and opened its beak to tear at its tormenter, but Middy clung tighter and the white nimbus around her grew.

"Let me go, Middy. I'm not strong enough," Drusilla cried before her face turned reptilian again.

Dred imagined Tally must be in excruciating pain to endure the shifts. She wouldn't be able to fight the creature much longer. He didn't know how to separate them without hurting Middy.

Just then Dred saw the creature's aura blink into total darkness, and he made his move. Those teeth tore into Midnight's throat, but rather than blood and flesh, there was only light. It exploded from her like a bomb, but she didn't let go.

It kept tearing at her, ripping holes in her flesh, but Midnight held tight. Dred could see her resolve and there was nothing that would pry her away from her intention, not even her own death.

Dred felt the lure of her goodness and he moved to stand behind her. To let her take whatever strength she could from him. He wrapped his arms around her and the creature both.

The deadly razor teeth turned on him, but Dred didn't fight back. If Middy could endure it, so could he. Better that the lamia tear his demonic flesh than Midnight's.

It was only moments after Dred lent his strength to Middy that the lamia splintered; it crawled like a slug from Tally's throat. As soon as it was free, Tristan brought his flaming sword down into its body. It screamed and thrashed, but Tristan pinned it to the wall with the sword and a magickal binding.

Martin Vargill emerged from the shadows onto the parapet with Barista in tow. Her skin went sallow as soon as she saw Dred and his wings glittering like diamond dust under the warm light of the sun.

"That's mine!" Vargill demanded, gazing at Dred's crown, which burned brightly with hellfire. He began chanting and drawing sigils in the dust and blood on the floor.

Dred held Middy's lax form in his arms and wouldn't put her down. Not even to smite Martin for all of the pain and terror he'd inflicted.

Tristan, however, was another matter entirely. "Take this one instead!" Tristan took his own golden crown and threw it at Vargill and the points pierced the flesh around his black heart in a perfect circle. Tristan used his magick to will the black essence back to his painting in Chaldonean Hall, where he would serve out his sentence for eternity.

Dred was too busy with Midnight to worry about what happened to his aunt. If he'd learned anything, it was that The Wheel turned in mysterious ways. He didn't need to punish her as much as he needed these last moments with Midnight.

His hands were on her face, stroking her throat where the wounds had healed, tangled in her hair, and his wings shielded them from the rest of the universe. Dred held her tightly against him; his lips were on her forehead, her cheeks, and her mouth.

"I love you, Midnight. I love you." He whispered it like a holy canticle—and for him, it was. She was his faith, she was his higher power, she was the universe.

Dred prayed that she'd wake up, that she'd hear him before he had to leave. His soul rebelled at the thought of leaving her, but he'd accepted it as the price for her life. Nothing was too much to save her, not even this.

Her eyes fluttered open, that wondrous light still burning there. She touched his cheek. "I thought you were dead," she whispered.

"I was," he replied truthfully. "But you're safe now. That's all that matters."

She looked to the burning crown on his head.

"What have you done?" she gasped.

"I've loved you, Middy. More than myself. More than the cause. More than anything in this world or the next."

"No," she cried out and fat tears rolled down her cheeks. "No, you didn't have to love me. We'd have been happy."

"You were going to die. I couldn't live without you." Dred kissed her again with the hope that she'd forgive him for leaving her. "Don't cry, Middy. I want you to live your life, do you understand me? Be happy, whatever that takes."

She shook her head. "Not without you."

"There's a potion you can take. You'll forget me. . . ." It broke something in him to say it, but he knew it was the right thing.

"No!" She shook her head vehemently. "I'll trade my soul, too. I'll do it right now."

"Remember the light inside of you? No, you're meant for something greater than me," Dred said as he began to untangle himself from her embrace.

"No," she screamed again and the building began to quake.

"Well, if this isn't a sodding mess, I don't know what is. You two have fucked this up almost beyond repair." Merlin's voice boomed through the structure.

Middy and Dred turned to the voice, Midnight trying in vain to put herself between the Bigger Boss and Dred. As if they were mortal enemies.

"Midnight, you have to control your anger. That's you shaking the ever-loving shit out of the building. If this structure falls, it will kill people on the mortal side as well as the warlockian. Settle down," Merlin demanded.

Caspian emerged from a shadow and put his arm around Barista as she was trying to leave. "Where are you going, love?"

She made a valiant attempt to stab him with the same ceremonial dagger that was smeared with Dred's blood. The end broke off like an icicle and Caspian laughed as if he was genuinely amused.

"Dred," Caspian began.

"You can't have him!" Middy demanded before Caspian could say anything else.

"I don't want him. Look at those wings! White? And after Labor Day." Caspian turned to Tristan. "You, on the other hand, you're coming with me."

Joy exploded inside her like a starburst knowing that Dred wouldn't suffer in Hell. She was happy he'd be in Heaven, Middy couldn't have lived with the knowledge that he'd traded his life and eternity for her, but her heart had splintered into a thousand pieces knowing he was still lost to her. Dred loved her. Wholly. Completely. Middy had no doubt she would have traded that just to keep him with her.

She looked away from Dred, still hungry for the sight of him, but unable to keep the devastation of loss from her eyes. She saw then that Tristan's wings had melted into a dark, inky blanket of shadows.

"What do you say? Chicks dig the black wings, man. I promise." Caspian winked at Tristan.

"Can I be a Crown Prince instead of a Duke?" Tristan asked as if they were playing dress up instead of talking about eternity.

"Sure, why not?"

"I'm in." He shrugged.

Caspian turned to look at Tally and wrinkled his nose. "I'm not sure what to do with her yet, but you," he said as he turned to Barista Snow, "I have just the thing for you.

I've designed a special Hell for those who try to interfere with true love." He snapped his fingers and she disappeared.

The lamia struggled against its bonds and Caspian shot it with blasts of fire until it quieted before he turned back to Dred.

"I guess it looks like you're on Merlin's team now. All that self-sacrifice and such." The Devil made a show of acting disgusted, but he winked at them both. "I'll tie this bitch up and ship her back to the Abyss," he said as he motioned to the lamia.

"Why not Hell?" Middy questioned, still avoiding the only question that really mattered to her: When she'd have to say good-bye to her husband.

"Are you kidding? I'm raising imps there." Caspian sounded offended.

"What about Tally?" she asked.

"What happens with her is up to you. You can still save her, but it will be damned uncomfortable. I'll catch you two kids later."

Caspian disappeared with Tristan and what was left of the lamia, leaving them alone.

Dred pulled her tightly against him. She clung for a moment before she sank to her knees and cradled Tally's broken body. "You know I have to try to save her."

Dred knelt down beside her and took her hand. "*We'll try.*"

The white nimbus of light that had surrounded Middy surged again with little effort. It was as strong and boundless as Middy's heart. She didn't need his strength this time, but she leaned into him all the same.

The light filled Drusilla Tallow and unlike the backlash with the baby gargoyle, Middy didn't have to endure any of Tally's pain. Her body simply knit itself back together, bones cracking and reshaping, muscle and fascia melding together.

As Tally became whole, iridescent white wings burst from Middy's back and a diamond crown appeared on her head.

Dred was gifted with the knowledge that her sacrifice, her ability to love and hope even in the face of her own death had earned her her place as a Crown Princess of Heaven. And he remembered Caspian's words about the pinnacle of her soul's journey.

Yes, this was what she was meant for. She'd bring healing and hope to the whole world, but she could still belong to him. His heart swelled with a deluge of emotions: pride, joy, hope, love.

Middy turned her attention to him, and he knew their connection told her everything he wanted to say but was unable to find the words for because he saw the same things reflected in her gaze.

Tally opened her eyes, tears streaking down her cheeks, and she clung to Middy much the same as the baby gargoyle had. She was so small, and though she'd been made physically whole, she was still broken.

Dred wanted to take Midnight in his arms and assure himself that this was all real, to tell her everything he felt even though she already knew. But Middy was working. Tally was her friend, but Dred knew she needed the comfort and safety that only a Crown Princess of Heaven could provide. Compassion flared. Dred had eternity with Midnight. He could spare a day to ease this woman's suffering.

"I know she needs you now. But you're mine tonight."

"Yours always," she whispered.

CHAPTER THIRTY-FOUR
A Wedding and a Wake

Midnight Cherrywood stood before a full-length mirror and this time, allowed Drusilla Tallow to do what she would with her dress *and* her hair. The other witch primped and tucked, fussed and snorted until finally she stood back, pleased with the results.

Middy's hair fell in a cascade of curls down her back and between her wings. Her dress was a pale ivory, and the bodice was wrapped in seed pearl lace. The rest of the dress fell fey and wispy; it seemed to move around her as if it were sentient.

"You know, being your maid of honor with only one functioning arm is a little more of a challenge than you'd think." Tally flapped her sling like a chicken wing, sending glitter flying into the space around them. She'd used her magick to embroider sequins all over it and doused it liberally with glitter in her usual Tally style.

Tally had come through the singular horror of being possessed by a lamia with nothing more than a broken arm. Middy had been able to heal the rest. All but the memories, and Tally wanted those, she said, so she'd remember to be thankful for what she had every day. She wondered if the arm had been left unhealed by the Powers That Be as a daily physical reminder of all that had happened. Middy knew Tally had a tough road ahead of her to prove herself worthy of her second chance.

Tally sniffed. "Oh, shit. I said I wasn't going to do this. Now, my mascara is running." She sniffed again. "You're so beautiful, Midnight. I don't know how you're going to keep your wings a secret or that glow, but you're beautiful."

"It's my wedding and I'll wear my wings if I want to. No one will believe they're real anyway."

Middy turned to the side and her wings looked as if they'd been doused in glitter like everything else that Tally got anywhere near.

Merlin had smiled on her and Dred both that day. She'd been made a Crown Princess of Heaven, which he'd told her had always been her destiny. Dred's, not so much. Merlin was sure he'd end up on the other side, but was happy to have him on the team, or so he said. Middy got credit for his redemption, hence the direct promotion to Crown Princess instead of Grand Duchess. There was a hierarchy, after all.

"I can't believe my mother isn't going to meet my husband until the reception," Middy added.

"I'm sure he'll charm the piss and vinegar right out of her." Tally hugged her. "Thank you for still being my friend. For still loving me."

"We're more than friends. You're my sister and I'll always love you," Middy said as she hugged her back.

"You know how people are going to look at me. I'm a pariah."

"Not everyone," Middy said. "Falcon has been staring at you anxiously all day."

"He just thinks I'm easy," Tally snorted.

"Make him work for it and he'll follow you like a puppy. All my brothers are like that."

"So, would it be wrong of me to use Falcon for a one-night stand?" Tally asked hopefully.

"First, you have my blessing. Second, just don't tell me about it." Middy grinned.

The orchestra began to play and Middy heard her cue. She stepped carefully from the bride's tent and moved to the red carpet where Hawk waited to give her away. Middy took his arm and as they walked, he spoke.

"Raven tried to talk him out of it."

"What?" Middy growled through clenched teeth and a smile.

"Yeah, told him to run and be free while he still could. Like he was reintroducing a rakehell back into the wild. They are an endangered species, or so Raven seems to think."

"It'll be even more endangered when I kick him in the balls. Is he trying to turn this wedding into his wake?"

"How did you get into Heaven again? You're a mean little crotch puppet."

"Tough love, baby." Middy grinned.

When she caught sight of Dred, her grin turned to a shy smile and even though she swore that she had nothing to cry about, her eyes filled with unshed tears.

He was a Heavenly sight, her warlock. He watched her progression intently and with open joy on his face. Dred wasn't wearing his wings, but he was wearing a suit of armor; shining armor. It was pure silver and fit him like a second skin. The heavy metal seemed molded to his very flesh and he moved inside it with ease.

He accepted her hand from Hawk's and bowed his head to the other warlock before getting down on one knee in front of Middy. She was aware of no one else but her handsome Crown Prince of Heaven.

Not the cleric, not Tally, not her brothers—no one but the man who was bent before her just as she'd asked on a night that now seemed an eternity ago. They didn't need the mortal words to bind them, but the ritual meant something to Middy. He stood when the cleric began speaking.

When she looked up into his eyes as they repeated their vows, she knew that Dred's shining armor wouldn't rust. He was everything a fairy-tale prince should be, and her Happily Ever After was real.

CHAPTER THIRTY-FIVE

The Credits

The credits are rolling and the lights have come up in the theater. Middy and Dred have their Happily Ever After with the capital letters and . . .

What happens to the rest of them? Where did the wedding take place? Important questions to be sure. Another peek wouldn't hurt.

Middy and Dred were married on the vast property of the Shadowins Estate. Middy's mother planned most of the wedding and Aradia paid the bill; both seemed quite pleased with the arrangement. Dred, did indeed, charm the piss and vinegar right out of his witch-in-law. She was so entranced with him that she was angry at Middy for calling him "Dred the Dastard" for all those years with no return scolding for "Miss Cherry-Would-If-She-Could."

Further, Aradia Shadowins decided since her only son had married, she was entitled to do as she wished. She'd put in her time as a highborn society lady and decided to install the gargoyle hottie from the Harpy Tea, Valerian, as a permanent fixture in her household. This decision was met with a great collective gasp by society, but it solidified her standing as an eccentric. Aradia and Valerian spend their time antiquing, reading eighteenth-century French poetry, and shagging like bunnies.

Raven is still concerned with the vanishing species known

as the rakehell and has made it his life's work to see that as many as possible are saved and reintroduced into the wild. Dred's black book has been the catalyst for many a successful release, but Raven blames Middy whenever she brings up the subject. She was the one who relayed Hawk's smart-ass comment from the wedding and it inspired him.

Dred's uncle, Roderick Snow, after being rescued from his own dungeon, has been seen keeping company with one Ginger Butterbean. Most recently they were spotted together at an Italian cooking class.

Merlin was kind enough to gift Dred and Midnight with a tract house on the same block of Heaven/Hell as the rest of their merry band. Middy has been convincing Grace of the joys of World of Warlock on the spelltop and they both have high-level paladins. Sera Ann wanders freely between residences and Middy made her a red cloak that she never takes off.

Dred still dresses up in his wedding armor for Middy, but sometimes, just sometimes, she likes it when it's black and he carries her off to be pillaged like a captive of an invading knight. Or Viking, even though they didn't wear armor, but that's okay with Middy. She likes the imagery just the same.

Dred likes his job, but he works from home a lot. Merlin thinks that Caspian is setting a bad example. Now that he and Dred are both doing it, Nimue has started to expect him to be home more, too.

Middy still allows him to pose for *Weekly Warlock*. She doesn't even mind the interactive program. She knows that she's the only one who has the real Dred, and all of the proceeds go to the Gargoyle Masque.

They'll be shooting for the *Weekly Warlock* calendar soon and Dred thinks he's convinced the Trifecta to take the spring months.

And they lived Happily Ever After.

AUTHOR'S NOTE

When I first read about the Loudun possessions of 1634, it captured my imagination. Possessed nuns and priests frosted with sex appeal and politically ambitious sprinkles? I knew that I was going to have to use the incident in a story. That's when Dred and Midnight began speaking to me. There was plenty of research material for me to sift through, but even with the help of one of the most brilliant search mavens in the world (thanks, Jess), we were unable to find information as to the state of the Ursuline convent today. To tell the story that these characters kept yelling in my ear, I've had to take liberties with structure and perhaps the very existence of the convent in the here and now.

The creature I used as the villain, the lamia, is a popular figure that appears in many mythologies. The lamia have been connected with Greek mythology as well as Christianity. Lamia are associated with succubi and specifically, Lilith. In all of the myths, they are devourers of innocent flesh, particularly children. Again, I've taken the information and used it for my own nefarious ends.

I hope you enjoyed Midnight and Dred as much as I did and come back for another helping of over-the-top fun with Falcon and Tally in *How to Seduce an Angel in 10 Days.*

Thanks for reading!

Did you miss HOW TO LOSE A DEMON IN 10 DAYS?

GOT DEMON?

Grace does. She's got more demon than she can saddle. In fact, she's got a sinfully sexy Crown Prince of Hell named Caspian. She's also got ten days to get rid of him or Bad Things shall ensue. See, her Russian mobster ex-boyfriend didn't take kindly to her smutty Mephistophelean contract. It's not that she's conspiring with fiends; that was his idea. It's that she's conspiring against him with outrageous devilry that runs the gamut from embarrassing to a dead hooker turned dominatrix demon gunning for his soul.

One should never trust demons, let alone shag them. They don't have hearts. Yet Grace is buying hers some slightly tarnished armor and hoping that once he's been shoveled into it, kicking and screaming, he'll find it's just his size. This damsel in distress needs a dark knight for a Happily Ever After.